2.00

"**A Major Event!**...a fast-paced page-turner of a science fictional mystery...original concepts and lots of pizzazz. It's going to be talked about and enjoyed!"
—*Publishers Weekly*

"**GOLEM**[100] is a novel that has no parallel...Alfred Bester has taken the concept of a sciencefictionally decadent civilization of the next century or so, and turned it into a super-demonology. In the process the English language has had evoked from it the most dazzling verbal pyrotechnics in its long and glorious history...an experience in poetic madness!"
—*A.E. van Vogt*

"When I was in my teens and twenties, Alfred Bester was doing as much as anybody to reshape science fiction...I speak for the whole field when I say that I'm glad he's back."
—*Larry Niven*

GOLEM¹⁰⁰

ALFRED BESTER

Illustrated by
Jack Gaughan

A TIMESCAPE BOOK
PUBLISHED BY POCKET BOOKS NEW YORK

A Timescape Book published by
POCKETS BOOKS, a Simon & Schuster division of
GULF & WESTERN CORPORATION
1230 Avenue of the Americas, New York, N.Y. 10020

ISBN: 0-671-82047-8

First Timescape Books printing March, 1981

Published in hardcover by Simon and Schuster.

10 9 8 7 6 5 4 3 2 1

TIMESCAPE and design are trademarks of Simon & Schuster.
POCKET and colophon are trademarks of Simon & Schuster.

Printed in the U.S.A.

For
Big Red
Who helped from the
beginning to the end.

Le chemin est long du projet à la chose.

1

There were eight of them who met in the hive every week to warm themselves and each other. They were charming beeladies, attractive and sweet-tempered despite—or perhaps because of—the fact that they were all secure and assured. (The less-privileged classes called them "high mucky-fucks.")

They were not all cut from the identical pattern like insect-type bees. They were intensely individual, human-type ladies even though they were living far in our future. After all, our heirs won't change all that much. Each of them had her own kinky eccentricity which is the true source of charm.

Each had a secret name, as indeed we all do, and that was their real reality. Perhaps I'm committing a heinous crime in revealing them—T. S. Eliot insisted that the secret name of a creature, "the deep and inscrutable singular Name," could and should be known to no one—but the bee-ladies knew them and used them, so here they are:

Regina, the Queen Bee. It has the old English law pronunciation, Re-JYN-a.

Little Mary Mixup, who can never get anything straight, including her hair.

1

Nellie Gwyn, who would have given the raunchy King Charles the Second an even harder time than her namesake.

Miss Priss, who still has a girlie-girlie lisp, and as a child was heard to say in praise of her schoolboy beau, "He's a perfect gentleman. When we cross the street he takes my arm and walks me so I shouldn't step in the shit."

Sarah Heartburn, flinging the back of her hand against her brow and declaiming in thrilling tones, "Go! GO! I must be a-LONE! I wish to—com-MUTE with myself!"

Yenta Calienta, who knows everything you have in your purse, your tote, your closets, your freeze. Yenta is always trying to make preposterous trades, like her broken hourglass for your antique mah-jongg set with one piece missing.

And the twins, *Oodgedye* and *Udgedye,* which mean "Guess who" and "Guess which" in Russian. Anton Chekhov used those words for dog names in one of his farces.

That adds up to eight. There was a sort of ninth, Regina's slavey called Pi, not because she had anything to do with the ratio of the circumference of a circle to its diameter (3.1416) but simply because she's a pie-faced girl.

You may want to know whether the bee-ladies were married or single or living in sin or frigid or having dyke affairs or swinging from the chandelier or whatever. The answer is a blanket yes because they lived in the famous or infamous Guff precinct. Much more about the Guff later. But keep in mind that they were all secure and assured in background—they'd all been through the posh colleges called "The Seven Sisters" —and in status and income. So when you meet them alone together with their hair down, so to speak, remember that you're seeing their Closet-Selves.

The rest of the world only met poised, attractive women who were insulated from the fears that beset the submerged majority who lived in the Guff; murder, mayhem, rape, robbery, and all other assorted violences too numerous to list. The dignity and charm of the eight ladies was preserved by living in strongly protected homes, using guaranteed, bonded transport, with iron-safe escort service at their call. The only real *crise* in their lives was the chronic boredom that insulation brings.

So they entertained themselves (with their hair down) by meeting as often as they could in Regina's big *avant-garde* apartment, which could hardly be called a hive, and yet they did behave like bee-ladies. They buzzed with gossip and jokes and chitchat. They played nonsense games. They did bee-dances now and then. They gorged on sweets when they were restless or tired or angry. And there were occasional sad moments when they butted heads to establish an informal dominance-order. Human-types do that along with many other creatures. We've been doing it ever since the first primordial DNA molecule told the rest of the DNAs who was boss and proved it.

Their latest amusement was diabolism. None of them took it seriously. None of them really believed in commerce with the Devil; riding broomsticks and pulling off their stockings to raise a storm and all that sort of nonsense. As a matter of fact, Regina had become interested in the game only because she was a direct descendant of Sir John Holt (1642–1710), the Lord Chief Justice of England.

Holt was a swinger when he was an undergraduate at Oxford and he ran out of money, as usual. He managed to swindle a week's free lodging by pretending to cure his landlady's daughter of an ague. The goniff scribbled a few words of Greek on a scrap of parchment and told his landlady to tie it to the girl's waist and leave it there until she was well.

Years later, when Holt was L.C.J., an old woman was brought before him charged with sorcery. She professed to cure fevers with the application of a piece

3

of parchment. Holt looked at the parchment, and you guessed it; the identical phony charm he'd faked years before. Holt burst out laughing and confessed, and the old doll was acquitted. She was one of the last to be tried for witchcraft in England.

So you can see why Regina was interested but never serious. It was more or less amateur theatricals, play-acting with overtones of a parlor concert, fun and games in a deliciously dark key. But the hell of this game was that without their knowledge or intent—repeat: *without their knowledge or intent*—these darling, good-humored ladies were actually generating a most damnable demon.

It was a polymorphous quasi-entity never before dreamed of in the entire history of witchcraft and devil lore, a monstrous Golem. No, not the well-known synthetic slave of Jewish legend, but a unique multiplication of the brutal cruelty that lies buried deep within all of us, even the best of us. Freud called it the "Id," the unconscious source of instinctive energy which demands savage animal satisfaction. Alone and separate, the Id in each of the bee-ladies was under control; but together, consolidated by the fun-diabolism, they all merged.

$$8 \times Id = Golem^{100}$$

Watch their first ritual.

* * *

"Now then, ladies, final rehearsal for raising the Devil. Got your scripts? Everybody ready?"

"Yes, but is this the realsie, Regina?"

"No, not yet. For real it has to be all of us together with stage effects. This is just the final tryout, one by one. Invocation, dear, you go first."

"Well, all right, *but* if *ANYONE* l!a!u!g!h!s—"

"No, no, Sarah. All Sincere City. Go."

Sarah Heartburn declaimed the Invocation.

4

"Wonderful! Wasn't she dramatic, ladies?"

"All heart. All heart."

"Sarah could invoke anything out of the woodwork."

"Aye, you mock me, but I felt a C*H*I*L*L when I was chaunting it!"

"The devil playing footsie with you?"

"'Twas NOT my foot, Nellie."

"Oops! Naughty, naughty."

"Now ladies, please! We must be serious."

"Doesn't Satan have a sense of humor, Regina?"

"Try a clean joke on him, Priss. Now let's get on with it. *Oodgedye*, you're next. Prayer."

Oodgedye read the Latin Prayer.

$$\frac{\begin{array}{r} \text{Sarah} \\ + \textit{Oodgedye} \\ -6 \end{array}}{0}$$

"Lovely. I never thought Latin could sound so beautiful. Congratulations, dear."

"Thanks, Regina. I only wish it made sense, too."

"I'm sure it will to the Devil. Now who's next? Mary Mixup with Pact?"

"No, me, Regina. Conjuration."

"Oh, of course, *Udgedye*. It's back to English before we get to the French. Ready?"

"Willing and able. Stand back, everybody. When I conjure I'm practically a fiend in human shape."

"Splendid, Ud, but don't get too intimate with Satan. He's not exactly reliable."

"You have to be guffing her, Regina, or else you don't know your way around hell."

"And what makes you think so, Nellie *dear?*"

"I know the Devil's big sell when he comes on with witches. He's got a built on him like a hot elephant."

"I hope you find out, Nellie. All right, Ud, conjure the hot elephant to come to hot Nell Gwyn."

Udgedye read the Conjuration.

$$
\begin{array}{r}
\text{Sarah} \\
+\ Oodgedye \\
+\ Udgedye \\
-\ 5 \\
\hline
0
\end{array}
$$

"Only sensational, Ud. You could sell tickets. Now it's Pact. Mary, dear, did you practice the medieval French?"

"I did my best, Regina, but it's a bitch."

"I offered to trade with you, Mary. Mine for yours. Even. Why didn't you swap?"

"What, Yenta? Hebrew for French? Some even trade! No, I took from some history experts."

"Aye! There is a *history* in all men's lives. Shakespeare. *Henry IV*. And what, pray, did the savants say?"

"They were kind of vague, Sarah. Nobody's sure how they talked way back then."

"How long ago was medieval, Mary? Like the time of King Charles the Second?"

"I'm not sure, Nellie. Maybe more like Napoleon or Joan of Arc. I always get them mixed up."

"How could you possibly?"

"They were both generals."

"Hmmm. Makes sense. At least to her."

"So if I sound funny-ha-ha and funny-peculiar, Regina, remember it's not my fault."

"We'll remember, Mary. Go."

Mary Mixup read the Pact.

```
          Sarah
        + Oodgedye
        + Udgedye
        + Mary Mixup
          − 4
        ─────────────
              0
```

"Marvy! Simply marvy, Mary. Joan of Arc couldn't have done better."

"Or Napoleon."

"Or even the general that heads the Glacial Army."

"He's tough to top."

"Why?"

"Because he's a she."

"Ladies! Ladies! We must be serious or we'll never raise the devil. You're next, Nellie, with Rituel."

Nell Gwyn read the Rituel.

```
          Sarah
        + Oodgedye
        + Udgedye
        + Mary Mixup
        + Nell Gwyn
          − 3
        ─────────────
              0
```

"Wonderful, darling! You rattled those arcane names off like a dance program."

"I suppose that makes me the Belle of Hell."

"Yes, I can see Satan asking for the next dance."

"Or yance, Priss."

"Really, Nell! We don't use five-letter words."

"But we think them, Priss."

"*You* think them, Nellie."

"No, love, I *do* them."

"Please, ladies, don't let's bicker. It's my turn now. I just adore Vision."

Regina rehearsed Vision.

                    Sarah
                + *Oodgedye*
                + *Udgedye*
                + Mary Mixup
                + Nell Gwyn
                + Regina
                − 2
                _____
                    0

"Applause, Regina! Applause! Applause!"

"Thank you. Thank you all. Time out for my sighs. Whoever had that vision was—"

"Aye, a W*I*T*C*H!"

"And one of the elephant's favorites, Sarah."

"I was going to say that she was a previous incarnation of me. Nellie. And now, last of all, our two Cabalists. One at a time, please. Priss?"

Miss Priss recited the first Cabala.

                    Sarah
                + *Oodgedye*
                + *Udgedye*
                + Mary Mixup
                + Nell Gwyn
                + Regina
                + Miss Priss
                − 1
                _____
                    0

"Fagin! Positively Fagin, Priss."

"Fagin? Who he, Regina?"

"The Merchant of Venice. I thought everybody knew."

"I didn't. Is that good or bad, being this Venice-type?"

"The highest praise, dear. I only hope our second Cabalist can do as well. She has the toughest assignment of us all."

"And don't I know it. Listen, I want a trade."

"Here we go again."

"What do you want to trade, Yenta?"

"Well, I've got the Hebrew down cold."

"How'd you do that?"

"I'm married to a rabbi."

"No! A Hebrew Jew rabbi? How voluptuous!"

"And she taught me. But I had a look at my face in the mirror while she was coaching . . . Ughsville! So I don't dare do it twice in a row. My face might stick that way."

"Maybe she'll like it better that way."

"Oh shut up, Nellie. I'm offering a trade. You trust me to get it right when we do the whole number together, and I'll hold the Hand of Glory."

"But we're going to spike it on a candlestick."

"I'll hold it instead. It'll be more sincere."

"You can't, Yenta. You'll be sick."

"I'd rather be sick than ugly. I'll hold it. Is it a deal, Regina?"

"But that thing is so hideous, dear. . . . Well, all right. It's a deal. Now, ladies, we've got the spells letter-perfect but we mustn't be careless. It'd be maddening if one niggling slip ruined everything."

"Are the fiends so fussy, Regina?"

"All my wicked books say so. It's a sign of sincerity to Satan. Now, are we ready?"

"Is it for real this time?"

"It is, with lights and props. Pi-face, light the Hand of Glory and give it to Miz Yenta. Light the incense and all the other horrid smells. All of us together around the pentacle. We chant in symphonic form. Take your tempo and entrance cues from me."

They formed a circle around the pentacle drawn on the floor, with the stately, gracious Regina sitting like a baroque jewel at the head of a ring; Nell Gwyn, all red hair, milky skin, opulent *poitrine;* Yenta Calienta, tall, dark, handsome, butch; Sarah Heartburn, piercing blue eyes under heavy brows set in a mobile face; the twins, *Oodgedye* and *Udgedye,* looking like a pair of succulent Greek slaves; Mary Mixup, wearing her fair hair like a helmet that needs adjustment; Miss Priss, who might have modeled for Tenniel's Alice in *Through the Looking Glass*.

"Now, ladies," Regina urged in her sweet, flowing voice, "you are no longer ladies. You are wicked witches. Really mean it when you chant. Want the Devil to appear. Yearn for him. Love him. Beg him . . . Now!"

* * *

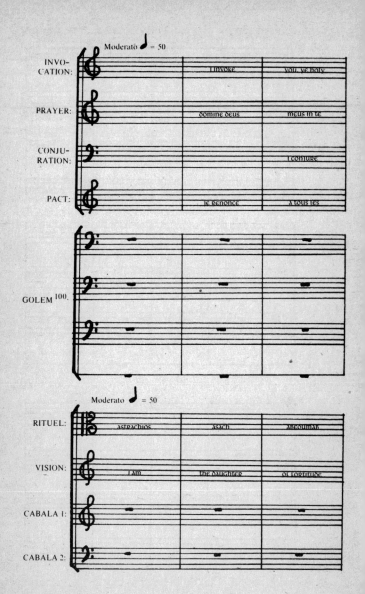

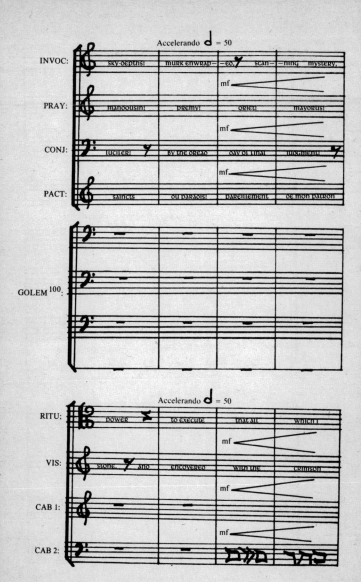

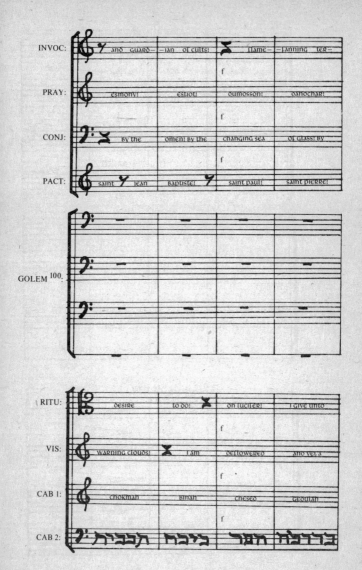

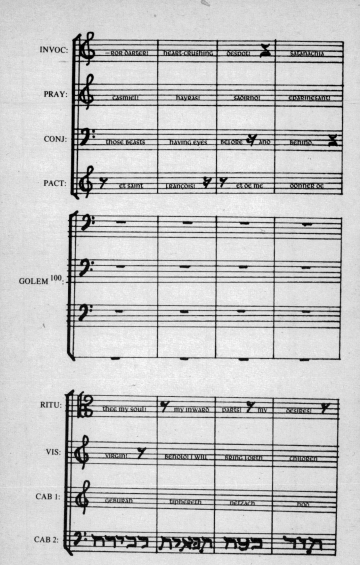

2

Adida Ind'dni was Subadar of the poisonous Guff, a
police precinct incorporating the territory of the old
Greater New York in the Northeast Corridor. Subadar
is a distinguished rank in the Indian military which had
been enlisted in most of the world's police forces by
the year of Our Lord 2175. Particular qualities of high-
caste Hindus—subtlety, sophistication, deep cultural
resources, and profound emotional reserves—ideally
suited them to the trying investigation of the psycho-
pathic and psychedelic crime that was a way of life in
the Guff.

Subadar is a title which can mean Viceroy, Governor, Captain, Chief, take your pick. Ind'dni was var-
iously addressed as Subadar, Captain, Chief, or
Mister. He responded to any and all salutations because he was too exalted in caste and rank to stand on
dignity and status. However, he did recoil from one
label which the twenty-second-century media had
pinned on him: "The Murder Mavin of the Guff." No
one ever dared address him as "Mavin Ind'dni."

The Subadar thought he had seen every fatal outrage
perpetrated and even created (for new sins were constantly being originated) in the heart of the Northeast
Corridor, nicknamed "the Guff" by its brawling in-

mates, but this horror was unique, and nauseated his sensitive Hindu soul.

She thrashed in the garbage and trash. She was bound, wrists and legs, with some sort of oozing rope. She was still alive and screaming. Ind'dni wished she would die quickly, for she was covered with a swarm of carpet beetles. These insects are used in natural-history museums to eat the last particles of raw flesh off skeletons preparatory to mounting them.

The beetles were busily, hungrily, single-mindedly devouring the flesh of the living woman. Bone showed already. Her eyes, nose, ears, lips, and tongue were gone, and she screamed. The beetles welcomed the blood that gouted from the gaps in her face with each cry of agony. Subadar Ind'dni shuddered and did the compassionate thing which would most assuredly imperil his distinguished position in the Guff, if reported. He seized a laser from the holster of one of the uniformed *polizei* and drilled a neat hole through the woman's skull.

There were grunts of relief from his homicide squad, and the Subadar knew that his mercy would not be reported, but an assistant muttered, "Evidence, sir?"

"Evidence verbal?" Ind'dni asked in his lilting *chi-chi* accent. "How accomplished? She could not speak, surely?"

"No, sir. But written?"

"Ah yes, to be sure. Written. But with what? You see her hands?"

"There aren't any left, sir."

"Just so. And the ears? Could she have heard questions? Assuredly not. No. Here we have only evidence factual, and—" Subadar Ind'dni broke off in astonishment. He was unaccustomed to astonishment, and he stared. His squad stared. In one instant, the beetles had disappeared. In that same instant, the binding strands disappeared. There was nothing left but one piece of evidence factual, the gnawed body of the dead woman.

"And how," wondered Ind'dni, "is this to be reported to Legal? The insects and the pinions were on her. Yes?"

"Yes, sir."

"We saw them disappear. Yes?"

"Yes, sir."

"We have all seen identical?"

"Yes, sir."

Ind'dni gazed around at his squad. All were obviously sincere and convinced in their reports. He sighed. "Then we have all seen and unseen the cause of this most cruel death?"

"Yes, sir."

"Just so. Do we believe what we have seen and unseen?"

"It isn't easy, sir."

"Easy? No. Impossible. Impossible to report to Legal. Perhaps best would be to report ourselves to lunacy."

Subadar Ind'dni sniffed curiously. His nostrils twitched. He was familiar with the hundreds of fetors that polluted the Guff, but this stench was new. It was unique. He was astonished again.

* * *

"Where's Satan?"

"Not here."

"Anybody see anything stirring in the pentacle?"

"Not a sign."

"Anybody feel anything? How about you, Sarah? Footsies from the Devil?"

"Not even a tickle, Regina. Alas. *Alas!* ALAS!"

"Drat! What a letdown."

"Maybe he wasn't home."

"Somebody should have been there to answer."

"Maybe he's unlisted."

"That shouldn't make any difference; it was person-to-person. Well, don't let's give up. We'll try again next week. All right?"

* * *

The hysterical calls to the Guff precinct complex were just so much gibberish. But when Subadar Ind'dni arrived with his squad, he understood why and was appalled.

The man was circling a pillar stub of the decayed opera-house portico; crawling, falling, rising, stumbling, crying piteously, shrieking, calling on Christ and cursing his gods. There was a gash in his belly that oozed blood and extruded intestine. One end of his gut had been fastened to the pillar, and as he circled and circled it was torn out of him, inch by inch, to garland the column with a bloody, grey hawser. He was driven to eviscerate himself by—

"What?" Ind'dni burst out. "By what, please? What? Never have I— Never. You see? We see?"

They saw a hulking gun-metal executioner that glittered and gleamed; that had shape and yet no shape. It was amoebic, amorphic, protean-flowing as it extruded legs, feet, pads, and hands; a dozen hands, a score of hands, a multitude of hands. Some glowed hot; so white-hot that their odor mingled with the stench of the victim's burning back as the sear of their roasting and prodding drove him around the pillar, pulling his gut out until he tore the Guff with his last screaming agony and shriveled into death. Then the hulk disappeared, leaving only its unique odor to pollute the Subadar's nostrils.

"Yes, I know it now," he thought. He was incapable of speech through his retching. "I recognize it. It is the *bouquet de malades,* the aroma of the mad." At last he managed to speak to his aides. "You saw? We saw? All?"

They could barely nod.

"And what was that we saw?"

They shook their heads.

"It was a man? An animal? A creature? Alive?"

They shrugged helplessly.

"Had it a face? Features? I saw none."

"Neither did we, Subadar."

"But it had feet. Many. They came and went like the thing itself. And hands. How many hands saw you?"

"Ten, sir."

"No, fifty, sir."

"More than that, sir. A hundred, at least."

"To be agreed. A hundred-hander, and some hands white-hot. You saw?"

"Yes, Subadar, but . . ."

"Ah. You say, 'Yes, but . . .' and then you cannot continue. Yes. But. But how can flesh glow white-hot, eh? And yet we saw. Flesh cannot glow like metal. But. We saw the hundred hands torture and kill. We saw the creature disappear, and living things cannot disappear. But it was alive and it did. But. But. But. How explain the 'But' to Legal? How explain to ourselves?"

* * *

"Well, we've failed again. Damn it, ladies, it's not working."

"Maybe that's our trouble, Regina. We're not damned . . . enough."

"Are we sure we got the chants right?"

"Letter-perfect."

"Maybe they're the wrong spells."

"I got them out of my wicked books, word for word."

"What about that Hand of Glory I've been holding? Genuine? Was the candle made from the fat of a virgin?"

"My Droney's word for it, Yenta. And the hand that holds it is truly the hand of an executed felon. My Droney has heavy clout at the morgue."

"How does he do it, Nell?"

"Bribes, Sarah."

"B*R*I*B*E*S? For what?"

"I thought everybody knew. My Droney's a dedicated necrophiliac, bless him."

24

"Ladies, no more chitchat, please. I think that's the real problem; we're not serious enough. We'll have to try again, and this time make it *sincere*."

* * *

They were stretched out in a neat row, ten of them lying supine in the rusting, rotting car dump; boy-girl-boy-girl, almost like a love-gig except that they weren't swinging on each other. They were dead.

"Most recent Lethal," Subadar Ind'dni observed, fighting for composure. "They still bleed, you perceive?" He sniffed and his delicate features twisted in disgust. He recognized the sinister *bouquet de malades*. "Yes. It is to be sure. Our Hundred-Hander again. Only such a monstrous thing could have contrived this."

The contrivance was simple and brutal. The genitals had been torn off each boy, living and conscious as the frozen contortions of the faces revealed, and thrust into the mouth of a girl. A breast had been torn off each girl and thrust into the mouth of a boy. Subadar Ind'dni took a deep breath and shook his head.

"To confess an admission," he told his staff, "I think I have lived in the Guff too long. When first I came to the Corridor, it was so much like my dearly remembered Bombay. I was so happy and at home. But there has been change and change and change. You agree, gentlemen?"

"Yes, sir. The Corridor *has* changed in our time."

"To be sure there must always be change and we must always, as civilizèds, adapt; but adapt to what? This? And the other Lethals of the Hundred-Hander? What is this hundred-handed monster that stinks of madness? Whose Lethals stink of madness? Is it of animal? Yes and no. Is it of vegetable? Yes and no. Is it of mineral? Yes and no. Is it of anything we have ever encountered before?"

"The answer is no, Subadar."

"To be sure. Is it motivated by any purpose we have ever discovered before?"

"No, Subadar."

"Is there anything on earth like this thing of hands and stench and madness and cruelty?"

"No, sir."

"Could it be alien from outer space, as in entertainment drama?"

"No, Subadar. Our communications section knows there's no life of any sort within light-years of our system."

"They know, or believe?"

"They know, sir. The five-hundred-meter radio telescope has been beaming out to the entire galaxy for two centuries . . . a human figure, binary numbers, atomic numbers, DNA structure, a diagram of our solar system . . . and no response. We're alone in our segment of the Milky Way galaxy."

"Most interesting. Then it is not alien from our galaxy, so it is alien of our own solar. It is living and impossible. It is incomprehensible fact. Inconceivable. Unknowable. Inexplicable. Yet it is fact. It is a new Guff madness."

"Yes, Subadar."

"Is it then required of us to master this new madness?"

"We must, sir. We're required by our duty."

"Ah yes. Our moral and legal obligation, but how to deal with this? Do we respond to each new madness of the Guff by going newly mad ourselves? Must we perform this adaptment to meet our responsibilities, to conform and be thought normally sane in a world that is of a raving madness?"

"We have to conform, Subadar . . . all of us."

"Then must we cling to our civilized values in secret and become Closet Sanes? What shall happen to us? What is happening to the Guff and the Corridor? I beg of you, gentlemen, tell me if you can. . . . What *is* the Northeast Corridor today?"

3

By now, of course, the Northeast Corridor was the Northeast slum, stretching from Canada to the Carolinas and as far west as Pittsburgh. It was a lunacy of violence inhabited by a swarming population with no visible means of support and no fixed residence. It was so vast and chaotic that demographers and the social services had given up all hope. Only the police continued the struggle.

It was a monstrous raree show that everybody denounced and adored. Living in the Corridor, and particularly in the Guff of the Corridor, was like being desperately in lust with a freaked-out Hottentot Venus. You hated it but you couldn't kick it.

Even the privileged class, like Queen Regina and her seven bee-ladies, who could afford to live protected lives in luxury Oases and, indeed, could escape to anywhere they damn pleased, never dreamed of leaving the Guff. The jungle magicked you. It was alive, by God! Its dementia churned up exciting new vices, sins, crimes, outrages. You never knew when you might be suddenly dead, but you always knew you were superbly alive.

There were hundreds of daily survival crises in the

27

Corridor. Cold was a major discomfort. Everybody was chilled and winter seemed to be stretching out into half the year. A popular revival movement preached that another Glacial Epoch was on the way, announcing the Second Coming. The mystic (?) year 2222 was to be the final freeze when all sinners would be called to judgment. The Scriabin Finkel stable of musicians had composed the Glacial Army's anthem: "Where You Beez Come God's Big Freeze?"

Even more exasperating than the lack of heat was the lack of fresh water. Most of the natural potable water had long since been impounded by Ibet (Industry Building a Better Tomorrow) so there was very little left for the suffering consumer of today. Rainwater tanks on roofs, of course, frequently siphoned off by thieving "HOjacks." Recycling and purifying. A black market. And that was about all, which meant that very few could bathe or launder properly, so the jungle stank. You could smell the Northeast's bouquet from ten miles out at sea.

Not to believe that everybody minded stinking as they skipped merrily over the rot in the streets, but a lot did, and their only recourse was perfumery. There were a hundred competing companies manufacturing perfume products, but the leader, far-and away, was the Corrugated Can Company which had had the good sense to diversify when the great perfume explosion burst.

CCC had the grace to admit, privately, that it had been neck-and-neck with their competition until Blaise Shima joined them. Then it turned into a no-contest. Blaise Shima. Origins: French, Japanese, Irish. Family: None. Education: B.Sc. Princeton, M.Sc. M.I.T., Ph.D. Dhow Chemical. (Dhow had secretly tipped CCC that Shima was a winner, and unfair-practice suits brought by the competition were still pending before the Business Ethics Review Board.) Blaise Shima, thirty-one, unmarried, straight, genius.

His sense of scent was his genius and at CCC he

28

was privately referred to as "The Nose." He knew everything about perfumery and its chemistry: the animal products—ambergris, castor, civet, musk; the essential oils distilled from plants and flowers; the balsams extruded by wounded trees and shrubs—myrrh, benzoin, storax, Peru, Talu; the synthetics derived from the combination of natural scents with the esters of fatty acids.

Shima had created all of CCC's premium sellers; "Vulva," "Assuage," "Oxter," (A much more attractive brand name than "Armpitto," which Kornbluth in Sales had suggested.) "Prep-F," and "Tongue War." He was treasured by CCC, paid a salary enormous enough to enable him to live in a super-luxury Oasis that was comfortably warmed. Best of all, CCC had the clout to win him a generous supply of fresh water, h. & c. No girl in the Guff could resist Shima's invitation to come up and enjoy a hot shower.

But Blaise Shima paid a high price for these comforts. He could never use scented soaps, shave creams, pomades, perfumes, depilatories. He could never eat seasoned foods or drink anything but glass-distilled water. All this, you understand, to keep The Nose undefiled by contamination so that he could smell around in his pure and sterile laboratory and create new masterpieces. He was presently composing a promising new product (working title, "Dil-d'Eau") but he'd been on it for two months without any firm results and CCC Sales was alarmed by the delay. There was a meeting of the board of directors.

"What the hell's the matter with him anyway?"

"Has he lost his touch?"

"Not a chance."

"After all, he *has* slowed down before. Remember that girl from Ipanema? She wiped him out. What was her name?"

"Ildefonsa Lafferty."

"She was a killer, from all reports, but Ildefonsa didn't hold him up this long. Maybe he needs a rest."

29

"Why, he had two weeks' holiday last quarter."

"What did he do?"

"Spent a week eating and drinking up a storm, he told me. He's got feisty appetites."

"Could that be it? Hangover?"

"No. He said he spent the second week purging himself before he came back to work. Sincere."

The chairman of the board, massive, magisterial, his skin resembling a crocodile's, broke in. "Is he having trouble here at CCC? Difficulties with middle management, perhaps?"

"Impossible, Mr. Chairman. They wouldn't dare annoy him."

"Is he sulking for a raise? Give it to him."

"He says he can't spend the money he makes now."

"Wait. Has our competition got to him?"

"They approach him all the time, sir. He just laughs them off. He's happy here."

The chairman considered. "Then it might be something personal."

"Agreed, sir."

"The usual woman trouble?"

"My God! We should have such trouble! In his private life, The Nose turns into The Stud."

"Family?"

"He's an orphan, Mr. Chairman."

"Ambition? Incentive? Should we make him an officer of CCC? I believe we have a vice-presidency open."

"I offered that to him the first of the year, sir, and he laughed at it. He just wants to play around with his chemicals."

"Then why isn't he playing?"

"What the hell's the matter with him, anyway."

"Which is how you started this meeting."

"I did not."

"You did."

"Not."

30

The chairman broke in again, his heavy voice sounding like a controlled roar, "Gentlemen! Gentlemen! Please! It would appear that Dr. Shima has personal problems which are stifling and/or blocking his superb genius. We must solve them for him. Is it urgent?"

"It is, Mr. Chairman. Sales has already booked over a million in advance orders for 'Dil-d'Eau.' It will be a disaster for our future credibility if we don't fill them, and I hate to think what it will do to Shima's reputation."

"I see. Suggestions?"

"Psychiatry?"

"That won't work without voluntary cooperation. I doubt whether he'd cooperate. He's a stubborn gook."

"Senator!" the chairman chided. "I beg you. Such expressions must not be used with reference to one of our most valuable assets."

"Mr. Chairman, you said our problem is to solve his problem."

"I did, governor."

"Then shouldn't we find out what it is first?"

"Your point is well taken, governor. Suggestions?"

"I think the first step might be to maintain a twenty-four-hour covert surveillance; all of the gook's—*Excuse* me! All of the good doctor's activities, associates, contacts, and so forth."

"Very good, senator. By CCC Security?"

"I would suggest not, sir. There are bound to be internal leaks and finding out would only antagonize the good gook—I mean *doctor!*"

"Outside surveillance, then?"

"Yes, sir."

"Suggestions?"

"We've used Skip-Trace Associates in the past, sir. They've always done an honest and efficient job."

The chairman considered, then arose and lumbered

31

out with the gait of a lazy crocodile. En route, he called over his shoulder, "Very good. Agreed. Meeting adjourned."

* * *

"Ladies, this is a dreary bore." The Queen Bee flowed with gracious exasperation. "Learning all those spooky spells and burning all those smelly smells, and absolutely nothing happens. No Lucifer. Not even an assistant demon. I vote for a change."

"Couldn't agree more, Regina," *Oodgedye* said. "Let's try something else, but no more Latin."

"And no more Hebrew. My face still feels backwards."

"Ladies, your cruise director speaking."

"We tremble with suspense, Regina."

"I'm more like trembling from the cold." Nell Gwyn's milky skin showed goose bumps. "I'm congealed, Regina."

"Pi-girl! More peat on the grate. Quick now. And put the kettle on the hob. We'll have coffee."

"Only recycled bathwater left, Miz Regina."

"It'll do. Ladies, my game-plan. What would you all say to an old-fashioned quilting bee?"

"A *what* bee?"

"A quilting bee. Women persons used to hold them ages ago. They got together every so often, just like us, and sewed patchwork quilts."

Sarah Heartburn was astonished. "You mean those BEAUTIFUL things were actually all !!!handmade!!! by H*A*N*D? I always thought museums produced them by spontaneous combustion."

"I always thought the word was 'spontooneous.' "

"Oh hush, Mary," Regina laughed. "Yes, they were sewn by hand and we can make one, if you like."

"I like, Regina." Yenta Calienta looked shrewd. "But which of us gets it when we're finished?"

"None of us. We'll sell it to a museum and buy gallons of lovely scent for all of us."

"Heaven! Count me in, brrr!" Nell Gwyn shivered. "Anybody else in favor? Hands, please. Not you, Pi, you don't get to vote. One, two, three, four . . . Six out of eight. *Oodgedye* and *Udgedye* dissenting, as usual."

"We're not dissenting. We're recusing."

"What does that mean? Is it dirty?"

"Another time, Priss. So what now, **Regina**?"

"The problem is cloth patches, Nell. Colorful ones, and real cloth; nothing recycled."

"No problem, Regina. My Droney has a fantastic collection of antique silk ties. There are lots of dupes he'll never miss. I'll pinch them."

"Beautiful, Nell. There's a fascinating design in one of my wicked books, and we'll start next session. Pi! The coffee! I must say, a quilting bee will be a relief from trying to get in touch with silly old Satan."

* * *

Skip-Trace Associates, Inc., was furious. It was the first time the firm had failed for a valued client, and somehow they felt they had been deceived. After two weeks the general manager threw the case back into CCC's lap, asking for nothing more than expenses.

"Why in hell didn't you tell us we were assigned to a pro, Mr. Chairman, sir? Our tracers aren't trained for that. We only handle deadbeats."

"Just a moment, please. What do you mean by 'pro'?"

"A professional rip."

"A what?"

"A ripjack. Gorill. Gimp. Crook. Geek. Goon."

"Our Dr. Shima a crook? Preposterous!"

"Look, Mr. Chairman, sir, I'll frame it for you and you draw your own conclusions. Yes?"

"By all means."

"It's detailed in this report anyway. We put a double-trace—that's two tails, shadows, ops—on Shima every day outside your shop. You didn't need us inside. When he left, they followed him. He always went straight home. No meetings, outside of girls. No contacts, outside of girls. No nothing. Yes?"

"Go on."

"We staked his Oasis in double shifts. It's got prime protection, so that was easy. He had dinner sent in every night from the Organic Nursery, which is a legit place on a pure-food-nothing-added gig. Our ops checked the delivery boys. Legit. They checked the meals—sometimes for one, mostly for two. Legit. No tincts, no chromes, no mords, no tinges, no nothing."

"Excuse me. I don't understand what you're referring to."

"That's all right, sir. It's street language; Guff talk for the squeams—that's drugs—they're tripping on these days."

"Thank you."

"Our ops tailed the girls who left his penthouse and checked them. All clean. So far all clean. Yes?"

"And?"

"Now here's the crunch. Couple of nights a week he leaves his place and goes out into the Guff. He leaves around midnight and doesn't come back until four, more or less, give or take half an hour."

"Where does he go?"

"Ah! That's the unch in the crunch. We don't know. We don't know because he shakes his tails like the pro that he is. He weaves through the Guff like a whore or a faggot cruising for trade, and he always shakes our ops. I'm not putting them down. They're good, but he's better. He's smart, shifty, quick, a real pro, and he's too much for Skip to handle."

"Then you have no idea of what he does or who he meets between midnight and four these several nights a week?"

"No, sir. We've got nothing, and you've got a problem. Not ours anymore. Sorry to let you down. Expenses is all we ask."

"Thank you. Now, contrary to the popular conception, corporations are not altogether callous. CCC understands that negatives are also results. In fact, it was Dr. Shima himself who taught us that. You have given us results, and I'm satisfied. You'll receive your expenses and the agreed fee as well.''

"Mr. Chairman, sir, I can't—"

"No, no. Don't feel that you haven't earned it. You've narrowed it down to those missing four hours. Now, as you say, they're our problem. I'm afraid we'll have to call in a rather strange specialist; but then, Dr. Shima has also taught us that strange problems require strange solutions.''

4

CCC summoned Salem Burne, the professional Warlock, which is to say, witchmaster. Mr. Burne always insisted that he was neither a necromancer nor a psychiatrist; he was a combination of both and called himself a psychomancer. He made the most penetrating analyses of disturbed people through his remarkable perception of somatic language and his acute interpretation of that silent tongue. The witchcraft he pretended to practice was merely a device to awe and disarm his patients.

Mr. Burne entered Blaise Shima's immaculate laboratory with a winning smile. Dr. Shima let out a howl of anguish.

"I told you to sterilize before you came!"

"But I did, doctor. Faithfully."

"You did not. You reek of anise, ylang-ylang, and methyl anthranilate. You've polluted my day. Why?"

"But Dr. Shima, I assure you that I—" Suddenly Mr. Burne stopped. "Oh. My. God," he groaned. "You're right. Unclean! Unclean! I used my wife's towel this morning."

Shima laughed and turned the ventilators up to full exhaust. "I understand. A natural mistake and no hard feelings, but let's get your wife out of here. I've got an office a safe mile down the hall. We can talk there.''

They sat down in the office and inspected each other. Shima saw a careful, controlled man approaching fifty, slender and smooth-skinned, moving and speaking with guarded polish, and yet always with light humor.

Mr. Burne saw a pleasant, youngish man, compact and muscular, with the balance of a middleweight boxer or, more likely, a karate champion. Cropped black hair, small expressive ears, high cheekbones, slitty eyes that would need careful watching, and a generous mouth and graceful hands that would be dead giveaways.

"Now, Mr. Burne, how can I help you? Mills Copeland, our chairman, said he'd be most obliged for the favor and I'm delighted to oblige him," Shima said while his hands asked, "Why in hell have you come pestering me, you damned quack?"

"Dr. Shima, I'm a colleague, in a sense. As I told you, I'm a psychomancer, a necromancer of psychiatry, so to speak. One crucial part of my diagnostic technique is the ceremonial burning of incense, but the scents are all rather conventional. I was hoping that your expertise might suggest something unusual for the ritual, which quite honestly is merely window-dressing.''

Shima was charmed by Burne's frankness. "I see. Interesting. You've been using stacte, onycha, galbanum . . . that sort of thing?''

"If that's their names. I'm no chemist. But they're all quite conventional, and my patients become unimpressed after too many exposures.''

"Most interesting. Yes. I could, of course, make a few suggestions for something different, even unusual, such as—'' Here Shima broke off abruptly and stared into space.

After a long pause, the psychomancer asked, "Is anything wrong, Dr. Shima?''

"Look here," Shima burst out. "You're on the wrong track."

"Am I? How?"

"It's the *burning* of incense that's conventional, and trying different odors won't help. Why not experiment with an entirely novel approach?"

"And what might that be?"

"The Odophone principle."

"Odophone?"

"It's a bastard term from Greek and Latin roots. (I wish I could get rid of my education.) There's a scale that exists among scents, similar to the scale in music. Sharp smells correspond to high notes, and heavy smells to low notes. For instance, ambergris is in the treble while violet is in the bass. I could draw up a scent scale for you, running a couple of octaves, and then it would be up to you to compose the ritual music and figure out how to play it."

"Dr. Shima! This is positively brilliant!"

"Yes, it is, isn't it?" Shima grinned. "But in all honesty I must point out that we're equal partners in brilliance. I could never have come up with the idea if you hadn't presented a most original and fascinating challenge."

They made contact on this generous note and talked shop enthusiastically. They lunched together (raw vegetables and distilled water for Shima) and told each other a little about themselves and their odd professions. They even made plans for the incense experiment in which Shima volunteered to participate despite the fact that he ridiculed diabolism and devil lore.

"And yet the irony lies in the fact that he is indeed devil-ridden," Salem Burne reported.

The chairman considered this, rather like a sleepy saurian, but could make nothing of it.

"Psychiatry and diabolism use different terms for the same phenomena, Mr. Copeland," Burne said, taking the sting out of his lecture with a light tone, "so perhaps I'd better translate. Those missing four hours are fugues."

The chairman was not enlightened. "Do you mean the musical expression, Mr. Burne?"

Burne shook his fair head. "No, Mr. Copeland. A fugue is also the psychiatric term used for an advanced form of somnambulism."

"What? Blaise Shima walks in his sleep?"

"It's more complicated than that, sir. The sleep-walker is a comparatively simple case. He is never in touch with his surroundings. You can speak to him, shout his name at him, even fire a cannon over his head, and he remains totally oblivious."

"Yes. And the fugue?"

"In the fugue, the subject *is* in touch with his surroundings, but always *within* his fugue, and *only* within the fugue. He can hear you and converse with you while he is inside his fugue. He has awareness of and memory for events that take place within the fugue, but nothing outside it. When he's outside his fugue, he has no knowledge of anything that took place within it."

"I'm beginning to understand. He's two different people?"

"Exactly, and neither knows nor remembers anything about the other."

"So when he's himself he can tell us nothing of what transpires during his lapses?"

"Nothing."

"Nor why he suffers them?"

"No."

"Can you?"

"I'm afraid not, sir. There's a limit to my powers. All I can say is that he's driven by something. A sorcerer might say that he's possessed by the Devil, but that's merely the cant of witchcraft. A physician might say that he's suffering from obsessions or drives, but that's merely the cant of psychiatry. The terminology is unimportant. The basic fact is that something is

39

compelling Dr. Shima to go out into the Guff, nights, to do—What? I don't know. All I do know is that this compulsion is the most probable cause of his creative block."

"Then what would you suggest that we do to solve the problem, Mr. Burne?"

"Since you've told me the constraints that make the situation delicate, Mr. Copeland, all I can suggest is that you pray."

"Pray? Good heavens!"

"To heaven, if you like, or to hell. Pray to anything you choose, sir. Perhaps best would be to pray for a miracle. Your problem is so unusual that you'll need a miracle to solve it."

"Surely you're not serious, Mr. Burne."

"I most certainly am, sir. Why? Don't you believe in miracles?"

"I'll believe in them when I see them."

"How odd, when we have a professional miracle-worker practicing in the Gulf today . . . Gretchen Nunn."

"Gretchen Nunn? Never heard of her."

"A most distinguished colleague, Mr. Copeland, although I've not yet had the honor of meeting her. I call myself a psychomancer because I work on the subliminal level. Ms. Nunn's skill is psychodynamics on the architechtonic level. She perceives designs and constructs in what seems to be utter confusion and devises miraculous solutions. She's a psytech. I suggest that you summon Gretchen Nunn and pray to her."

* * *

"Regina! What a heaven design for a quilt!"

"But what is it?"

"The Seal of Solomon."

"The seal of who? Whom? Whose?"

"King Solomon, Mary. You must remember his name."

40

"Oh, of course. He had a thing with Libra."

"That's Sheba, darling. We used to sing sexy songs about them at school."

"Not sexy Solomon this time, Nell; wizard Solomon from my wicked books. We put in enough time memorizing his wicked spells."

"In obscene languages."

"What does his seal do, Regina?"

"It's heavy magic that's supposed to like make Satan do a number."

"Oh Lord! Not that false alarm again!"

"Perish the thought. No, this is just something different from those kitsch designs you see in the museums; cutesy cottages and schools and barns and birds and flowers; that whole Pennsylvania Dutch schmeer. We'll repeat it in big squares. Pi, light all the lamps. Come, ladies, to work, to work."

* * *

But one does not summon Gretchen Nunn, not even if you're the chairman of CCC. You work your way up through the echelons of her staff until you're finally granted an audience. This involves much backing and forthing between your staff and hers, and ignites a good deal of exasperation, particularly in applicants who are pressed for time. Consequently, Mills Copeland was understandably provoked when at last he was ushered into Ms. Nunn's cluttered workshop.

Gretchen Nunn's business was working miracles; not miracles in the sense of the extraordinary, anomalous, or abnormal brought about by a superhuman agency, but rather in the sense of her extraordinary perception and manipulation of reality on the supraliminal level. She was a master of psychodynamics. In most situations she achieved the impossible begged by her clients, and her fees were so enormous that she was considering going public on the Big Board.

Quite naturally, the chairman had taken it for granted that this mysterious psytech would look like one of Macbeth's Witches of Endor, or Merlin in drag. He was flabbergasted to discover that Ms. Nunn was a Watusi princess with velvety black skin and aquiline features. She was in her late twenties, tall, slender, and ravishing in crimson. The chairman's irritation vanished. Ms. Nunn dazzled him with a smile, indicated a chair, sat in one opposite and said, "My fee is one hundred thousand. Can you afford it?" Her accent was a lilting Jamaican.

"I can, Miz Nunn. Agreed."

"Not yet. Is your difficulty worth it?"

"It is."

"Then we understand each other so far. I prefer to —Yes, Alex?"

The young secretary who had slipped into the workshop said, "Excuse me. LeClerque insists on knowing how you made the positive diagnosis of his wife's one-month pregnancy."

"LeClerque? The impotent one?"

"Yes, Miz."

Ms. Nunn clicked her tongue impatiently. "He knows I never give reasons; only results. I made that clear."

"Yes, Miz, but he *is* agitated. Naturally."

"Has he paid?"

"Check cleared this morning."

"All right, I'll make an exception in his case. Psychometry gave me the clues. Pregnancy behavior unmistakable. Strong emotional revaluations. I checked with ultralight. Her face showed the banded pregnancy mask under the skin, and she isn't using the pill. Tell LeClerque, but no sympathy, Alex. Always cool and professional."

"Yes, Miz. Thank you, Miz."

She turned to the chairman as the secretary backed out. "In case you're alarmed, LeClerque is a code name known only to the client and my staff, which can be trusted. I never reveal a client's true identity."

"I understand."

43

"And you heard me? I only give results."

"Agreed, Miz Nunn."

"Now your difficulty. I'm not committed yet. If that's understood, go ahead. Everything. Stream of consciousness and free association if necessary."

A half hour later, she illuminated the room with another dazzling smile. "Thank you. This one is really unique; a welcome change for me. It's a contract . . . if you haven't changed your mind."

"I haven't, Miz Nunn."

"Consider for a moment, sir. Perhaps telling me about it has sorted it out in your mind. Then you'll no longer need me. That happens sometimes."

"Not this time, Miz Nunn," Copeland said with massive conviction.

"You still believe you need me?"

"Definitely."

"Then it's a contract, Mr. Tinsmith."

"What? Tins—? Oh. Of course. Thank you, Miz Nunn. Would you like a deposit or payment in advance?"

"Not from CCC."

"Expenses? Shall we arrange that now?"

"No. My responsibility, Mr. Tinsmith."

"But what if you have to—That is, if you're required to—"

She laughed. "My responsibility. I never give reasons and never reveal methods. How can I charge for them? That's why my set fee is so high. Now don't forget, sir, I want the Skip-Trace and Burne reports."

A week later Gretchen Nunn took the unusual step of visiting the chairman in his office at CCC. "I'm calling on you, sir, to give you the opportunity of withdrawing from our contract. There will be no charge."

"Withdraw? Why?"

"Because I believe you're involved in something more serious than anticipated."

"But what?"

"You won't take my word for it?"

"How can I? I must know."

Ms. Nunn compressed her lips, then sighed. "Since this is an unusual case, I'll have to break my rule. Look at this, please."

She unrolled a large map of the Guff sector of the Corridor and flattened it on the chairman's conference table. There was a star in the center of the map. "Shima's Oasis," Ms. Nunn said. There was a wide circle scribed around the star. "The limit to which a man can walk from the Oasis in two hours," Ms. Nunn explained. "Two hours out, two hours back, four in all. This is a maximum plot allowing nothing for any events that might interrupt the walk."

"I understand."

Twisting trails straggled out from the star toward the boundary circle in all directions. "I got this from the Skip-Trace report. This is how their ops tailed your Dr. Shima."

"Most ingenious, but I see nothing serious about this, Miz Nunn."

"Look closely at the trails I've plotted, sir. What d'you see?"

"Why . . . Each ends in a red cross."

"And what happens to each trail before it reaches the cross?"

"Why nothing. Nothing at all except that they're rather corkscrewed. Wait . . . They start as dots coming from the star and then change to dashes."

"And that's what makes it serious."

"I don't understand, Miz Nunn."

"I'll explain, sir. Each cross represents the scene of a Lethal-One."

"What! Murder?"

"The dashes represent Homicide's backtracking of the actions and whereabouts of the murder victim just prior to death."

"Murder!"

"They could trace the victim's actions back just so far and no further. Those are the dashes. Skip-Trace

45

could tail Dr. Shima from his Oasis just so far and no further. Those are the dots. The trails join up. The dates match. What's your conclusion, sir?''

"It must be coincidence! It has to be!'' the chairman shouted. "This brilliant, charming young man, with everything in the world that anyone could wish for . . . Lethal crime? Murder? Impossible!''

"D'you want more factual data?''

"No I do not, madame. I want the truth. Proof positive without farfetched inferences from dots and dashes.''

"Very well, Mr. Tinsmith. You'll get your proof poz.''

5

So Gretchen Nunn began assembling proof poz. She
rented the professional beggar's pitch alongside the
Oasis entrance for a week. Shima seen twice a day but
no contact. She hired the Glacial Army Revival Band
and sang hymns with it before the Oasis. No success,
and the Army complained that her rendition of
"Where You Beez Come God's Big Freeze?" had cost
them a thirty percent drop in contributions.

She finally made the connection after she'd pro-
moted a messenger job with the Organic Nursery. The
first three dinners she delivered to the penthouse, she
came and went unnoticed. Shima was entertaining a
series of girls, all scrubbed and sparkling with gratitude and luxuriating in the welcome warmth. When
she made the next delivery he was alone, and he noticed her for the first time.

"Well, well, well," he smiled. "And how long has
this been going on?"

"Sir?"

"Since when has the Nursery been using girls for
delivery boys?"

"I am a delivery *person,* sir," Gretchen answered
with dignity. "I've been working for the Organic Nursery since the first of the month, sir."

"Strike that 'sir' bit, will you? I'm no dignitary."

"Thank you s— Doctor Shima."

"How the devil d'you know I've got a doctorate?"

She'd slipped. He was listed at the Oasis and the Nursery simply as, B. SHIMA—PENTHOUSE, and she should have remembered. The man was lightning-quick. As usual, she made the mistake work for her. "I know all about you, sir. Dr. Blaise Shima, Princeton, M.I.T., Dhow Chemical. Chief Scent Chemist at CCC. Publications: *Aromatic Hydrocarbons, Volatile Oils and Dye Chemis*—"

"Have a heart," he broke in. "You sound like *Who's Who*."

"That's where I read it, Dr. Shima."

"You looked me up in that dumb catalogue? Why, for God's sake?"

"You're the first famous person I've ever met."

"What gave you the lunatic idea that I'm famous, which I'm not?"

She gestured around. "I knew you had to be famous to live like this."

"Very flattering, but it's my decorator who's famous. So you can read, can you?"

"And write, sir."

"Unusual for the Guff. What's your name, love?"

"Gretchen, sir."

"Watch that 'sir,' Gretchen. What's your last name, love?"

"People in my class don't have last names, s— doctor. It doesn't seem fair."

"And a social philosopher, too. Most unusual. Will you be the delivery b— person tomorrow, Gretchen?"

"Tomorrow is my day off, doctor."

"Perfect. Bring dinner for two."

So the affair began, and Gretchen Nunn discovered, much to her astonishment, that she was enjoying it tremendously. This was not the first time she had ever used pleasure for business, but this was the first time that she herself had been genuinely pleasured. She made a mental note to examine the psychodynamics of her reaction at some future date.

Blaise was indeed a brilliant, charming young man; always entertaining, always considerate, always generous. With affection and gratitude for the novelty she was giving him he gave her (remember, he believed she came from the dregs of the Guff) one of his prized *bijoux*, the five-carat diamond he'd synthesized for his doctoral dissertation at Dhow. She responded with equal style; she wore the cabochon in her navel and promised that it was for his eyes only.

Quite as a matter of course he insisted that this Guff flower scrub up each time she visited, which was a bore. In her income bracket, she could afford more black-market water than CCC's generous allowance to their pet. However, one convenience was that she could quit her job at Organic and attend to other contracts while she was investigating the Shima problem.

She usually left his penthouse before midnight and always staked out across the road from his Oasis until two. She picked him up this night as he was leaving a half hour after her. She'd studied the Salem Burne report and knew what to expect. She overtook him quickly and spoke in an agitated voice, using the lowest Guff diction which is blurted without pause or punctuation, "Hey man mistuh mistuh man mistuh!"

He stopped and looked at her kindly, completely without recognition. He was almost unrecognizable himself. The bright, alert, playful Shima was gone. This was a glassy creature who moved and spoke with the phlegm of a tortoise.

"Yes, my dear?"

"If yuh gone this way man kin I come too man mistuh I scared out late mistuh."

"Certainly, my dear."

"Thanks mistuh I gone home yuh gone home man?"

"Not exactly."

"Where yuh gone to nothin' bad is yuh man I doan want no part a bad mistuh."

"Nothing bad, my dear. Not to worry."

"Then what yuh doin' man I like mean what huh?"

He smiled secretly. "I'm following something."

"Yuh follow somebody who?"

"No. Something."

"Like what kine something mistuh?"

"Inquisitive, aren't you. What's your name?"

"Gretch like for Gretchen how they Guff say you man?"

"Me?"

"Got a name mistuh?"

"Name? Of course. I—I'm—Yes, I'm Wish. You may call me Mr. Wish. That's my name." He hesitated for a moment and then said, "I must turn left here."

"Thas dig Mistuh Wish I left here too man."

She could see that under the glassy exterior all his senses were prickling, so she reduced her prattle to a low background. She stayed with him as he turned and twisted through streets, alleys and lanes, always assuring him that this was her way home, too. She doubted whether he was really aware of her until, at a rather sinister-looking refuse dump, he surprised her by giving her a fatherly pat and cautioning her to wait while he explored its safety. Mr. Wish disappeared and never reappeared.

"I replicated this experience with Dr. Shima seven times," Ms. Nunn reported to the CCC board. "They were all significant. Each time he revealed a little more to diagnosis without realizing it. Burne was right. It *is* a case of fugue, and a classic one."

"And the cause, Miz Nunn?"

"Pheromone trails."

"What? Pheromone? What's that, please?"

"I'd thought you gentlemen would be acquainted with the term, being in the chemistry business, among others."

"But we're not scientists, Miz Nunn."

"Quite. I see I'll have to explain. It'll take some time so I beg that you do not require me to describe the induction and deduction that led to my conclusion."

"Agreed."

"Thank you, Mr. Copeland. Now surely you've all heard of hormones, the internal secretions which excite other parts of the body into action. Pheromones are external secretions which excite other individuals into action. It's a mute chemical language."

"Could you be a little more explicit, Miz Nunn? This is rather difficult for us."

"Certainly. The best example of the pheromone language is the ant. Place a lump of sugar somewhere outside the nest. A forager will come across it, feed, and return to the nest. Within an hour the entire ant colony will be single-filing to and from the sugar, following the pheromone trail first laid down by the discoverer."

"Consciously?"

"Not known. It may be as deliberate as the bee-dance, which indicates direction and distance of food, or it may be quite unconscious. All we do know is that the pheromone is a compelling stimulant."

"Remarkable! And Dr. Shima?"

"Is compelled to follow human pheromone trails."

"What? You mean *we* leave them as well?"

"Indeed yes. It's accepted that women leave unconscious pheromone trails which excite and attract men."

"Amazing!"

"It's been established for some time. So now, perhaps, you can understand that your Dr. Shima goes into fugue and is forced to follow certain pheromone trails."

"Ah! An *outré* aspect of The Nose. It makes sense, Miz Nunn. It really does. What trails is he compelled to follow? Women?"

"No. The death wish."

"What!"

"The death wish."

"Miz Nunn!"

"Why the surprise, sir? Surely you're all aware of this aspect of the human psyche. Many people suffer from an unconscious but powerful urge to self-destruct. Some psychiatrists claim that we all do. Apparently this leaves a pheromone trail which Shima senses . . . I would guess only in certain cases . . . and is forced to follow."

"And then?"

"Apparently he grants the wish."

"Impossible!"

"Preposterous!"

"What's she saying?"

"That the gook grants the death wish. He kills the ones that want to die. Lethal-One."

"I do, gentlemen."

"Apparently! Apparently!" the chairman stormed. "Dr. Shima? Murder? Ridiculous! I demand proof positive of such a monstrous accusation."

"Very well, you'll get it, sir. There are one or two things I must wrap up with him before I close the contract, and in the course of that, I'm afraid he's in for a shock."

* * *

"This is cruel and unusual punishment to my hands," Mary Mixup complained. "Did they really have to push needles with their finners in ancient days?"

"Aye, they DID! But the hand of little employment hath the daintier sense. *Hamlet*. ACT V, sc. 1. Let's quit."

"I'm with you, Sarah. I'm fed up with this number."

"Me too, Yenta. Let's take a vote. All in favor of dropping the quilting bee? Hands, please. Not you, Pi. Six out of eight. Carried." Nellie Gwyn grinned. "*Oodgedye* and *Udgedye* recusing, as usual."

"We're not recusing. We're dissenting."

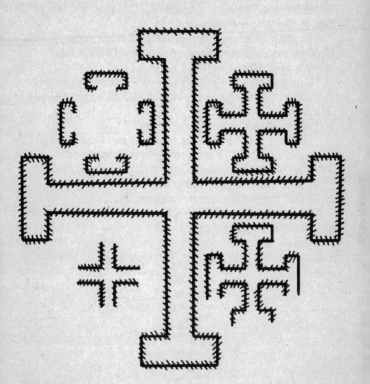

"So now what, Regina?" Priss asked.

"Oh dear. I'm out of entertainment ideas. Perhaps another call to Lucifer?"

"Why not?" Yenta grumbled. "Maybe we can get him to finish this dreary quilt."

"Regina. Ladies. Attention. Red-hot news. My Droney says we're calling up the Devil all wrong."

"We are? How, Nell?"

"Droney says we're in the twenty-second century. We have to drop the medieval schtik and communicate in a modern language."

"After all our memorizing! Why?"

"He says maybe Lucifer hears us but when he tries to return our call, he goes to the wrong century."

"That's an idea. Fiends can make mistakes, too."

"Sure. They're only human."

"What language does he suggest, Nell?"

"Computer binary. Droney programmed the whole bit for us. I've got it here. Look . . ."

$$
\begin{array}{c}
2,047 \\
1,799 \\
2,015 \\
1,501 \\
1,501 \\
1,025 \\
1,501 \\
1,501 \\
2,015 \\
1,799 \\
2,047
\end{array}
$$

"What in the name of—He has to be guffing."

"No, ladies, this is madly modern magic. The computer automatically translates the decimal into binary oneses and zeroses which form a sinister, evil, dirty rotten cross which no self-respecting demon can resist."

"What do you think, Regina?"

"It's worth a try, but I don't think we should just sit

around cold. Let's give it the full treatment. We'll put the kitchen computer in the pentacle and kneel around and really want it to happen. Pi-girl! Bring the lights and the smells and the computer.''

* * *

```
1 1 1 1 1 1 1 1 1 1 1
1 1 1 0 0 0 0 0 1 1 1
1 1 1 1 1 0 1 1 1 1 1
1 0 1 1 1 0 1 1 1 0 1
1 0 1 1 1 0 1 1 1 0 1
1 0 0 0 0 0 0 0 0 0 1
1 0 1 1 1 0 1 1 1 0 1
1 0 1 1 1 0 1 1 1 0 1
1 1 1 1 1 0 1 1 1 1 1
1 1 1 0 0 0 0 0 1 1 1
1 1 1 1 1 1 1 1 1 1 1
```

"My goodness! Will you look at that tape!"

"Better make that 'My badness,' Priss."

"But all I see is ones and zeros."

"Yes, that's the binary, Mary, but look at the design the zeros are making."

"Why! It's the wicked cross from the Seal of Solomon; the one we started to quilt."

"Right. My Droney's a genius."

"Will it really summon Satan?"

"If a computer can't, nothing can."

"Shush, ladies. We must be worshipful. No whispering, please."

"The computer can't hear us, Regina."

"But perhaps Lucifer is listening. Now be devout, you witches. Want! Yearn! Will!"

6

___

When Gretchen Nunn told the CCC board that she had
one or two things to wrap up with Blaise Shima before
she closed the contract, that was a half-truth from a
woman half in love. She knew she had to see him
again, but her motives were confused.

Q: To discover whether she really could love him
despite what she knew about him?

Q: To find out whether he really loved her or was
merely playing with a Guff flower?

Q: To tell him the truth about herself?

Q: To tell him the truth about himself?

Q: To close her contract with Mr. Tinsmith in cool,
professional style, and to hell with the personal relationships involved?

A: She didn't know. Certainly she didn't know that
while she was preparing a shock for Mr. Wish, she
was due for a bombshell herself, delivered quite casually by Shima.

"Were you born blind?" he murmured that night.

She sat bolt upright in bed. "What? What?"

"You heard me, Gretchen."

"Blind? Me blind? You must be mad. I've had
twenty-twenty all my life. Better."

"Ah-so. Then you didn't know. I suspected that might be it."

"You're not making sense, Blaise."

"Oh, you're blind all right," he said calmly. "Only you've never known because you're blessed with something far more extraordinary than sight; you have extrasensory perception of other people's senses. You see through other people's eyes. For all I know, you may be deaf and hear through their ears, and so on through all the senses. It's a fantastic faculty. Absolutely fascinating. We must explore it sometime."

"I never heard anything more absurd in all my life!" she said angrily.

"I can prove it if you insist, darling."

"Go ahead, Blaise. Prove it."

"Come into the lounge."

In the living room, he pointed to a vase. "What color is that, Gretchen?" "Pearl, of course." A carpet. "What color is that?" "Elephant-grey." "And that lamp?" "A sort of ice color with a black shade."

"Q.E.D.," Shima smiled. "It has been demonstrated."

"What's been demonstrated?"

"That you're seeing through my eyes."

"How can you say a ridiculous thing like that?"

"Because I'm color-blind. That's what gave me the clue in the first place."

"No!"

"Yes."

"Blaise, if you're guffing me I swear I'll—"

"This is no guff, love, it's a fact."

"No!"

"But yes." He took her in his arms to quiet her trembling. "It's a fact. The vase is green. The rug is amber and gold. The lamp is crimson with a burgundy shade. I can't see the colors, but the decorator told me and I remember."

She let out a little moan.

"Now why the terror, love? You're blind, yes, but

you're blessed with something far more miraculous than sight. You see through the eyes of the entire world. I envy you. I'd change places with you anytime."

"It can't be true!" she cried. "It's too horrible! Blind? A cripple? A freak? No!"

"It's true, darling, but don't think of yourself as a cripple."

"But when I'm alone I can see."

"Alone? When are you ever alone? When is anybody in the crowded Corridor ever alone?"

She tore herself away from him, snatched up her shift and ran out of the penthouse, sobbing hysterically. She ran back to her own Oasis nearly crazed with terror and despair. In her familiar apartment she recovered a little poise and resolved to put the disaster to the test. Either Shima was right and she was doomed, or else Shima was trying to destroy her. But why? Because he thought she was a Guff flower to be played with and tortured?

She dismissed her entire staff with curt orders to leave and spend the night elsewhere. She stood at the door and counted them out as they left, all bewildered and unhappy. She slammed the door and looked around. She could still see as well as ever.

"The lying son-of-a-bitch," she muttered and began pacing furiously. She raged through the apartment. Well at least she'd learned one lesson; interpersonal relationships always betray you. She'd made a fool of herself. But why in God's name did Blaise shaft her like this? Killing her outright would have been kinder. Was he trying to make her kill hersel—

She smashed into something and was thrown back. She recovered her balance and looked to see what she'd blundered against in her fury. It was a gilt harpsichord.

"But . . . But I don't own a harpsichord," she whispered in astonishment. "How did it—?"

She started forward to touch it and assure herself of

its reality. She smashed into the something again, reeled and clutched it. It was the back of a couch; her own tufted couch. She looked around in confusion. This was not one of her rooms. The gilt harpsichord? Vivid Brueghels hanging on the walls? Jacobean furniture? Linenfold paneled doors? Crewel drapes?

"But this is the Raxon apartment below me. I know it. I've visited. I must be seeing what they're seeing. I must—Oh my God! Was he telling the truth?"

She closed her eyes and looked. Through a veil she still saw the Raxon apartment. And dimmer and fading out of focus she saw a confusion of apartments, streets, peoples, actions, forms, colors. She had always seen this sort of montage, but had always thought it was the total visual recall which was a major asset in her extraordinary grasp on the psychodynamics of reality. Now she knew the truth.

She began to sob again. She felt her way around to the front of the couch and sat down, despairing. "My God! My God! My God! A freak! I'd rather be dead . . ."

When at last the convulsion had spent itself, she wiped her eyes courageously, determined to face her own freak reality and cope with it. She was no coward. But when she opened her eyes, she received another shock. She saw her own living room, the familiar remembered room, but now in tones of grey. And she saw Mr. Wish standing in the open door, smiling glassily at her.

"Blaise?" she whispered.

"The name is Wish, my dear. You may call me Mr. Wish."

"Blaise! For God's sake! Not me! You couldn't follow me. I left no death-wish trail for you."

"We've met before, my dear. I remember, but I'm afraid I've forgotten your name. More important matters on my mind, you understand. But now, suddenly, you've become very important to me."

"I'm Gretchen. Gretchen Nunn. And I have no

death wish." "Nice meeting you again, Gretchen," he said with crystal courtesy. He took two steps toward her. She jumped up and ran behind the couch.

"Blaise, listen to me. You are not Mr. Wish. There is no Mr. Wish. You're Dr. Blaise Shima, a famous scientist. *Aromatic Hydrocarbons* and . . . and . . . You're Chief Scent Chemist at CCC and you've created many popular perfumes . . ."

While his frozen smile remained fixed on her, Mr. Wish began drawing objects from his pockets; a rope knotted into a hangman's noose, a laser burner, a small pressure bulb labeled $(CN)_2$, a glittering scalpel, an antique 8 mm.-caliber palm-pistol. He arranged them neatly on the end table alongside the couch.

"Blaise," she pleaded. "I'm Gretchen. Your Gretchen from the Guff. We've been lovers for two months. You must remember. Try to remember. You told me about my eyes tonight. Being blind. You must remember that."

"Different people choose different ways of dying," he said pleasantly. "After all, it's their final choice, so they have every right to be particular. I try to provide every road. Here they are, my dear. Which would you prefer? Take your time. Don't be afraid. I'll help you kill yourself. I'll make it easy for you."

"For Jesussake, Blaise! You're suffering from blackout. Fugue. Split personality . . ."

"If it's the rope, we'll find a firm support for it, something that can hold . . . a hundred and twenty pounds, yes? That's my estimate. If you want to snap your neck, I'll fetch a chair and you can jump. If you'd like a slow strangle, I'll tie your wrists for you. I'll grant any wish."

"Blaise, you're inside a crazy creature driven by a pheromone, but I left no suicide trail. I couldn't!"

"If you prefer gas, here's cyanogen. Just press the button and take a breath. Some prefer to drink poison. We can bubble the gas into a glass of water and, Hey! Presto! Hydrocyanic acid that kills like a thunderbolt.

One sip and your wish is granted. Clever of me, eh? Two deaths in one package.''

"My God, Blaise, I've never wanted to die."

"Yes you do, my dear. Delighted to grant your wish. How about a nice warm bath and this?'' The scalpel flashed a cut through the air. "Your wrist, or the carotid in your neck. Just think, your last bath. You'll never have to worry about water again. And see? Two guns. Bullet or burn. Now really, you couldn't ask for anything more, could you? Mr. Wish is here to help.''

"No!"

"You called."

"No!"

"And I came to you."

She backed away from his hypnotic smile. Mr. Wish made no move. He stood quite still, and his assurance was terrifying. It was an inexorable statement. He knew she wanted to die. He knew she would not be able to resist one of the instruments of suicide. He knew that if he waited patiently, he would help and watch her die. He stood quite still, with the massive assurance of death itself.

"Christ!" she cried. She took a step, hesitated, then dashed past him to the door with a clear chance of escaping him, only to slam into two grinning goons standing shoulder to shoulder in the doorway. Suddenly she was aware of brilliant color in the room. They grabbed and held her while she squealed and struggled helplessly.

They addressed Mr. Wish over her head in the Guff Blurt, "Hi ole buddy boy buddy man."

"Blaise! Help me!"

Mr. Wish ignored her. "Oh. It's you again," he sniffed.

"Hey ole buddy boy buddy man got youself a real type bije this time huh buddy man."

"And upass loaded with goody goodies huh man we dig buddy."

"Make up for last three nowhere numbers you got our thanks buddy man Guff thanks buddy boy go home now man bye bye buddy."

"Why don't I ever get to watch one die?" Mr. Wish exclaimed petulantly. "They call me. I come. I bring everything and anything they could need. I do all the work, and you always send me away. It's not fair!" He seemed on the verge of tears.

"Now man no beef man we got to protect our good buddy bird dog who lead us to bije goodies."

"It's not fair!"

"And if anything bustass you man like take the rapsville you our setup ole buddy."

"I still say it's not fair."

"Home now buddy man rest of rip belong us so no fight buddy boy because we edge-up on you."

"We know who you but you don't know who us see man we blow whistle on you but you nowhere blow whistle on us."

"I know who I am," Mr. Wish said stiffly. "I am Mr. Wish, the donor of death, and I think I have the right to watch them kill themselves." He was now genuinely indignant.

"Sure man sure buddy boy sure next time belong you strictly you."

"That's what you always say."

"Asshole bond this time no guff this time now split buddy boy go home safe you."

"I don't like you, not one little bit," Mr. Wish said resentfully and headed for the door, ignoring the spasming Gretchen who was trying to scream through an iron hand over her mouth. The goons ripped her naked and let out a yell of delight when they saw the diamond in her navel. Mr. Wish turned at the door and saw the jewel, too.

"But . . . But that's mine," he said in a small bewildered voice. "That's only for my eyes. I— Gretchen promised she—" Abruptly the confusion vanished and Dr. Blaise Shima spoke in a voice accustomed to command. "Gretchen? Gretchen! What the hell are you doing here? What's this place? Who are these—Get your hands off her!"

Salem Burne's karate guess had been correct. Shima shot into action like a battering ram, but the goons were Guff-fighters of vicious experience, and it was a dangerous scene for Shima until the two suddenly exploded air and collapsed, one after the other. He stood, panting and shaking, and looked down at them. They were dead. He looked at Gretchen Nunn. She stood, nearly naked in her ripped shift, the silent laser burner in her hand.

He tried to speak. "I—"

"Thank you, Blaise. Hello, Blaise."

"Hello, Gret— Darl— I—" He tried to catch his breath. "I d-don't know where I'm at. I . . . I'm not used to this."

"Come sit down."

"They're dead, aren't they?"

"Burned through the back. Sit here with me."

"This is one hell of a time to relax."

"Sit!"

"Yes'm. I . . . Thank you. I . . . You know, I've never seen a Lethal before. It . . . It isn't as bad as I imagined."

"Yes it is. Turn so we can't see them. We have to be quick, Blaise. You've got to be protected."

"Protected? Am I in trouble?"

"Bad trouble. I'm going to give it to you fast. Can you listen?"

He nodded.

"Then just listen. No questions." She gave it to him fast, and his bewilderment gave way to shock and dismay. "Now you understand," she finished. "There can't be any connection between Mr. Wish and Dr. Shima."

"But . . . But there has to be a connection. If I killed any of—"

"No!" she broke in sharply. "I don't think so. I

63

really don't think so, Blaise. But I must admit that I really don't know for sure. I believe it was those two who did the Lethals; you were just the Judas-goat. God knows how they ever started following you. We'll never know that either, but the Guff is full of unknow-ables. Now get out of here and go home. I've got to call the precinct."

"Gretchen . . ."

"No. Go."

"Why this for me?"

"Because I love you, you dumb son-of-a-bitch, and it was one hell of a way to find out."

"But you'll be alone. Blind."

"Yes, we both have our crosses. You carry yours; I'll carry mine. Go. I'll have sight again as soon as Homicide arrives."

"I—"

"Blaise, if you don't get out of here, I swear I'll scream. Take that suicide junk with you. Leave me the burner; I'll need it for my story to Homicide. Right now I need a few minutes to write the story, so I beg you, go!"

"Tomorrow?"

"If you want to."

"I want to."

"Then tomorrow, if I can get us out of this bind."

"Someday," he said slowly, "someday I'll figure out how to thank you. Right now I'm feeling out-classed, and it's a new sensation. I— You're wasting your time on me. Be sure to safe the door after me."

He left, and his immediate grey sight dwindled away from her, but she was able to secure the door and call the precinct. Then she felt her way back to the tufted coach, sat quietly and composed herself, preparing her story. The background noises of the Oasis and the Guff were comforting. The kaleidoscope of extrasen-sory sight no longer frightened her; it had become in-teresting. Understanding is half the battle.

"Blaise is right," she thought. "I've never noticed

it before because we're rarely alone in the Guff. . . .
There are always enough eyes around for me to see
through. . . . But when I'm isolated in a room with
one person, then what? They can't see themselves, so
I couldn't see them. Why didn't I realize?"

She thought hard. Then: "Reflections, probably.
They must have seen themselves and given me flashes
. . . There are mirrors everywhere to multiply light in
this energy-starved age. And I think I must have been
soundtracking without realizing it . . . I know when
I've been in bed with Blaise it's been that and touch-
tracking . . . Fascinating, how we can conjure ourselves into rejecting reality . . .

"That consultation with Mills Copeland . . . Yes, I
saw him when staff was in the room, through their
eyes, but when we were alone together? Remember
hard, Gretchen! Hmmm. No, I didn't really see him
. . . Only flashes when he happened to see a reflection
of himself . . . He was mostly just a voice. . . . I
wasn't aware, I've never been aware, because I
thought I was concentrating on the problem. . . . This
must have happened hundreds of times before, and I
never realized . . . It's one hell of a handicap, but now
that I understand I can handle it and make it work for
me. . . ."

The fact that she had left a pheromone trail of self-
destruction for Mr. Wish to follow was also something
she no longer denied. It was simply another fact. She'd
been shattered, and the child in her had tried to escape
the child's way. Run away and end it all. Death is the
simplistic solution; the final way out.

"Yes, for children," she murmured. "Blaise jokes
about getting rid of his education. I want to get rid of
the child in me, but it's no joke." A fresh fear struck.
"Will knowing who and what I really am make any
difference to him? That 'outclassed' remark he made
. . ." Then, after a moment, "But who am I, really?
Yes, it has to be love when you stop knowing who you
are. At least that question's answered."

A clammy chill swept over her. "My God! It's cold in here, all of a sudden. I should put something on. No, the hommies have got to find me like this if my story's to stand up."

The hommies found her like this ten minutes later, in the tatters of her shift, her skin raked, the burner in her hand. She was grateful for the full illumination their eyes gave her. She was grateful for the gentle courtesy of the reputedly formidable precinct Subadar. She wondered whether Mr. Ind'dni's soft chivalry inspired the awe of the rogues and vagabonds of the Guff. She did know that Ind'dni was short for his full name, which ran to seven impossible syllables.

Physically, Ind'dni was indeed awesome to the rogues and vagabonds of the Guff; tall, spare, ascetic, obviously incorruptible—skin the color of antique amber—trimmed jet-black beard—straight black hair going grey in curious streaks—eyes like lanterns—a voice with the timbre of an oboe. Gretchen was delighted to converse with this remarkable man, even though she knew it would be an ordeal.

"May I sit here, Subadar?"

"Anywhere you so please, madame."

"I don't want to look at them."

"I quite understand."

"Thank you, Subadar."

"Only too happy to accommodate most distinguished colleague, madame." The homicide squad was muttering and exclaiming behind them. Gretchen was too concentrated on the lie she was going to tell to notice that the element of surprise was missing from their exclamations.

"What did happen, madame?"

"Those two goons. They broke in."

"Please, so careful, madame. It is well known how cautious you are. Broke in? Broke and entered in legal sense? With force and arms? *Vi et armis,* as Legal would say. How?"

"You're right, Captain Ind'dni. I must be professional and precise. Not broke and entered in the legal sense. I'm afraid the door had been left unsafed.''

"Most unusual for you, madame. Yes? In your profession. It is permitted to ask how transpired?"

"I'd sent my staff out for the night."

"Entire staff? Most unusual."

"And in the excitement the door was forgotten."

"Which is to say, the lock was forgotten?"

"Yes."

"By yourself?"

"Yes."

"It is permitted to inquire cause of unusual excitement?"

"It was a step I'd never taken before."

"Yes. Why taken, please?"

"I'm working on a difficult and complicated contract, Captain Ind'dni. I needed time alone to think it through."

"Precise nature of said contract?"

"I'm sorry. I can't tell you."

"To be sure. Professional ethics. Understood. And then the two entered? Through unsafed door?"

"Yes."

"Time of said entry?"

"About thirty or forty minutes ago."

"So much for method. Sorry to learn that entry security of this Oasis is not what it should be. Now, motive?"

"Isn't it obvious, Captain Ind'dni? Rape and robbery."

"In that order? How very curious."

"No, I'm wrong. Forgive me, Captain. I'm still upset."

"To be understood."

"I assume it was for the rip first. When they found me here, the rape was added."

"Much more reasonable assumption, madame. And then?"

"There was a struggle."

"Evidence of same most explicit."

"Yes, I was lucky. I managed to survive."

"One against two?"

"Yes."

"And they armed?"

"With this. Take it, please."

"Thank you, madame. You seized it from them?"

"I was lucky, or they were careless."

"And killed your assailants?"

"In self-defense."

"Lethal-Just, to be sure. Describe them, please."

"Is that necessary, Captain Ind'dni? You have only to look at them."

"But surely you are humorous, madame. You know there is nothing to see."

"What!"

"You are so surprised? How very odd."

Gretchen leaped up and turned. The squad broke its cluster and permitted her to look.

Two clean skeletons lay on the floor. The bones were dry and polished. There was not a particle of flesh. There was not a drop of blood.

She was speechless.

"Like that woman in the dump," one of the squad muttered. "Only no beetles this time."

Subadar Ind'dni cut him off with a sharp gesture. To Gretchen he said smoothly, "Surely not accomplished with this burner, madame? Flesh drills, yes. Penetration drills, single or several, yes. But complete disintegration? And of flesh and blood alone? You will understand my astonishment."

"I . . . Yes, Captain."

"I am acquainted with every form of Lethal by violence, madame. Surely you are, too. Never before have I seen anything of this sort. Have you?"

"I . . . Never . . . Until now."

"And yet you allege this is your work. I have very special cause to beg for very careful answer. This is your work?"

"I . . . Yes."

68

"It is permitted to inquire how accomplished? This is most important, madame; more important than you know."

"It is permitted."

"Thank you. Then . . . ?"

But he had given her enough time to gather herself. In those few moments she had accelerated and improvised everything she would say in the next half hour.

"Unfortunately, I can't tell you, Captain Ind'dni."

"No? Why, madame? Again I must warn you. This is of much importance and danger; more danger than you know."

"The weapon I used is new and secret. In fact, it is the crux of the contract on which I'm working. No one has seen it yet and no one may see it. That's why I had to dismiss my staff tonight."

"Ah. And you used contract weapon on your assailants? Not the laser you presented to me?"

"Yes."

"Producing this effect?"

"Yes."

"You have never used it before? Elsewhere? At another time? Be very careful, madame."

"Never. That's one of the things I was trying to puzzle out tonight; how to test it in secret."

"And then came this most opportune rip." Subadar Ind'dni's tone was tinged with irony. "I congratulate and thank you, madame. Frankly, I found it difficult to believe that you had fought off two assailants, disarmed them, and killed them with their own laser. You are most formidable lady, but not physically."

"Forgive the clumsy lie, Captain Ind'dni. I'm trying to protect the contract, and I'm rattled."

"To be understood, madame. Alas, protection no longer possible. I must have the contract weapon."

"It's out of the question."

"It is not my choice, it is constraint of Legal. Weapon must be produced. You know that, madame."

"I'm sorry."

"You are adamant?"

"I must be."

"You place us both in most difficult position."

"I know mine."

"Then consider mine. I am dealing with most distinguished colleague of great honor and respect. That is the one hand, but here is the second. I am required by Legal to gather all existing evidence, both factual and verbal, to complete case for prosecution."

"Of course."

"But you will not produce lethal weapon."

"I can't."

"Then what am I to do? Your refusal requires me to follow homicide procedure."

"I suggest you do whatever the procedure requires."

"Then you are under arrest, madame."

"Lethal-One? Lethal-Two? Lethal-Just?"

"You persist in making difficult case doubly compounded, madame. Never before have I—You are above suspicion, but the—No. No. The charge will be none of them. I charge you in an invented category. It is . . . What to name it? Ah. Yes. It is Felony-Five."

Gretchen burst out laughing. She had brought it off. "Bravo, Captain Ind'dni! Have you improvised a procedure to go with a Felony-Five? Will I be confined? Can I get bail?"

"I continue to invent in face of most unkind laughter. You are under extended house-arrest. We will call it Guff-arrest. You may continue professional practice, but you will not leave Guff under any circumstances without *hukm* (which is Hindu for sanction) from me."

"Thank you, Subadar."

"Although I am not of your quality, madame, I do have resources. I warn you that I will uncover this most secret contract weapon, if it exists."

"*If* it exists? You doubt my word, Captain?"

"I do not apologize. Disbelief is the Bombazine syndrome, but that is not the case now. You are, alas, involved in one of a series of most malignant outrages, of which I hope you have no knowledge.''

"This *is* a surprise. What outrages, Captain Ind'dni? I haven't heard of any lately.''

"They are not yet matters of record.''

"Why not?''

"Because they are too *outré* for belief.''

"I see. At least I think I understand. All the same, I thank you for your courtesy, Subadar. I'll do everything I can to cooperate. This is a damned nuisance, isn't it?''

"Most sadly I agree, madame. And I am afraid that both of us will be much sadder when I have finally all questions firmly answered.''

"When you do, I hope you'll tell me,'' Gretchen prayed fervently. Her psytech skill at construction and design had taken a temporary leave of absence. Emotion will do that to the human animal.

7

After her final report (which most definitely was not the truth, the whole truth, and nothing but the truth) to Chairman Mills Copeland, Ms. Nunn received his thanks and check and went directly to the scent laboratory, which she entered without announcement. Dr. Shima was doing demented things with flasks, pipettes, and reagent bottles.

Without turning, he ordered, "Out! Out! Out!"

"Good morning, Blaise."

He spun around, revealing a mauled face. "Well, well, well," he smiled. "The celebrated Gretchen Nunn, I presume? Voted 'Person of the Year' three times in succession?"

Her heart leaped; there wasn't a hint of resentment in his tone. "No, sir. People in my class don't have last names."

"Strike the 'sir' bit, will you."

"Thank you, s— Mr. Wish."

He winced in agony. "Don't remind me of that incredible insanity, Gretchen. I—How'd everything go with Homicide?"

"Oh, I snowed them."

"And the chairman?"

"I snowed him, too. You're off the hook."

"I may be off the CCC hook but I'm not off my own. D'you know, I was seriously thinking of having myself committed this morning."

"What stopped you?"

"Well, you, partly."

"Only partly? I'm indignant. You gave me to believe that I had you in my thrall."

"And I got involved in this patchouli synthesis and . . . and sort of forgot."

She laughed. "You don't have to worry. You're saved."

"You don't say 'cured.' "

"No, Blaise, not any more than I'm cured of my freak blindness. We're a pair of freaks, but we're saved because we're aware. We can cope now."

He nodded unhappily.

"So what's your plan for today?" she asked cheerfully. "The battle royal with patchouli?"

"No. To tell the truth, I've just been going through the motions. I'm still in one hell of a mess, Gretchen. I think I'd better take the day off."

"Perfect. Bring two dinners. No funny business; we've got to have a war council. We're both in one hell of a mess."

* * *

"You've told me everything?"

"Everything, Blaise."

"Nothing left out by oversight or undersight?"

"Not even by second sight. I'm in the fact business, man."

"So am I, ma'am, but I'm a chemo and you're an intuitive, which means I'm cerebral and you're visceral."

"Are you claiming I think with my gut?"

"Certainly. You must know that you really do *feel* the answer to a problem first. Then your mighty brain produces a proof construct."

"And how do you work?"

"Exactly opposite. After I find a fact, I try to translate it into feeling. That's how I create perfumes."

"Then tell me this, mighty creator, is a Lethal-One fact or feeling?"

"It could be pure rut for all I know. Listen, if the war council is starting, kindly get off me."

"Yes, you think best vertical."

"What gave you that idea? Psychodynamics?"

"I know how you make love."

"Which leaves me in doubt. No more jokes, Gretch. I want to be profound."

"Proceed cautiously."

"We ought to hate each other."

"Yes? Why?"

"Because we think exactly opposite. You're psych-oriented and I'm chem-oriented. We're opposite poles, but that makes us an ideal team; a sort of psychemo—What are you laughing at?"

"I just thought of some twentieth-century pejoratives we could call us."

"Don't shock me, I beg."

"Blaise, I never."

"Gretchen, you always."

"Only professionally."

"Oh? Who told me just this morning, no funny business? What a way to refer to love!"

"And who forgot to bring two dinners?"

Shima took a beat and then muttered, "My very good friend, Mr. Wish."

Gretchen cut the comedy. "Right on, man. Thank God you can joke about that."

"Gallows humor," Shima said without humor.

There was another pause. At last Shima faced the firing squad. "You think this mess is connected with Mr. Wish?"

"Think? I know. It has to be."

"Your gut speaking?"

"Yes."

"So we can't just slough off the skeleton mystery as another Guff maggot and let it go at that?"

"How can we? Take a hard look at what's hanging over us. I'm prime suspect in a Lethal-One. What's more, I'm guilty as hell."

"Not of a Lethal-One. Lethal-Just."

"What difference does that make? Both our careers are hanging." Gretchen took a breath. "Even if I do justify the Lethal to Ind'dni, it'll become public record and I'll lose my reputation for guaranteed discretion, which is a big part of my sell. Ind'dni will be forced to bring in Mr. Wish publicly, and where's your career?"

Shima thought that over. "You're right. Either way it's a bummer. But believe me, Gretch, if you have to involve Mr. Wish to save yourself, I'm game."

She kissed his back. "What I love about you, Blaise, is that I like you. You're a nice guy. Thanks for the offer, but the Wish truth won't answer everything for Ind'dni. Don't forget those damned skeletons."

"I wish I could; but surely they'll be the Subadar's problem, not ours."

"Wrong. They're still our problem. Who did that to the goons? How? Why? Will it be done again? All that's Ind'dni's problem, yes, but answer this: Was the outrage really meant for me or for you?"

Shima stared at her. "You mean, could the goon butchery have been a goof?"

"Yes. It could have been intended for us. And if so, will it be tried again, so how can we cop out?" Gretchen grimaced. "We've got to defend ourselves, but don't ask me against what."

Shima frowned. "Then let's fall back and regroup. Ind'dni mentioned other malignant outrages?"

"He did."

"Not specifying?"

"He said, 'Not of record' because they were too *outré* to be believed."

Shima shook his head. "They'd have to be damn fantastic to be considered *outré* in the Guff today."

"He gave me the feeling that they were worse than what happened here."

"And you don't know what happened here?"

"Not a clue."

"You did safe the door after I left?"

"I did."

"Then how in God's name did he get in? Jesus-Mary-and-Joseph! Incredible! You saw nothing?"

"Nothing."

"Then you couldn't see through his eyes. That means he's blind. Impossible!"

"He or she . . ." Gretchen hesitated. "But blind? I don't know. I'm feeling for something else."

"Feeling. You felt nothing while you were waiting for Homicide?"

"Nothing. I—Wait. There was a sensation of cold for a few moments, but I was half-naked, and anyway, we're all used to drafts and chills most of the time. 'Where You Beez Come God's Big Freeze?' "

"Cold. Hmmm. Impossible entry and sudden cold. Did you hear anything?"

"Not a sound."

"Any other sensations?"

"None. No, wait. A strange odor, I thought."

"That's my department. What kind of odor? Sweet, sharp, cloying, pleasant, unpleasant?"

"Strange and sickening."

"Entry. Cold. Silent. Sickening smell. And then consumed the flesh and blood of the dead goons?"

"Every particle. The bones were clean."

"And then left through the safed door, but leaving it safed. Impossible exit. *Punkt.* And where are we? I'll tell you where this half of the psychemist is . . . Nowhere! So much for data-power. What were those pejoratives you had in mind?"

"You jump around so, Blaise." Gretchen giggled in relief from the tension. "The Jig and the Jap."

"Uh-huh."

"Why aren't you laughing?"

"Am I supposed to? I don't know what a Jig is. I'm a sort of Jap, yes? You're a Jig?"

"Uh-huh."

"What's a Jig?"

"A Black."

"Why is it funny?"

"Because it didn't used to be."

"How long ago?"

"Couple hundred years."

"It hasn't improved any with age. All right, Miz Jig, your turn."

"This can't be data'd, my dear Jap. It has to be felt'd."

"I usually start with an empiric equation."

"Very handy at times, but in this case where would we put the equals sign? No, we have to feel it."

"I don't know what to feel."

"But you do feel something?"

"Christ! Yes!"

"Only you don't know what it is."

"I don't."

"Thank you, sir. That's where I'm headed."

Shima looked so bewildered that Gretchen explained. "Your gut responds to situations, yes?"

He nodded.

"What I'm saying is, the situation may be new, unexpected, a surprise, but your gut can accept it and respond along familiar paths because it feels that the unexpected *can* be knowable."

"Jeez, Gretch, this high altitude is making my ears ring. I think I understand. You're saying that we respond to events *provided* we sense that they're within the parameters of life as we know it or *can* know it."

"Yes, and that's the crux."

"Proceed cautiously."

"Where are we when we don't know and understand our responses?"

77

Shima examined her face as he would an unexpected precipitate which had surprised him in a flask. "Then. The. Event. Is. Un-know-able," he said slowly. Suddenly he took fire. "By God, Gretchen, you've got it. Psymetrics forever! We aren't dealing with anything animal, vegetable or mineral . . . anything known or capable of being known . . . We're involved with something completely alien; outside of any possible parameter."

"Yes. That's where I was headed."

"And arrived in triumph."

"Thank you. Time out for a question?"

"Ask it."

"Something alien from outer space?"

"Nonsense! There's nothing viable in the galaxy that's on visiting terms with our solar system. All our probes have demonstrated that. No, we're dealing with a native, viable, home-grown entity which is entirely alien . . . A sort of Golem."

"You mean Rabbi Loew's monster?"

"No. That's the classic Jewish version of the artificial creature used as a servant."

"Then what do you mean?"

"I'm going back to the original legendary Golem. The original Golem, according to Talmud tradition, was Adam in the second hour of his creation, when he was alive, but a shapeless mass without a soul."

"Shapeless and without a soul. Hmmm." Gretchen considered, then nodded. "So we can't know what this Golem is, what it wants, or why it wants."

"We don't even know *how* it wants and achieves. That would account for the impossible entrance and exit and everything in between. My God, we don't even know whether it *does* want."

"It must want something, Blaise. What about the cannibal bit and the other things Ind'dni hinted at?"

"You think our Golem may be responsible for them, too?"

"My within thinks so. Viscera speaking."

"Then no argument." Shima was tremendously excited. "This is fantastic, Gretch! Unique! We don't know whether it has senses in our terms or appetites in our terms. Its senses may be functioning on Ångstrom wavelengths above or below the limits of our own spectrum."

"I buy that, Blaise, but if it's alive or quasi-alive, it must have appetites. That's just another word for life."

"D'you think it's alive in our sense, Gretchen?"

"You tell me what life is, doctor, and I'll answer your question."

"I wish I knew. I wish somebody could define life. What a magnificent challenge this is! I—" Suddenly Shima deflated and let out a shuddering sigh. "But it's made me forget the reality of our situation. To tell the truth, Gretch, deep down inside I'm scared, really scared. I feel like I'm in a nightmare and can't wake up . . . That filthy Golem . . ."

"Easy man, I feel the same way. It's an intellectual challenge, but an emotional nightmare."

"Then how do we wake up? As you say, we don't know where to put the equals sign in any equation because there's no equation to balance. All unknowns."

"Except the outrages," Gretchen added.

"And the danger. That alien Golem 'it' may be anywhere doing Christ knows what, and—and this is what tears me—it might be coming through that safed door anytime . . . even now."

Gretchen nodded quietly. "Yes. If it came once, it may return again . . . after you or me or both of us or Mr. Wish."

"You mean that alien something may have been tailing Mr. Wish?"

"It's possible. Anything's possible. We don't know. We're Ground Zero in the nightmare."

"Then what do we do?"

"Find the Golem, and zap."

79

"D'you really think the danger is that close?"

Gretchen looked hard at Shima. "I do, Blaise. Every nerve in my bod is tingling; not only for us, but for others. Subadar Ind'dni kept harping on the danger. There's something new and diabolical loose in the Guff."

Shima shook his head. "It's like a plague that's got to be wiped out, but we don't know what it is, why it is, where it is, what it wants."

"The Black Death didn't know or want anything; it just *was*."

"Agreed, and that's a hell of a good analogy, Gretch. Since we know nothing about this Golem we should handle it like an alien disease. That means locating a vector which will lead us back to the plague reservoir. Then we can zap."

"Yes, that's the hard-science way."

"Let's look at the possible vectors. It may be following me."

"Or you as Mr. Wish."

"It may be after you."

"Or you and me together."

"It may have some connection with the goons."

"A possibility." Gretchen thought for a moment. "Maybe the most likely."

"It may be functioning at random."

"In which case we're helpless. No design or construct could lead to it."

"Wrong, lady. Even randomness has a pattern where life is involved."

"Isn't that a contradiction in terms?"

"Isn't the thing we're tackling a contradiction?"

"Damn it, you're right, Blaise."

"Strange problems require strange solutions. As you said, the most likely vector candidate is its possible past connection with the goons. That means we'll need Subadar Ind'dni's data on other outrages."

"Which means going to him." Gretchen scowled.

"I don't like it, Blaise. He's shrewd, experienced, intuitive. He can be dangerous."

"What you really mean is that you don't want to run the risk of his connecting me with Mr. Wish. I thank you, lady, but I'll have to take my chances. We join up with Ind'dni. Have we got a reason?"

"Easy. I'm volunteering cooperation because Guff-arrest is bad for my business. I want to help him crack the case as quickly as possible."

"He'll buy that."

"Only if we're completely honest with him, Blaise."

"Including Mr. Wish?"

"No, we reserve that."

"Then your weapon fable will have to stand."

"Yes."

"What else must we be honest about?"

"Everything he can check, and make no mistake, baby, he'll check everything about us."

"It's risky."

"Yes, but not for me; for Mr. Wish. Are you still game?"

"By God, I am, lady. Yes. Now how am I supposed to assist you? In psychodynamics?"

"Me? Ask you for help in my specialty? Unbelievable. No, as a chemist."

"To do what?"

"Help me get an I.D. on the goons through a chemical analysis of the remains."

Shima thought that over, then nodded. "Yes, it might work."

"Ind'dni will be too courteous to tell you that you're wasting your time. He has his own forensic experts on the precinct staff. But he won't know that it's a fake. Just another sincere civilian trying to get into the Sherlock Holmes act."

Shima nodded again. "They do it all the time."

"And while you're staging your phony chemical analysis, I'll be sifting for information by indirection

. . . anything that's likely to help us shape up an—"

"Empiric equation?"

"I was going to say 'equals sign,' but what's the difference?"

"Lay down and I'll show you."

8

0

3 1 4 1 5 9 2

"What in the world is that, Nellie?"

"The latest heap-big magic from my Droney, Regina."

"?WHY? does he keep *trying* to get into OUR ACT?"

"He's just trying to service the Queen Bee and her ladies, Sarah."

"Sorry, Nell, not interested." The twins were disgusted. "His binary bag was a bust. We reject."

"No more binary. This, sisters in the hive, is The Price!"

"What price?" Yenta was definitely interested.

"The price we have to pay the Devil."

"Oh, no! Not Mr. Wrong Number again."

"Wait a minute." Mary Mixup was bewildered. "That's a price, Nell? Those lines?"

"Of course. You must know. You see lines like that on every package in your markethon."

"WE, madame, do !NOT! market in person."

"Then when you unwrap them after they're delivered."

"I, madame, do NOT unwrap in P*E*R*S*O*N. I leave that to the (UGH!) Pi-persons (YCH!)."

"Then you'll have to take Droney's word for it, Sarah. These lines are read by the shop computer and translated into the price you pay. Then they're all added up and put on the bill that's sent to your bank computer."

"Which pays, kicking and screaming," Yenta growled. "That part we all know in person."

"Droney says maybe Lucifer hasn't shown because we neglected to tell him the price we're willing to pay for a personal appearance."

"And this is it, Nell?" Regina was amused.

"Yes. Isn't it *fabelhaft?*"

"That's up to my bank." Yenta was not amused.

"No, no. The bank doesn't pay. We do."

Mary was bewildered. "We do? Us?"

"In person. Yes."

"How much?" Yenta demanded.

"Droney wouldn't tell me. All he said was, 'Satan isn't paid with money.' "

Miss Priss was offended. "Shame on him."

"Regina, what d'you think? Should we try it?"

"I honestly don't know, Nell," Regina laughed. "Are we supposed to run these lines through the house computer? I don't think it can read this sort of message."

"Droney says just put it in the pentacle and burn it."

"Well, all right. It can't do any harm to try, but let's add our evil symphony to attract Lucifer's evil attention. Pi-girl! Lights and smells, please. Witches, gather 'round and please be sincere."

"How?" Yenta was wary. "Are we supposed to chant, 'Thick line, thin line, space, thin line, thin line . . . ?' That'll be worse than Hebrew."

"No, dear, no ritual. Just the lights and smells and our dedication. We must want. Really want. Want Satan to appear. Want to pay this price, whatever it is in your own mind."

* * *

"What took you so long, Gretchen?"

"I lost the Subadar."

"Lost him!"

"Correction. He lost me."

"But he was very much with us when he gave permission to run the analysis. He couldn't have been more cooperative."

"And then he disappeared."

"He twigged your ploy?"

"No, he was called out by another outrage."

"Ugh! Our Golem?"

"Probably."

"Don't tell me."

"Nothing to tell. Merely a man flayed."

"Flayed!"

"Skinned alive. And in a safed room."

"Dear God!"

"Ind'dni told me he was still conscious when they broke in."

"I can't stand this."

"Neither can Ind'dni. He was shaking when he came back to the precinct complex. He's a sensitive soul, Blaise. I like him."

"I think he's in the wrong business."

"Everybody in the Guff is in the wrong business."

"Did you get anything from him?"

"Nothing."

"Not even through the magic of psychodynamics?"

"Absolutely nothing. Maybe he was too badly shaken."

"I don't blame him. Skinned alive. Christ!"

"He went mystic on me. Talked about Saturn, the youngest of the Titans. (You think *you're* excessively educated!) It seems that Saturn killed Sky with a sickle and from the drops of Sky's blood which fell to earth sprang the Furies and the Giants."

"This is a cop talking?"

"Indeed yes. He's quite a cop, our Subadar. Where was I? Oh yes. Saturn was warned by his Earth-Mother that he would be deposed by one of his children, so he swallowed them whole, one by one, as they were born."

"This I remember. Goya did one hell of a painting of that scene. He made Saturn look like one of our ravening Guff psychotics."

"Ind'dni said that Zeus was the youngest of Saturn's children. He was saved by his mother and overcame Big Daddy and exiled him, guarded by the Hundred-Handers."

"The what?"

"The Hundred-Handers. Wild, huh? Out of sight. Ind'dni couldn't describe those mythical weirdos. He said they had no shape or form."

"No shape, no form. Sounds like our Golem."

"Ind'dni seems obsessed with his Hundred-Hander."

"And that's what you fished out of him, baroque gems from Thos. Bulfinch?"

"That's what I got."

"It scares me. It really does, Gretchen."

"Why?"

"Because I'm beginning to believe that Ind'dni has second sight."

"You have to be guffing."

"No. His Greek obsession ties in with something I found in the goon bones."

"You can't be serious. Your phony analysis found something?"

"It wasn't phony; couldn't be. The Subadar's forensic mavins were all over me, and those dudes are good. I didn't dare fake; had to go the sincere route."

"And?"

"And now I'm really spooked."

"Yes. But why?"

"Because I found another gem from Ind'dni's mythology."

"Come on, Blaise! What did you find?"

"Promethium in the bones."

"Promethium?"

"With an I. U. M."

"Like Prometheus? The hero-type who stole fire from the sun and gave it to man and got zapped by Zeus?"

"The same. It was named after him by the jokers who found it 'way back in the nineteen-hundreds."

"What is it?"

"One of the rare earths. I have to talk technical, Gretch, because there's no other language to describe it. It's a lanthanide, a radioactive element with a half-life of thirty years. That means—"

"I know about half-life, Blaise. That's the time it takes for half the atoms to disintegrate. Yes?"

"Good for you. Promethium's symbol: capital "P" small "m," Pm. Atomic number, sixty-one. It's a fission product of uranium. I found its chloride, which is a pink salt."

"In the bones?"

"In the bones."

"And this is a clue?"

"Damn right it is, because there are no rare earths —repeat: *no rare earths*—in the normal bone salts."

"Never?"

"Never."

"Not even hardly ever?"

"Never."

"Then this is something abnormal."

"Definitely, and it may be a vector; only I don't know what it is or where it leads."

"Let me think a minute. Strike that. Let me feel a minute."

"Feel free."

After an extremely long minute, Gretchen asked, "Any of this Pm stuff in our normal, healthy Corridor pollution?"

Shima shook his head. "No."

"So the goons couldn't have absorbed it accidental-like?"

"No."

"Then they acquired it deliberate-like? A conscious act?"

"Probably."

"Is it used in food or drink?"

"Not a chance."

"Even as a preservative, fortifier, adulterant, aphrodisiac, health-advertising gimmick?"

"No way, Gretch. Too rare for commercial use of any sort. Too damn expensive."

"Expensive." Gretchen meditated. "Yes, that's the operative word. What would your normal, healthy, all-American goon use that was expensive?"

"Easy. Drugs."

"Q.E.D. This could be your vector."

Shima nodded. "Maybe. The only trouble is, I never heard of any tinct, chrome, mord, tinge, any junk that uses Promethium, and I have to know all the squeams in the scent business."

"Then that makes your lead even stronger. It must be something new on the market, so we don't have to waste time on the street level, chasing connections. We go right to the top."

Shima nodded again. Then he got up and began wandering absently around her workshop. Of course she couldn't see him because they were alone together, but she could track him by sound. At last he said, "You go right to the top, love. I'm going to try another line."

"Like what?"

"Cover the chemical supply houses. They know me. They'll give me what we want."

"But they don't handle junk, do they? I mean, it's legit these days but it's still *infra dig* for anybody with class."

"Of course not, but you don't find Promethium in any of the street squeams. That means it must be added to produce a new junk trip. And that means it's got to be bought from a legitimate house, and they keep careful records."

Gretchen nodded. "Sounds promising." Then she grinned. "Hey, bubie, got any Pm in your lab? Maybe we should try it ourselves."

"So happens I do; about a hundred grams of the hydride. But how is that going to lead us to the Hundred-Hander Golem?"

"Oh, it can't, but maybe we can trip, hundred-hand-in-hand into a psychedelic future, forsaking all others, and—"

"And voted 'Squeamies of the Year.' Knock it off, Gretch. You're not even slightly funny. That damned Hundred-Hander thing may catch up with us at any moment and skin *us* alive."

Gretchen sobered.

Shima patted her. "So *dozo* you take care, hear? We've got our empiric equation at last. Pm plus squeam plus goon I.D. equals Hundred-Hander-Golem-Thing. So let's move it and, for God's sake, don't talk to the rough boys on the corner."

"Yes, but you take care, too. There's another danger for you."

"Me? What danger?"

"Ind'dni."

"The Subadar a danger to me? How? Why?"

"Ind'dni suspects that you're involved with his Hundred-Hander. That's why he was so cooperative. He was doing some subtle fishing himself."

"For what?"

"Your connection with the goon butchery."

"Subtle, hell! I *am* connected."

"Not the way he's thinking."

"How is the Hindu thinking?"

"That as a genius-type chemist *you* may be responsible for the Golem."

"What? The Frankenstein bag?" Shima burst out laughing. "Preposterous!" Suddenly he sobered as an idea struck him. "But good God! Is it possible that Mr. Wish is responsible?"

"Anything and everything's possible in the Guff."

9

Gretchen knew the P.L.O. Oasis by sight. Everybody in the Guff did, although very few were ever permitted entry. It was one of "The Sights." Shaped like a pyramid; surrounded by plastic palms in glittering mica sands; fountains at the four corners—not jetting up precious water but chlorobenzene (C_6H_5Cl) as amateur HOjacks discovered to their disgust—it was quite literally an Oasis.

"All it needs is camels," she thought as she walked up to the gate set between the paws of a pint-sized sphinx. It was guarded by a squad of Liberation guerrillas wearing traditional desert-fighting khaki and carrying antique automatic rifles at the ready. She was stopped at gunpoint.

"Who you?" they demanded.

"Shalom aleichem," she answered.

"Who you?" The slam of cartridges into rifle chambers meant business.

"Gretchen Nunn. Shalom aleichem."

"You speak Jew. You Jew?"

"Vudden? Frig mir nicht kein narrische fragen."

"You? Jew? No."

"Ich bin a Yid."

"You no look Jew."

"Nudnick! Ich bin Falasha Yid."

There was a blank pause. Then a face brightened. "Ah? Ah! Black Jew. I hear. Never see. You pretty black Jew. Come in." To the rest of the squad. "She okay real Jew. Let her."

Gretchen's first ploy had worked. She was passed into an enormous hall of unspeakable filth and fetor, echoing with the bilious belches of twenty tethered camels. There were tents. There were naked children playing in the mica sands who stopped and stared at her. There were veiled women in black, tending small fires of dried dung, who stared but did not stop. The cathedral ceiling was clouded with acrid smoke.

A bearded sheikh in splendid robes advanced and greeted her. "Shalom aleichem."

"Aleichem shalom."

"Good morning, Miz Nunn. How nice of you to pay us a call."

"Good morning, sir. I'm afraid you have the advantage."

"Sheikh Omar ben Omar. No, we've never met but of course you are one of the Guff celebrateds. Ours the honor, Miz Nunn."

"Yours the grace, Sheikh Omar."

"I see you are acquainted with our polite forms, and I thank you. Will you take coffee?"

Over the ceremonial coffee taken cross-legged in a tent, alone except for hordes of urchins peeping in, and after the endless courtesy exchanges, Gretchen began inching up on her business with a confession of her deception of the Oasis guards. Sheikh Omar laughed.

"Yes, they reported to me that a Jew was entering, which is why I gave you the Israeli greeting. We recruit and train our guards for strength, not I.Q. I'm amazed that even one of them has even heard of the Falasha. Our guards are, after all, an equivalent of the old Mafia 'soldiers.' "

"Just as you, of course, are the powerful new Mafia."

Omar gracefully shrugged off the compliment and continued to delay the impending business with a scholarly diversion. "Yes, the Falasha," he chatted. "Black Jews from Ethiopia. They claim to be descended from Solomon and Sheba who was black, it is said. More coffee?"

"Thank you."

"Actually, they were simple natives converted to Judaism long before Christ. Then some went over to the new Christianity, and many more later found the True Faith. A vacillating people. Our dear friends, the Israelis, had much trouble with the Falasha when they were founding their magnificent nation."

Gretchen smiled to herself; her second ploy was gearing into action. When the Palestine Liberation Organization had at last taken over the United Arab Republic, it was just in time to see the last of the fat-cat rich oil reserves exhausted. The P.L.O. very sensibly switched to opium culture and the illegal sale of its derivatives. This was fat-cat until drugs and addiction were legalized; then the bottom fell out of their profits. The one nation still denouncing drugs and fighting furiously to have them outlawed was stiff-necked, puritanical Israel. This made Israelis the beloved of the P.L.O. Mafia.

"So perhaps it would be best to continue the deception, Miz Nunn," Sheikh Omar said. "I'm sure our soldiers have spread the word already. We won't contradict them. We do not take kindly to strangers, but we do to Jews. It will make matters easier for you."

"Yours the honor."

"Yours the grace. And now, if you will forgive my impetuosity, what matter has brought the celebrated Gretchen Nunn to our humble Oasis?"

"A most unusual contract. It requires that I ask El Plo a question."

"El Plo! You actually have come for an audience with El Plo?"

"With the PloFather himself. Yes."

"Unheard of! Will I not serve?"

"All honor to you, Sheikh Omar, but I'm afraid not. The information I need must come from the very top."

"May I ask the nature of the contract which requires this unusual step?"

"It is crash security, but I will put my faith and trust in your honor, Sheikh Omar, and be as frank and open as possible."

"Mine the honor indeed."

"And yours the grace. The contract concerns a unique lethal weapon. Its like has never been known before. I can't reveal anything about the weapon while I'm negotiating ironclad patents, but I will confide that I used it secretly on two Guff goons in my investigation of its potential."

"Not two of ours, I hope." Sheikh Omar smiled thinly. "And the results of your investigation?"

"Oh, Lethal-One, of course," Gretchen said casually. "Uniquely lethal. Subadar Ind'dni is very much upset."

Sheikh Omar smiled again.

"But there were strange side-effects which I must explore and explain for the patent application. I need El Plo's help for this."

"No more? You merely want to ask questions?"

"Nothing more. Just a few questions."

"And they are?"

"You will hear when you ask them for me, as I hope you will honor me by so doing. I would not dream of daring to speak to El Plo myself."

"Yours the grace, Miz Nunn. Please to wait."

While she waited in the tent with the uproar and stench of the Great Hall battering her, Gretchen speculated on the appearance of the formidable PloFather of the Mafia. Her secondhand sight gave her no clue. She was debating between a massive gorill who had

94

lethaled his way to the top and an acidulous accountant who had bookkeeped his way to the top when Sheikh Omar ben Omar at last returned, looking rather awestruck.

"It is granted," he said. "I would never have believed it possible. Please come with me."

"Must I veil my face?"

"No longer necessary, Miz Nunn. The years have accustomed us to the strange ways of the infidels."

He led her up steep ramps to the top of the pyramid where they were passed by four guerrilla guards and entered a pyramidal chamber. Gretchen was a bit short of breath.

It was an enormous room, carpeted with glowing rugs and hung with priceless tapestries depicting the conquests of Islam. A long, low, inlaid conference table stretched the length of the room with embroidered cushions on the floor flanking both sides for the cross-legged conferees. At the far end a group of magnificently robed sheikhs clustered around a regal ebony chair. Their heads were bent reverently as though they were listening to sacred whispers.

Sheikh Omar indicated a cushion at the near end of the conference table and Gretchen squatted down on it. He remained standing and cleared his throat. The sheikh cluster looked up and spread slightly, but Gretchen still could not see the PloFather in the chair.

"The Falasha woman is here," Omar announced.

One of the sheikhs bent down attentively, then straightened. "El Plo instructs the Jew bitch unbeliever to stand that she may be seen."

Gretchen started to rise, but Omar's hand on her shoulder restrained her. He looked down at her. "El Plo instructs you to stand that you may be seen," he said and then removed his hand.

Gretchen arose. The cluster of sheikhs spread a little wider to permit El Plo to see her, and she had her first view of the legendary PloFather. She saw an ancient little figure, almost a stick-figure, sitting twisted in the regal chair. The hands were gnarled and knotted with arthritis. The hair was white, long and sparse, exposing bald patches. The face was—What? Veiled? A woman? El Plo a woman? Gretchen was incredulous.

After a long interval of examination, a gnarled finger wavered up like an insect's antenna and then dropped. A sheikh bent, listened to the veiled mummy, then straightened.

"El Plo says you first crossed our path in '71."

By now cued in, Gretchen waited for Sheikh Omar to transmit. Then she replied, "Yes, the Oberlin contract. I did not know that the P.L.O. was involved when I signed. I'm sorry if I inconvenienced you. It was not intended, I assure El Plo."

The transmission of her reply was transmitted to El Plo. Then, roundabout, came, "Why did you not then withdraw?"

"I was committed to the contract."

"In '72 you caused the extinction of an entire P.L.O. assault cell."

"Yes, that was the Graphite contract. That time I knew the P.L.O. was involved and warned the cell to clear out. I gave them good and sufficient notice, but your soldiers were either stupid or stubborn. I didn't come out of that unscathed. I was in hospital for two months. I—" Suddenly she broke off and her mind blazed: *Yes. Blinded in the crossfire. The medics thought and I thought that I'd recovered my vision, but I didn't. My extrasensory sight took over, and none of us realized it.*

But El Plo was continuing, "You were offered double your contract fee to drop the Graphite engagement. Why did you refuse?"

"I was committed to my honor and I do not accept bribes."

"In '74 you were instrumental in the escape of a P.L.O. girl to join a dog of a Christian unbeliever."

"I was."

"Where is she now?"

"I will not say." Gretchen heard Omar gasp along-side her.

"Do you know?"

"Yes."

"But you will not say?"

"No. Never." She heard Omar gasp again.

"You are committed to a contract?"

"No. To grace."

There was another long pause. Sheikh Omar mur-mured, "I'm afraid you're in for it now. I'm powerless to protect you."

The veil before the mummy face fluttered slightly. A sheikh bent to listen to the whisper, then straightened. "El Plo is pleased with your defiance. El Plo is pleased with your strength. El Plo says both of you should have been born men."

"I thank El Plo."

"El Plo asks what you need."

"Information."

"What will you pay?"

"Nothing. I ask it as a favor."

"Does El Plo owe you favors?"

"No."

"Nevertheless it is granted. Ask."

"Thank you. The P.L.O. deals in all drugs. Is there a new squeam just reaching the Guff streets which uses an extremely rare earth metal called Prome-thium? P-R-O-M-E-T-H-I-U-M."

The double transmission seemed to take an age. At last came the reply. "No."

"The P.L.O. knows the sources of all drugs. Is it possible that a new junk is being concocted privately by a squeamie?"

Again a long delay. Then: "The answer is no. Our *Enforceurs* would know within a week. They have not reported anything new made privately or commer-cially."

Gretchen sighed in disappointment. "Then that's all. I thank El Plo. You have my honor and my grace." She turned to leave.

"Stop, please." The projected whisper came as faint and yet as penetrating as a snake's hiss. Gretchen stopped and turned in surprise. El Plo was actually speaking directly to her.

"You are no Falasha. You are Gretchen Nunn, a woman of clout and respect."

"Thank you, El Plo."

"You have earned it."

"You honor me."

"If you were offered a contract by the P.L.O., would you accept?"

"You have your own organization, El Plo."

"Would you accept?"

"Why would you need me?"

"Would you accept?"

"As a bribe?"

"Not as a bribe. Would you accept?"

"I cannot answer a question unless I know why it is asked."

"You have rare courage, independence, and ingenuity. You also have the rarest of all, earned arrogance. Would you accept?"

Gretchen began to sense the indomitable will that could not be deflected, concealed within that mummy stick-figure. Suddenly she was reminded of Tzu-Hsi, the last Dowager Empress of Imperial China, who maneuvered, murdered, bedazzled, and betrayed her way from slave-concubine to the Celestial Throne.

She replied very carefully. "I will accept and fulfill any and all contracts provided they are not intended to harm anyone or anything directly. I am not a destroyer. Unfortunately, I cannot foresee all possible results, but that's my accountability, not the client's."

"Yes, yes, yes," came the hiss. "I am pleased with you. Much pleased. I will arrange for us to meet again, and you will be pleased, too. You may go now, Gretchen Nunn.''

After Sheikh Omar ben Omar had seen her out of the Oasis with much courtesy and many compliments, Gretchen took a deep breath and shuddered.

''My God! That woman makes me feel like a child again.''

* * *

Shima thought he knew every practicing pharmacy, chemist's and drug dispensary in the Guff—after all, that was part of his profession—but this grotesque was a surprise to him.

It was a tottering brownstone in Canker Alley plastered with ''Bldg Condemned'' stencils as old as the Emancipation Proclamation. A corroded sign, well-hung on a crazed gallows arm, read: RUBOR TUMOR. The letters were bordered with explicit and exaggerated erogenous zones. A small crowd of street-geeks loafed around the shop window which was a rear-projection screen displaying blurry hard-porn action that must have been at least a century old. Some of the geeks were wearily trying to get a gig going and not succeeding. Shima entered RUBOR TUMOR, serenaded by a shrill voluntary of catcalls. He took a lightning survey.

''Gloryosky!'' he exclaimed. ''This place has to like date from the twenty-hundreds. It's a damned museum.''

There were vats, casks, carboys, volumetric flasks, alembics, retorts, beakers, graduates. ''Not ripped yet?'' he wondered. ''Why? How?''

There were honeycombs of antique nostrums in their original glass bottles with the original labels. The empty bottles alone were worth a fortune as Collectors' Items: 2-Propynyl Pepsi; New Improved Oxy-Shasta$^+$; Nova Tab; 7-CH$_3$·S·C$_3$H$_7$-Up; Club (K° + hv) Soda; Frescathiol; Dr. Brown's Phenylene Tonic;

1,3-Hexadine-5-yne Sprite; 4-n-hexyl-resorcinol Dr. (Pepper$_3$)^2; Coca (R·N$^+$) Cola;

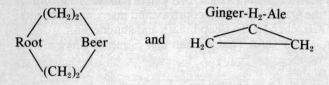

There was a bottle of Ultra-Wink-Erektall, its glass interestingly purpled by light and time. Shima tried to pull it out of its comb cell to examine it for evaporation (glass does evaporate), and his hand was instantly zapped by a charge a hell of a lot more painful than a slap on the wrist.

"And that explains the No-Rip bit," he muttered, rubbing his hand. "If I tried to grab through the warning, I make it six-two-and-even it'd cost my arm. Whoever runs this pharmacy isn't going to lose anything, wherever he is." Shima raised his voice. "Hello, the pharm! Anyone home? Mr. Rubor? Mr. Tumor? Or Miz?"

A faint reply oozed out of the walls. "Hello. This is your Pharman. How can I serve—FLAP-RRR-FLAP —This is your Pharma-FLAP-RRR-FLAP-RRR-an RRR Phar FLAP RRR erve you FLAP RRR Hello—"

"Christ Almighty!" Shima swore in amazement. "This is a goddam twenty-hundred computerized drugstore, and it's still functioning."

"Arman-FLAP-Pharman-RRR—Hello. This RRR—"

"Well, sort of functioning, but it's still a miracle. I wonder how it generates its power."

"Pharma-RRR—"

"I want a prescription," Shima shouted, "if you can respond. Can you respond, Pharman?"

"Shillings ten cash in-put slot-FLAP-RRR—"

"Shillings? My God, that coin hasn't been around since the I.R.A. quit back in—"

100

"FLAP-RRR-ten cash RRR-slot."

A sort of turnstile coin slot was flickering in a spasmodic signal, demanding payment. Shima inspected it perplexedly. There was no coin in use in A.D. 2175 that could possibly fit it. He was about to turn away in disgust when inspiration suddenly visited him. He lifted a foot and smashed the payment slot with his heel.

"Advantages of higher education," he grinned. In undergraduate days a mallet was hung from the dormitory pay CB phone to save wear and tear on the feet.

"FLAP-RRR-FLAP- Not programmed to give change. You may RRR two prescriptions. FLAP. This is your RRR Man. How can I FLAP you?"

"I want a special prescription."

"Name Remedy FLAP Narcotic Physic RRR Nostrum RRRRR Salve Poultice FLAP Bane Poison RRR Toxicant—"

"I want the same prescription ordered from Rubor Tumor before."

"Name FLAP person client."

"I can't but I can tell you that the prescription was special. It contained PROMETHIUM. P-R-O-M-E-T-H-I-U-M."

"Contained PROMMMMMium."

"Yes. A lanthanide rare-earth metal."

"Group FLAP of periodic table. Atomic number G1. Atomic weight RRR. Fission product of uranium. FLAP FLAP FLAP Request prescription profile records."

"I request prescription profile records."

After a pause, a new clear woman's voice spoke briskly. "Prescription profile records. Shillings ten input."

Shima kicked again. "Got you coming and going," he mused.

"Beginning year two one hundred, profiles—"

101

"No," Shima broke in. "Start with current profiles and report in retro."

"Shillings ten in-put."

"Got to install a mallet," he growled and kicked.

The brisk records voice began reporting filed prescriptions in retro by date, number and ingredients. Shima listened patiently to the long recital, somewhat surprised that this ancient, demented pharmacy did so much business, and wondering what the customers used for shillings. "They couldn't all use the kick trick," he thought. "The coin slot wouldn't be standing." At last he heard the magic abracadabra: "PROMETHIUM CHLORIDE. Fifty grams."

"Stop! That's it," he shouted and kicked before he could be requested for another shillings ten. "Name and address of person client."

Pause. Then: "Burne, Salem. The Number of the Beast. Hell Gate."

"Well, I'll be damned," Shima said slowly. "I. Will. Be. Damned."

* * *

What idealistic Ibet (Industry Building a Better Tomorrow) had done was construct the equivalent of the Zuider Zee dam across the Hell Gate channel and continue it across the Hudson River. (Also known as the North River because it was west of ancient New York City. Either early cartographers had rotten compasses, or else they hated Henry Hudson.)

The dam had a threefold purpose: (1) Block the salt water tiding in from the Atlantic and keep the fenced Hudson sweet; (2) Reserve the Hudson's waters for industrial use; (3) Provide a spillway into upper and lower New York harbor for the boiling wastes from the nuclear power plant built on top of the dam.

Those exasperating eco-dreamers had demanded why the water life of the harbor was being destroyed for an energy never granted to the public, and why the heat couldn't at least be used to warm the chilly Guff.

Patient Ibet kindly explained that the cost made it impractical, and what the hell did the destruction of all littoral and oceanic life for a few hundred square miles matter when a Better Tomorrow would solve everything?

One interesting side-effect of the Hudson–Hell Gate dam was that the reservoir had raised the water level by ten feet, drowning thousands of homes and creating a scattering of tiny islands and hillocks around its shores; a sort of artificial Venice. There were a few hundred private homes still standing or newly built on these island hillocks. No. 666 Hell Gate was one of these privileged homes.

It was no Venetian *palazzo,* but more of a stone fortress rather like a miniature castle with window-slits suitable for defending archers. As Shima sculled up to the landing pier he was impressed and oppressed by the implicit menace. Gretchen was, too.

"I can easily see our Golem-Hundred-Hander-Thing coming out of this place, Blaise."

He nodded. "All it needs is a hunchback calling Burne 'Master' and bringing him the wrong brain."

She smiled. "Pity it's such a lovely day. There ought to be thunder and lightning."

"Probably Burne's got that staged inside."

But quite to the contrary, the reception rooms of 666 Hell Gate were a delightful surprise. They were styled in the Quaker and Shaker tradition: random-width pine plank floors, sawbuck tables, Moravian armchairs, grandfather clocks, walnut ladderbacks, painted dower chests, pewter, Steigel glass, silver Argand lamps, beautifully framed Colonial Primitives.

"All this barn needs is hex signs," Shima muttered enviously. It was quite obvious that the quack, Salem Burne, lived even far more luxuriously than the distinguished Blaise Shima, B.A., M.A., Ph.D.

"Our afternoon ritual has just begun," the attendant murmured, "but you may enter. You will find unoccupied couches."

He slid a silent panel aside and the two entered what seemed to be an enormous grey velour womb without any discernible walls or ceiling. There were velour couches scattered around in the smoldering darkness with vague forms reclining on them.

"Is it group therapy?" Gretchen whispered.

There were dancers in the center of the womb, dozens of them, nude and painted luminously into vampires, ghouls, cacodemons, succubi, harpies, ogresses, satyrs, furies. They wore confusing contrasting masks, front and back. They glowed, writhed, entwined, and contorted to the music.

Shima sniffed. "By God!" he whispered. "He's composed a scent symphony with the Odophone scale I gave him."

They tiptoed through darkness to a vacant couch and sat to watch and listen and sense.

The nebulous shape of the psychomancer moved silently from couch to couch. Sometimes he bent, sometimes sat, sometimes knelt; always he murmured to the reclining figures. He was a solemn version of the traditional property man in the traditional Japanese theater who moves around onstage, dressed in black, and is presumed to be and accepted as invisible. He came at last to the couch where Gretchen and Shima were seated.

"Dr. Shima, what a pleasant surprise," Burne said softly. "And this, to be sure, must be my exalted colleague, Gretchen Nunn. Overwhelmed to meet you at last, madame."

"Thank you, Mr. Burne. Or should it be 'doctor'?"

"Never in the presence of the genuine Dr. Shima. I know my place. And how do you like your Odophone music, Dr. Shima?"

"I'm really impressed, Burne. It blends beautifully with the ballet and orchestral music. How do your patients respond?"

"Completely, as you can see. Their barriers are broken down. They run on and on about the witchcraft of

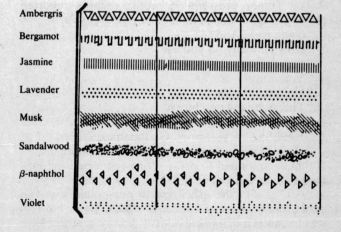

scent, dance, and music while their bodies speak volumes. I can't thank you enough, doctor."

"You're welcome, I assure you. I never dreamed that that notion would turn out so well."

"Thank you. Forgive me if I seem to rush you, but my ritual patients are waiting. You and madame are telling me, without words, that something extremely urgent brings you here." Burne shot a look at Gretchen. "The fugue?"

She returned his look. "Yes and no. I'm sorry, but we must reserve that."

"Understood, Miz Nunn, but as a friendly colleague, I must warn you that your somatic speech is telling me that it's something deadly."

"It is."

"Then?"

"Blaise will tell you."

"Mr. Burne," Shima began carefully, "it's been necessary for us to track down a rare-earth metal called Promethium. Omni-Chem reported to me that they alone handle it and have made only one sale; to Rubor Tumor, a retailer in Canker Alley in the Guff. Rubor Tumor prescription profile records reported only one sale of Promethium chloride—to you."

"Quite true. And?"

"How and why do you use it?"

"I don't."

"You don't!"

"Not at all."

"Then why did you buy it?"

"It was bought for a patient at her request."

"Her? She? A woman?" Gretchen exclaimed.

"Most of my patients are women, Miz Nunn."

Shima continued to press. "She requested the Promethium specifically?"

"Not at all. She asked me to compound a novel, exotic, and malevolent incense which, when burned, would exude a diabolical odor. I did my best to oblige a regular and most profitable client—I'm always direct and honest with you, doctor—and concocted a disgusting gallimaufry which Rubor Tumor filled for me. I threw in a score of outlandish chemicals which I found in the books, including Promethium chloride.''

"And gave it to her?"

"Of course."

"Mr. Burne, I hate to ask this but I'm forced to—"

"Please, doctor," Burne interrupted. "You and Miz Nunn are telling me in no uncertain manner that you're facing a crisis. Certainly I must break with ethics for the sake of colleagues. All I ask is that you pledge not to reveal the source of your information."

"It's pledged for both of us," Gretchen said.

"And above all, not to Subadar Ind'dni."

Gretchen and Shima stared.

"How the devil—" Gretchen burst out and then clapped a hand over her mouth.

Burne smiled at her. "Someday, madame, I may teach you the subtleties of somatic speech." Then he gave Shima an odd look. "The patient is Ildefonsa Lafferty. She is listed in the Guff directory."

Shima gasped. Gretchen searched his face for a long moment while he fought for composure. "It's nothing . . . Nothing at all," he stammered, fully aware that he was deceiving neither of them. "I . . . It's simply that I was wondering how to—How to ask Mr. Burne how he—How he pays Rubor Tumor. There aren't any shillings these days."

"With frozen CO_2 slugs," Burne smiled. "It's all right, doctor. I will never reveal Ildefonsa Lafferty's confidences. You may tell Miz Nunn as much or as little as you both think best."

10

"You'll have to tackle her alone, Gretch. I won't see her. I don't dare."

They were pacing the Guff's "Strøget," the long, exclusive shopping boulevard which was sternly protected by private police. All traffic except pedestrians was prohibited. Only shoppers with Class A identification were admitted.

Shima was deeply disturbed. Gretchen was trying to soothe him and satisfy her curiosity at the same time.

"Now what's all this, baby? You had a thing with Ildefonsa Lafferty. Yes?"

"The Girl from Ipanema. Two years ago."

"Does Ipanema signify anything?"

"That was a pop tune centuries ago about this girl on the beach who never looked at the guy who loved her. Lovely tune."

"Was Ildefonsa lovely?"

"I thought so."

"Then why the *crise de nerfs?* You've had go-rounds with loads of women."

"Before I met you, and not all that many."

"D'you feel the same about the others? Won't. Don't dare."

"I can't even remember their names."

"Then what's so special about Ms. Lafferty?"

"She murdered me."

"Was it love?"

"For me, yes."

"And still is?"

"I'm still dying, if that's love."

"Love shouldn't kill."

There was a long pause while they strolled, threading their way through the crowds of shoppers. Suddenly Shima began murmuring in a low voice with his head averted, as though making a shameful confession, "When I was a kid in Johnstown, P.A., back in the forties, I—"

"Johnstown! The forties? That was the time of their fifth flood."

"Yeah, but that's not what I'm telling you. My Grandfather—I called him Grandy—decided he wouldn't live long enough to see how I'd turn out, so he invented a fiendish forecast of my future."

"What?"

"He gave me a fifty-franc gold piece."

"Franc?"

"Uh-huh. Grandy was the French side of the family. Back then the fifty-franc gold piece was the equivalent of . . . oh . . . maybe a hundred of today's computer credits. A fortune for a kid."

"How was that fiendish?"

"The coin was a counterfeit."

"My God! Did he know?"

"Sure. It was deliberate. That was the forecast; to see how I'd behave after I discovered it; try to pass it, sell it, exchange it, ask him for a genuine coin, squeal on him to the fuzz, whatever."

"What did you do?"

"Nothing. When I found out the gift was a phony I was hurt and disappointed, but I never did anything. I put the fake away in a drawer and never mentioned it.

Grandy was very sad. He said, '*Ah, le pauvre petit.* He will never be able to cope with the hard knocks.' "

Shima fell silent. At last Gretchen asked, "And that adds up to . . . ?"

"I thought, I wanted, I believed that Ildefonsa was making a genuine gold gift to me, and I gave whatever gifts I had in return."

"Ah! Including a pet diamond?" Gretchen snapped jealously.

"I try to give you more than the diamond. I tried to give her more, but she was a false coin. A counterfeit. I've put her away in a drawer. I can't take her out again."

"So underneath that bright, brilliant, witty facade, you're just a poor, romantic schnook."

"I can't take the knocks, which is why I've spent my life hiding in labs. If there's one thing for sure, it's Newton's Third Law of Humor. For every joke, there's an equal and opposite hurt."

She kissed his cheek. "I'll be extra gentle and kind to you, I promise, and I'll tackle this Ildefonsa bitch alone."

"She's an Ipanema hard-case, Gretch. She won't be easy to crack. She feels nothing. I know."

"One way or another I'll get what we want. You just keep her locked up in that drawer and throw the key away."

* * *

Ildefonsa Lafferty was assault prone. Gretchen took her in with one lightning rake of the eye, as only women can, and itemized her coldly. Dyed red hair, but manifestly a natural redhead, as the milky skin, brows, lashes, and Mount of Venus proclaimed through the transparent white shift. ("Flaunty display. Trashy!") Not tall. Juicily rounded. Thrusting plummy breasts. ("Should lose ten pounds.") Assured. Defiant. Glowing with—What? ("*Chutzpah!*") Hateful. ("How could Blaise ever have—?")

110

"So? What d'you see?" Ildefonsa challenged.

Gretchen accepted the *défi*. "That you're an open invitation to rape."

"Thank you, but flattery will get you nowhere. Come in. Gretchen Bunn, is it?" (Gretchen had been carefully and accurately announced by Oasis Security downstairs.) "Come in, Gretchen Bunn."

("Blaise was right; this one won't be easy.")

Ildefonsa led Gretchen out of the mirrored foyer into the enormous living room. It looked odd and interesting. There were illuminated vitrines filled with curious collections; sundials, ear trumpets, walking sticks, matchbook porn, French letters, death masks, dog collars. But there was no noting details in the presence of this volupt. Her crimson glory outshone everything, and she was only too aware of it. Gretchen was pleased to see that despite her overpowering assets this *fata Morgana* moved awkwardly. ("Badly coordinated—except in bed, most likely.")

Answering Gretchen's opening rape reply, Ildefonsa said, "I chase them into the horizontal first and accuse later, but only if the performance is below standard."

"I can believe that."

"You better believe it."

"And I'm sure your standards are exalted."

"Why not? I've earned them." Ildefonsa contemplated Gretchen indifferently. "I'd say you're an open invitation to a climbing plant."

"Yes, I would enjoy being wrapped around."

"By what? Men? Women? Beans? Grapes?"

"I never could dig a gig with chlorophyll, Miz Lafferty. Men only."

"At least that's the plural. There's hope for you, Miz Funn."

"It's Nunn. Gretchen Nunn. Hope for me? You think my horizons should be enlarged?"

"Let's say enhanced and enyanced."

"So you know Guff Blurt."

"I've heard enough to know the score."

111

("This sex contest will get me nowhere; she's too old a hand at it. Try the humble approach.")

"You're right, Miz Lafferty, I—"

"Call me Ildefonsa, child."

"Thank you, Ildefonsa. I've intruded because my horizons should be enyanced."

"By me? Sorry, child, I don't dig the dyke gig."

"No, not that way. I've come to the Venus Mantrap for advice."

"Venus Mantrap? Don't be insolent. There *is* a brain inside this beautiful red bod."

("Oops! She has a redheaded temper. Careful!")

Gretchen smiled. "Red *is* beautiful. I have to back the black numbers."

"That figures." Ildefonsa gave her a token smile, then broke into song in a peanut-whistle voice: "*It take a long, tall, brownskin gal to make a preacher put the Bible down . . .*"

Gretchen applauded enthusiastically. "Heavensville! Wherever did you learn that bijou?"

"From a long, tall, brownskin stud."

"It's a perfect line for me. Thank you. You know, this *is* my lucky day. I knew it would be when I hit six on the black three times running this morning."

"Three sixes. Adding up to eighteen. Quite a score."

"Or six hundred sixty-six?"

Ildefonsa shook her head. "You're a dreamer. No stud in this world can score that."

"If any stud could score six sixty-six, you'd be the one to make him."

"Don't be jealous of your betters, child."

("Safe. She doesn't connect me with 666 Hell Gate. I've kept my promise to protect Burne. Now let's get what we need from her.")

"Not jealous, Ildefonsa. Envious."

"I don't blame you."

"I don't have your kind of luck with men."

Ildefonsa snorted. "Luck!"

"So that's why I followed my lucky number to 18 Canker Alley and the Rubor Tumor Pharm."

"The Rubor Tumor Pharm? I don't know it. Rubor Tumor. What a yummy name."

"But you must know it, Ildefonsa."

"Are you calling me a liar, child?"

"No. Wait. I asked them for a prescription that would turn men on."

"You can't mean it."

"But I do. Rubor Tumor told me that they'd put together that kind of prescription for you."

"That *is* a lie. I don't need that sort of thing." Ildefonsa wrinkled her milky brow. "It's a crazy mistake. Or else they were guffing you. I've never been there. I didn't even know about the Pharm until you told me just now. It has to be a guff."

"Rubor Tumor claims they compounded some sort of sexy incense for you that turns men on."

"What? Incense? Sexy incense?"

"So they said, and that's why I'm here . . . to ask you what it is and how you use it . . . if you'll be kind enough to tell me. I need all the help I can get."

"But I never—" She stopped in mid-sentence, thought, then burst out laughing. "Of course. That must be it. He must have told them the incense was for me." She gave Gretchen a genuinely friendly look. "Thank you, Gretchen. I haven't had a good laugh in ages."

"But he, Ildefonsa? Who? I don't understand."

The redhead was so delighted that she did a complete *volte-face* and was almost affectionate. "Never you mind who, lovey. That's a secret. But I can tell you that the incense wasn't intended to grab men, it was meant to grab the—No, I won't tell you; you'd never believe it. I'll show you. We're meeting in the hive this afternoon, and I'll bring you along. A new face will be entertaining and, who knows, you may even join up. I have the feeling that you're just our type."

113

"Wait a minute; you're going too fast. What's all this? Meeting? Hive? Entertaining? To who?"

"All will be known shortly, Gretchen, including the quote sexy unquote incense," Ildefonsa giggled. "No questions now. I'll give you lunch, and then you'll come along with me to the hive."

* * *

It was an *avant-garde* apartment in the chic, nostalgic style of the Communist era of Old New York City in the 1930s. A fortune had been spent transforming it into a converted brownstone flat with naked linoleum-covered floors, fruit and vegetable crates and barrels for furniture—designed and built by Antique Plastique, Inc.—monk's-cloth drapes over the windows, oil lamps constructed of piled books, a battered player-piano, old wooden kitchen tables covered with front pages of *The Daily Worker,* posters of Marx, Lenin, the Kremlin, and Moscow University tacked to the walls. This simulation of left-wing poverty was an extravagant luxury; hardly a hive.

The bee-ladies were already assembled when Ildefonsa Lafferty ushered Gretchen into the lounge. They looked up with surprise and delight.

"Nellie, dear, you've brought a new face. How wonderful! Will she join our commune?"

"That's up to her, Regina. This is Gretchen Nunn. Gretchen, our Queen Bee, Regina." (The name on the registry board of the Oasis had read; Winifred Ashley.)

"Good afternoon and welcome, BB," Regina said in a lovely, mellifluous voice. She was a large lady in a flowing gown, gracious and aristocratic.

"BB?" Gretchen asked.

"My dear, do forgive me, but you're such a ravishing Black Beauty that the nickname just tripped off my lips. Let me introduce your new friends. You've met Nell Gwyn of course. This lady is Mary Mixup." Regina indicated a slender fair girl with her hair cut like a helmet and the body and legs of a dancer.

114

"Hello, BB," she said. "So nice meeting you. I would have thought that Regina would give you more a name like Trojan."

"How do you figure that, Mary?" Nell asked.

"They were both horses, weren't they? Not that BB's a horse."

Nell nodded. "Makes sense. To her."

A small, compact woman, dark, with vivid blue eyes and an emphatic manner, stepped forward. "I can't WAIT to be introduced, BB. I MUST clasp your hands and welcome you. ALAS! Alas! alas! Too, TOO im-PET-uous."

"Sarah Heartburn," Regina smiled. "Our favorite diva. And this lady is our conscience, Miss Priss."

Miss Priss looked like "Alice in Wonderland" to Gretchen. Her girlie-girlie lisp seemed to be half a stammer and was most winning.

"Nice to be properly introduced, BB. I hope you'll join us. A new person will put them on their best behavior. Their manners are shocking. And their language!"

"I've been known to use Guff Blurt myself," Gretchen smiled.

"Where did you get that marvy *tuta*, BB?" a tall butch-type demanded. "I've got one not half so good. I paid a fortune, and it doesn't fit the crotch worth a damn."

"Please, Yenta," Miss Priss said. "We shouldn't use five-letter words here."

"Six in 'crotch,' Priss," Nell Gwyn said.

But Mary Mixup was doubtful. "Six?" She counted on her fingers. "C-R-O-U-C-H. You're absolutely right, Nell."

Regina laughed. "The *tuta* misfit is Yenta Calienta, BB. She'll probably try to set you up for a swindle. And these are our twins, *Oodgedye* and *Udgedye*."

Two identical women; jet-black hair, white, white skin, dead ringers for the beautiful Greek slave in *Monte Cristo,* smiled and nodded to Gretchen.

"Hi, BB. I'm *Oodgedye*."

"No you're not. You're *Udgedye*. It's my turn to be *Oodgedye* this week. Hi, BB."

"They swap identities," Nell explained to Gretchen. "I've got a bet on with Yenta. I say their husbands will spot the switch. Those two are look-alikes but they couldn't be identical in bed, could they?"

"Of course not, Nell. No two women are."

"Then I lose the bet?"

"No, it's a standoff."

"How do you figure that?"

"The psychodynamics of human behavior. Their men have probably spotted the swap but they're enjoying it, too, so they keep their mouths shut. The cute question is whether the husbands have told each other, and I wouldn't bet on that."

Nell Gwyn looked at Gretchen with awe. "Help, Regina! I've gone and brung an intellect-type bee into the hive."

"How lovely for us. Do make yourself comfortable, BB. Let's get acquainted, Pi-girl! Coffee!" Back to Gretchen. "We're all grateful for the introduction of someone clever. We're running out of entertainment ideas."

"That's what brought her, Regina. She wants to know about one of our games."

"Does she, Nell? Which?"

"She doesn't know yet. I brought her along to show her."

"This is getting complicated," Regina laughed. "You'd best tell us yourself, BB."

Gretchen was perplexed; whether to go along with the lie she'd told the redhead or tell the truth. She opted for the lie.

"There's a pharm in Canker Alley called Rubor Tumor."

"Is that dirty?" Miss Priss wanted to know.

"Why should it be dirty, Priss?" Nell inquired.

"They're five-letter words."

"They *are* suggestive, Priss," Gretchen smiled. "Rubor and tumor are characteristics of tumescence."

"What a brain! She's staggering."

"Can anyone understand the words BB's using?"

"It doesn't matter," Gretchen smiled. "Many times the words just pop out—I don't know where from— and I don't understand them either. Maybe I've got an unknown twin who's switching identities when my back is turned."

"Oh, I like her. I LIKE her. She has the soul of the true creative artiste."

"Do *you* use words like that on *him* when my back is turned?" *Oodgedye* (or *Udgedye*) shot at *Udgedye* (or *Oodgedye*).

"Here's our coffee," Regina interrupted tactfully as the Pi-faced slavey wheeled in a trolley. "Serve our guest first, Pi."

The trolley was wheeled before Gretchen who was overwhelmed by the centerpiece: a block of clear ice with a single rose frozen in it. After she had received her coffee, the trolley went to the Queen Bee, who first passed her hands gracefully over the face of the ice and then dried them with a napkin. Only then did she receive her coffee.

"A fingerbowl!" Gretchen exclaimed to herself. "This is luxury on a fantastic scale. I'm glad Blaise isn't here. He'd be perfectly furious."

"And now, BB dear, what's all this mysterious, complicated business of pharmacies and games?"

"Oh, it's nothing, Regina. Rubor Tumor told me that they'd concocted an exotic incense for your Nell Gwyn. I jumped to the conclusion that by exotic was meant erotic. I went to see her this morning to ask her about it."

"But why, BB?"

"She thinks she has problems, Regina."

"Erotic problems, Nell?"

"That's what she thinks."

"A Black Beauty like you, BB?" Yenta broke in. "I'd trade—"

"Not now, Yenta dear," Regina interrupted. "We all have our private problems and we mustn't intrude. What happened, BB?"

"Nell laughed and said no, the incense wasn't intended to attract men, it was for something else but she wouldn't say what. Then she gave me a lovely lunch and brought me here to find out for myself."

Regina chuckled. "Raising the Devil, of course."

"What? The Devil?"

"I told you you'd never believe me," Nell said.

"One of the entertainments we've been playing, BB. Trying to raise the Devil with diabolical incantations and ceremonies. We've read all the wicked books and memorized the sinister spells. Nell got us all the evil smells—that incense is one of them—and we've tried over and over again . . ."

Miss Priss made a face. "The worst part was that disgusting 'Hand of Glory,' BB. Filthy! Obscene! The hand of an executed criminal holding a candle made from the fat of a vee-eye-are-gee-eye-en. Ugh!

"And that's all it was, Regina? Just a game of trying to raise the Devil?"

"That's all, BB."

"The incense was only intended to magick him?"

"That along with all the other stage-effects." Regina gave an amused sigh. "All the work we put in!"

"Just the eight of you?"

"That's all, unless you count Pi, but she refused to play with us. Too frightened, I think." Regina smiled tolerantly. "Her class still believes in the old superstitions."

"Perhaps other guests to assist?"

"None, dear. We play our games in private."

Gretchen grinned. "Any luck? Any sort of diabolical epiphany?"

Nellie Gwyn was awed again. "The words she uses! Will you listen to her!"

118

"Nothing, BB. Not a sign of Satan, although Sarah claims she felt a twinge when she was rehearsing the Invocation."

" 'Twas NOT a twinge. It was a THRRRILL! A huge cloudy symbol of a high romance. John Keats."

Gretchen hesitated, then decided to gamble. These bee-ladies were all so openly friendly toward her. She pursed her lips and shook her head judgmatically. "You know," she said slowly, "I really can't believe it."

"Can't believe what, dear?" Regina asked.

"That the ceremony had no results, exotic or erotic. The incense is elaborate and expensive enough to raise something, even if not the Devil."

"If she means what I think she means," Nell Gwyn began, "we can strip a man naked and—"

"And that will do, Nell," Regina said firmly. To Gretchen, "I wish you were right, BB, but nothing happened. Nothing."

"ALAS! Alack! Wellaway!"

"Are you sure, Regina?"

"Quite sure."

"And so say we all."

"*Oodgedye* and *Udgedye* not dissenting."

Inchoate designs and constructs began to prickle Gretchen—the architechtonic instinct intruding— These eight ladies were all so adorable and amusing and friendly, but what realities lay underneath? "Newton's Third Law, courtesy of Blaise Shima," she thought. "For every charm there is an equal and opposite—What?"

Aloud, she said, "D'you know, Regina, I'd like to see for myself."

"Our wicked ritual?"

"Yes, as an observer."

"But it's just a fun game, BB."

Gretchen's tone transposed to the serious. "It may be more than just a fun game, you know."

"Nonsense!"

"No, listen, all of you. Perhaps something *is* happening, but you don't notice because you're all too close to the ceremony. You know the old saw about not being able to see the forest for the trees? Why not let me watch?"

Miss Priss became so uncomfortable that her stammer was pronounced. "B-but we c-couldn't let a stranger watch us, c-could we, Regina?"

"BB isn't really a stranger, Priss. She's our new friend . . . most *simpatico* . . . We all feel that and welcome her."

"W-Well, that's true. All r-right. But sh-she is new and she'd m-make us self-conscious."

"ME, madame? S*A*R*A*H self-conscious? !NEVER!"

"Perhaps Priss *is* right, Sarah," Regina said graciously. "All the same, BB may be right, too. We may have been too busy with the ritual to notice any results."

Nellie Gwyn was skeptical. "But I thought the Devil wouldn't just sneak in like a kid after-hours; I thought he'd prance in like a Regency Buck with black fire and diabolical laughter."

Gretchen smiled. "Maybe the Devil makes an entrance in his own style, Nell."

"BB is right, *right*, RIGHT. A quiet entrance is grrreat T+H+E+A+T+E+R!"

"That backwards Hebrew is enough to make anyone blind and deaf to anything," Yenta growled.

Again, the twins joined the majority. "BB's making sense, Regina. We've been too busy to notice any action. We vote to let her observe."

"We can't do it that way, *Oodgedye*."

"I'm *UD-gedye*."

"Oh, of course. Sorry dear. We must make BB a part of the ceremony so that we'll all feel comfortable. But how? All the parts are taken."

There was an intense pause while all the gears tried to mesh. Then Sarah Heartburn arose majestically and stood like a statue of Justice, but without the blindfold and scales. Gretchen choked back a burst of laughter and Regina winked at her.

"Ladies, mark me! Aye, MARK ME, I say . . ."

"Watch out for that lamp, Sarah."

"*I* have the so-lieu-see-on of the D?I?-L?E?M?M?A."

"Don't keep us in suspense."

"And what, pray, is T+H+E+A+T+E+R without S!U!S!P!E!N!S!E? 'Tis the divine torture. No matter. Here is my solution. Let BB hold 'The (Ych!) Hand of Glory' (Pfui!) Now, *mesdames,* what have you to say to THAT?"

There was a round of applause.

"Bravo, Sarah," Regina laughed. "You've found the answer. Now come, we must all be serious and sincerely dedicated to evil. Pi-girl! Clear away the coffee things. Bring out the pentacle and the lights and smells. We're going to raise the Devil again."

11

"And nossing she hoppen, Gretch?"

"Nossing."

"Damn!"

"No damnation. No demoniac laughter. No Satan."

Shima cocked an eye at her, then bellowed, "GEW-ERKSCHAFTSWESEN! OZONHALTIG!"

"What the hell's *that?*"

"My notion of demoniac laughter," he grinned.

"Sounds more like a libretto in search of Richard Wagner. You didn't really hope I'd tell you that the Devil actually appeared, did you?"

"Certainly not, but I was hoping for something realistic like goon-type geeks hanging around and cashing in. Any heavies in this Winifred Ashley's apartment house?"

"Impossible. It's a beautifully protected Oasis."

"Corrupt servants, maybe?"

"The pie-faced girl's the only servant, and she's too timid to be suborned by anyone or anything."

"The bee-ladies did use Salem Burne's Promethium incense with the rest of the sorcery?"

"Yep. Nellie Gwyn . . . that's your Ildefonsa Lafferty sexpot . . . kept shooting me funny looks and mugging and Regina was peeved because Nell wasn't sincere and dedicated enough to Lucifer.''

"Did the bee-ladies get any vibes from the Pm stuff?''

"Nope.''

"You?''

"Nope.''

"Will you kindly tell me how that Pm got from their séance into your goon bones?''

"Easy. Our Golem carried it.''

"Was it there?''

"No.''

"How did it get it?''

"Not known.''

"How did it carry it?''

"Not known.''

"Why did it carry it?''

"Unknown.''

"Will you lucidly tell me what the Hundred-Hander-Golem thing has to do with your bee-ladies and their playtime witchcraft.''

"I haven't the foggiest.''

"Could it be sort of hanging around, out of sight?''

"Maybe.''

"Why?''

"No idea.''

"Where?''

"Same answer.''

"This is frustrating, Gretch. I thought we were closing in on some kind of answer.''

Shima was so deflated and depressed by the disappointment that the words of his grandfather flashed through her mind. *"Ah, le pauvre petit. He will never be able to cope with the hard knocks."*

She tried to comfort him. "Maybe we are, Blaise. Maybe it's there, only I haven't spotted it yet. I'm going back to the hive.''

"Will they let you?'' he asked indifferently.

123

"They invited me. I've been accepted."

"D'you actually want to waste your time?"

"As a matter of fact, I do, for two reasons—I must and I want to."

"Must?"

"Psytech is bugging me, Blaise. My gut is sending up signals that there may be some sort of rotten construct deep down inside these women."

Shima's interest kindled. "As rotten as our Golem-Hundred-Hander-Thing?"

"Maybe. I don't know. That's what I must find out."

"Hmmm. And you said you want to?"

"Yes. I really like them, Blaise. On the surface they're all characters; funny, different, refreshing."

"All except Ms. Ipanema," he said gloomily.

"Maybe she isn't to a schnook who used to be in love with her and keeps the memory locked in a drawer, but women see each other differently. She's a delicious caricature."

"Sure, of humanity."

"No, Nellie's human, all right; she's just the school-girl's idea of the *femme fatale*." Gretchen did a lightning pastiche of Ildefonsa's rattle-rattle undulations.

Shima laughed. "But I always thought that type had to be tall, dark, and handsome . . . like the Yenta Calienta number you described."

"No way. She's a dyke."

"Then what about the actress-*manquée?* Passionate, you said, with burning blue eyes."

"Sarah Heartburn. Strictly for laughs. You can't be a clown and be fatal."

"The black-and-white twins who look like a pair of succulent Greek slaves?"

"*Oodgedye* and *Udgedye*. Too cold-blooded and stubborn. They're always dissenting and objecting and refusing and recusing."

"And switching."

"Miss Priss lisps and stammers. Very fetching, but

124

the Alice in Wonderland bit is far from fatal. Mary Mixup's just a darling dumb bunny.''

''That's the one with fair hair like a helmet and a dancer's bod?''

''Uh-huh. You've got to have a mind to make a man fall down in a dead faint.''

''Regina has a mind.''

''Too dignified and stately.''

''You said she gave you a wink.''

''Oh, she has a sense of humor but it's evah sew refayned. I'm not putting her down. She's a gracious and generous queen, and she's madly in love with Lord Nelson.''

''Lord . . . ? Oh. The admiral.''

''Horatio, Lord Nelson. He had a wild thing with Lady Hamilton which was a *scan. mag.* in the seventeen-hundreds. Regina spent an hour reading me Nelson's love letters to Emma Hamilton.''

''And the pie-faced slavey is out?''

''Absolutely. Now what is all this, Blaise? You couldn't possibly be interested in the construct of a *femme fatale*.''

''Just curious about the hive, is all.''

''The hell you're just curious. Come on, man.''

''You see through me as usual.''

''You're transparent.''

''I was feeling out the possibility that one of the bee-ladies might have an outside connection with Guff gorills.''

''I see. Yes, one might.''

''Who? Pi?''

''No. Me.''

''You!''

''Sure. I'm a bee-lady now, and I keep pretty rotten, low-down company in my business.''

''Like me?''

''Like Mr. Wish.''

Shima took a deep breath, held it, then let it out in a grunt. ''I wish you wouldn't joke about that.''

"All right, no more funnies, but we can't escape the fact that there's a damned incomprehensible network that's got us all twisted up in it; you, me, Mr. Wish, goons, Promethium, Ind'dni, the beehive, and Golem[100]."

"Golem-one-hundred? Why d'you call it that?"

"Because it seems to be a polymorph and can assume a hundred different forms."

Shima sighed. "I wish we could take off for Mars, Mother of Men."

"If you want to run away from the hard knocks, baby, why not Venus, also a very far planet?"

"*Ah, le pauvre petit?* Yes, you're right," Shima acknowledged with a wry smile. He pulled himself together. "So what's our plan of op.? You go back to the hive for more witchcraft, yes? And I? Ich? Moi?"

"You get cozy with Subadar Ind'dni."

"Oh I do, do I? Like why?"

"Like for data. I want to find out whether there's any sort of connection between the hive séances and the Golem[100] atrocities. In time. In space. Even the most doubtful link. Oh, and keep that Pm jazz in your lab under lock and key. And install burglar alarms."

"Alarms? Why, for God's sake?"

"Maybe this Golem creep is a junkaroola, too, in its own charming fashion."

"On Promethium?"

"Only a maybe, Blaise; just hoping for anything. It might get hungry for fresh supplies and visit CCC to tap the till. Turn your Pm into a trap. You might catch something interesting.

Shima shook his head wearily. "If that goddam polymorph thing could get in and out through your safed door, how in hell can I trap it?"

"What? The late, great Blaise Shima, B.A., M.A., Ph.D.? Brilliant inventor of my secret contract weapon which Subadar Ind'dni would give his eyeteeth to prove phony? Not capable of devising an infallible trap for a freak thing that defies all common sense?''

"In a word, no.''

"Damn right you can't. Nobody can . . . yet. I seriously doubt whether we can zap it if we're ever ingenious enough to catch up with it, but we can worry about that when and if we do. Right now we're looking for connections, any link, and you may trap a Guff geek who—surprise, surprise—may turn out to be a Pm pusher.''

* * *

By the turn of the 21st century the population of Old New York City was nine and a half million. By the turn of the 22nd New York had become the Guff precinct of the Corridor, and its swarming population could no longer be counted; only estimated. The guesses ranged from ten to twenty million.

Every member of those millions entertained the belief that he or she was unique. Subadar Ind'dni's Computer Section in the Precinct Complex entertained more realistic ideas. In their experience there were hundreds of thousands of look-alikes among the millions, ranging from rather similar to all-fours replication.

The chief of the section was cynical. "Take any Guff turkey and program him for the machine, and his software would match at least a hundred others.''

"Ah,'' Ind'dni replied gently. "Perhaps *en gros*, but it is our function to discover the small uniquedoms that distinguish one look-alike from all her others.''

He was nettled and dismayed by seven fantastic outrages perpetrated against seven look-alikes by the polymorphic Golem[100].

* * *

No one knew how or when this new troubleshooter first appeared or who had hired him. The Wall Street

Complex was so convoluted with management disso-
ciation that pretenders had been known to draw payment vouchers without having been hired for any job.
It took months for Accounting to catch up with them
"through channels."

He could cure any and all of the ills that plagued the
Big Board think-tanks. (When the computers stop realtime thinking, fortunes can be imperiled in minutes.)
He was no electronic genius. He was simply a mechanic who worked out of an uncanny intuition, a sort
of symbiotic sympathy with the tantrums and foibles
of the temperamental electronic brain trust that controlled the market. He had foibles of his own.

Example: He would appear without request or com-
plaint (through channels) carrying his complicated
toolbox, and everybody judged that a thunderstorm
was approaching. Lightning can throw computers into
fits.

Example: You could chalk a line tracing the 440-volt
input cables under the Exchange floor from the course
he habitually walked. He was drawn to the field generated by the high voltage.

Example: Without knowing it, he generated a
strange field of his own. Anyone who came into physical contact with him had his or her I.Q. quadrupled
while they remained in contact. He spread temporary
genius like a plague. The irony was that he was never
infected himself. He was always and forever a nice,
slow, intuitive maintenance man.

Her roomie told her about this new freak and she
was intrigued. She was a dumbbell and knew it, but it
had never bothered her because no one seemed to
mind. Yet once, just once, she wanted to experience
what it would be like to have the kind of giant intellect
that could absorb whole tapes, one after the other,
remember them, and talk about them afterward.

She took to dropping in on her roomie for lunch at
the Exchange Buffet, and on this forenoon with purply
clouds looming in from the west and half the Guff

128

racing to set containers on rooftops, he was already in the Exchange. He had the front fascia of a particularly hysteric IBM modulus removed and was buried half inside, silently soothing it before the storm broke.

She tapped the small of his back for attention and what she thought would be a vampire stare or a thrilling laying-on of hands. There was a lightning flash out in the Guff and a lightning echo inside herself, followed by a strange thunder in her head. She heard her voice murmur, *"Vengon' coprendo l'aer di nero amanto e Lampi, e tuoni ad annuntiarla eletti . . ."*

She was frightened. An alien intruder had taken possession of her mind. All this while her first tap was still on his back. Then: *"Sumer is icumen in, lhude sing cuccu! Groweth sed, and bloweth med, and springeth the wude nu—Sing cuccu!"*

And: *"Not until after artists had exhausted the possibilities of the ukiyo-e portrait did Japanese print designers begin to try their hand at natural scenery."*

And, *"In einer Zeit des Professionalismus und des brillanten Orchesterspiele hat die—"*

And then he pulled out of the IBM unit and grinned at her. He was entangled with affectionate electric cables and looked like a one-man Laocoön Group: *"Laocoön. (lā ok a wän) n. Gk. Legend. A priest of Apollo at Troy who warned against the Trojan Horse and, with his two sons, was killed by serpents sent by Athena . . ."*

He grinned again, pulled her into the IBM with him, and enjoyed her screaming spasms as he introduced himself and the leads of 220 volts into her body. *"Volt. A unit of electrical potential difference, abbreviation V or . . ."*

* * *

She saw him just behind her as she walked into Theaterthon for the performance of "Total-Twenty." He was vivid. "My God!" she thought. "He could play John What's-His-Name who shot that old president, Abe What's-His-Name. Fascinating type. Must be an actor."

She received her cue-bead and plugged it into her ear. First Overture was playing. She didn't care for music without light and was tempted to unplug the cue-bead, but she was afraid she might have an early entrance, so she suffered. She looked around for another glimpse of the grabby John Wilkes Somebody, but he had disappeared in the crowd. "Full house tonight," she thought. "Should be an exciting performance. Can't wait to see the total tape."

First Overture ended. The cue-bead announced, "Second Overture. Places and beginners, please. Places and beginners, please." This was in the ancient English tradition and was meaningless. There were no places and no beginners simply because no one in the house knew when his part would begin, and there certainly were no places. There was no stage; just a great soundproofed hall milling with the performing audience, now silent, awaiting their computer cues as "Total-Twenty" began, but still circulating in a gentle minuet, nodding, smiling, murmuring to friends.

She knew that the script dialogue was being spoken by the scattered performing audience. As often as not, an intimate two-scene was being played by audactors separated by a hundred feet and a hundred people. Once there was a shout raised by audactors all over the hall, but she had not been cued for that. There were no sound effects. That and the music was sync'd onto the tape along with the visuals.

The computer spoke sharply through her cue-bead, "Line coming. You are accosted by a flash-gimp. You tell him in level tones. 'Juck off, geek.' Repeat. In level tones. 'Juck off, geek.' On cue. Three. Two. One . . ."

The cue-bleep sounded. She delivered the line, wondering who and what she was, who the geek was (that John Wilkes actor?) and what "Total-Twenty" was all about. But that was the fun and games of Theaterthon, that and the delight of discovering what visuals were being sync'd to your voice on the total tape.

She was cued for a confident "Don't worry about me. I can take care of myself." Then (passionately): "The show MUST go on!" Then (frightened): "But why are you looking at me like that?" Then a long scream followed by: "Oh, you beast! You BEAST!" Later a groan. Much later (broken-voiced): "It was horrible. I don't want to talk about it."

John Wilkes What's-His-Name came out of the crowd to her. He said nothing, but his vivid actor's face told her that he had been drawn by the melody of her voice and the perfection of her performance. He smiled and put his hand on her shoulder. She understood what he was saying. She smiled back, magnetically attracted, and put her hand on his.

Then, still silent, still smiling, most theatrically, he ripped her naked. She tried to struggle, to scream, to beg help from the flabbergasted spectators, but he took her, most dramatically, most thoroughly, there on the floor of Theaterthon.

* * *

She had done something worse than criminal; she had done something stupid. This well-bred virgin from one of the best families, easily passed into the Strøget by the cautious guards, tried to shoplift a bijou which she could have bought. It was an exquisite teardrop of limpid amber. Enclosed in it was a tiny, glinting dragonfly. She had never stolen anything in all her life, and the strange surging in her loins was thrilling. She had never stolen anything in all her life, so of course she was clumsy.

The safe system nailed her immediately and she lost her head. She didn't try to brazen it out, talk her way out, protest that it was a silly mistake, offer to pay. No. She ran. The Strøget guards didn't bother to chase her. They merely broadcast an alert and her description. She would never be passed out of the boulevard. She would never get out of the criminal courts.

And in her panic she did what comes natural to a well-bred virgin; she took refuge in the Church of Jude, Patron Saint of Impossible Causes. It was empty except for a tall priest in a black gown standing before the altar. He might have been St. Jude himself. He turned as she tore past the nave imagining a hundred armed guards in hot pursuit. She fell to her knees before the priest in prayer for sanctuary and concealment. Jude blessed her with the sign of the cross, lifted the skirt of his cassock, and dropped it over her. Then she discovered that her face was pressed against an enormous nakedness, and her loins surged again.

* * *

The one good thing that the Guff aristocracy had to say for Industry was that it had turned New York's stepchild, Staten Island, into a free port. It's true that this had been swindled in order to receive energy conglomerates from the solar with a minimal ripoff by customs, but there were wonderful consumer side benefits. One of them was the Freeport Restaurant offering an exotic cuisine.

There is a frigid Venusian glowworm about the size of an eel. It glows even brighter at Terran temperatures and when poached and served in a *mirepoix bordelaise* moistened with Pouilly wine, the entire platter emits a frozen light and neon fragrance. *Anguille Venerienne* tastes like a Siberian snowball.

There is a Martian mold which must be scraped up from below the frostline. (And who was the blessed idiot who first dared taste it?) *Terfez Martial* is served like caviar and is so fabulous that the Black Sea sturgeons are protesting, and the U.S.Q.R. (formerly the U.S.S.R.) is denouncing Staten Island.

Did you know that stones can make an exotic seasoning? Yes indeed. Take one pound of Widmanstaetten asteroids. Grind to the size of cracked pepper; sprinkle on roasted fresh corn. (Butter, salt, pepper, &tc. should be forsworn.) There is a marriage with the sugar in the corn that produces a remarkable taste salmagundi which organic chemists are still trying to puzzle out. Curiously enough, it doesn't work with ordinary refined sugar, which makes Kansas very happy. Cuba is also denouncing Staten Island.

The Freeport Restaurant is enormous, of course, and its exotic kitchen is larger than most conventional restaurants, but there is a smallish club room for the discerning gourmets which is more difficult to enter than the vaults of the Bank of England. Here Madame brought her guests and was disturbed to discover that her customary waiter was not in attendance. This one was a new and strange person. She did not deign to speak to him, but summoned the *mâitre d'hôtel*.

"Where is my Isaac?"

"I am so sorry, madame. Isaac is at another station tonight."

"But where? I am accustomed to Isaac. A dinner could be only a meal without Isaac."

"He is stationed out in the main dining salon this week, madame."

"He is out with the mere! But why? Has he disgraced himself and earned punishment?"

"No, madame. He has lost a bet."

"Lost? A bet? Explain yourself, sir."

"With reluctance, madame. The waiters were playing *vingt-et-un* in the kitchen . . ."

"Gambling!"

"*Oui,* madame. Isaac lost everything to the new man. Then he bet you."

"Me!"

"*Oui,* madame. For a week. And he lost again. So Isaac is outside, and the new man has you."

"Outrageous!"

"But it is a compliment, madame."

"Compliment? How?"

133

"Your gracious generosity is well known."

"It will not be known to this new person."

"Certainly, madame, as you wish. Nevertheless you will find him the quintessence of courtesy. Now, may I *piquer* your palate with a *tour de force* created only this day by our superb chef?"

"What is it?"

"Queue de Kangourou aux Olives Noires."

"What?"

"Which is to say, stewed kangaroo tail with black olives. Olive oil. Brandy. White wine. Stock. Bouquet of bay leaves, thyme, parsley, orange peel, much crushed garlic and stoned black olives. It is flamed with the brandy to burn off excess fat and to strengthen the flavors. It is unique and magnificent."

"Good heavens! We must try it."

"You will not regret it, madame, and you will be the very first to be served. If you approve and consent, it will be honored with your name."

The *maître d'hôtel* bowed, turned and snapped his fingers. The quintessence of courtesy appeared. He did have a most refined and elegant bearing, Madame thought.

"Clear for the *Queue de Kangourou*," the *maître d'hôtel* ordered, pointing to the table centerpiece.

The new man who had won her bowed apologetically to Madame, stood close alongside her and cleared the center of the table with quick, graceful hands. He made just enough room for her body which he lifted, placed prone on the table and embarked on a refined and elegant retrorape the while he filled the stunned guests' wine glasses with quintessential courtesy.

* * *

There was a vintage streetcar rallye at the Sheep Meadow racetrack and the pits were gaudy with trolleys, charabancs, trams, and even beautifully restored

134

United Mine Workers' coal and ore carts. The pits were also decorated with the hundreds of women attracted to racing and death. They were all of a type; dressed *pour le sport* and sporting a to-hell-with-everything-else look.

She sat on an empty drum between the *Madison & Fourth Avenue* and the *Étoile Place Blanche Bastille* pits, giving equal time and attention to the Guff and Parisian crews who passed her constantly as they borrowed gear and advice from each other. They were oddly alike in their soiled *tutas* and really only to be distinguished by a favorite tool carried in a back pocket; spanner, S-wrench, maul, pliers, a Stillson, a monkey. The pit foremen were above carrying tools. The drivers' *tutas* were white and immaculate.

She was amused by the one with the pinch bar dragging down his back pocket. Pinch bar was either Paris or Guff—he spent so much time in both pits that she couldn't decide—young enough to be smooth-faced, yet obviously fully matured in frame and muscle. She was amused because each time he passed he didn't give her a "*Très jolie*," or a "Bije babe, doll." He banged the drum with his pinch bar. It emitted a resounding bass boom and sent tingles up her spine.

It was a Le Mans start. The streetcars were in position on the track. The drivers and seconds (now in traditional motormen and conductors' uniforms) lined up opposite. The starting gun cracked. The motormen and conductors dashed to their trolleys, scrambled in and took off in a frenzy of clanging bells while the pit crews and the women cheered and screamed. Then came the bass boom and the tingle, and there he was, pinch bar in hand, smiling silently at her. She smiled back.

He dubbed her shoulder lightly with the bar and drew her to the backup *Étoile Place Blanche Bastille* car and took her inside. She was delighted until he revealed that he was a woman and proceeded to ravish her, using the pinch bar as a dildo. Her screams merged with the cheering and screaming and clangor of the race.

* * *

GoFer was the camera test-pattern for "Studio Twenty-Two-Twenty-Two" at WGA. She sat patiently on a stool while the cameras dollied in and out on her skin and adjusted their color correction to its glowing tones. She was a crow, but her red hair and skin were magnificent. When she wasn't posing for the cameras, she ran errands for the Studio 2222 staff, so naturally she was called Miz GoFer. No one outside the WGA accounting department knew her real name.

She sat quietly on her stool waiting to go for coffee, food, props, costumes, anything. She was bored. She wasn't particularly interested in any of the 2222 shows. WGA was owned and operated by the Glacial Army Revival Movement and its programming was devoutly Judgment Day. "Where You Beez Come God's Big Freeze?" (Copyright 2169 by Scriabin Finkel Music Company, a division of Glacial Music Corporation.) All the Good Guys were trustworthy, loyal, helpful, friendly, courteous, kind, obedient, cheerful, thrifty, brave, clean, and reverent. All the Bad Guys got shot down in flames by God, and died, bitterly regretting their rotten Guff behavior.

There was an animal trainer on the set. She assumed that because he had a King Charles spaniel cradled in his arm, and anyway Studio 2222 was heavy on animals, pets, and the pure love of a boy for his dog. Only this man looked like he should have had a tiger cradled in his arm. He was gigantic and powerful enough to give an orangutan second thoughts about tangling with him.

The powerhouse came over to her stool and gave her a deadpan nod. She nodded back. High as she was perched, her head barely came up to his chest. She could hear the slow roar of his breathing, and it

136

sounded like surf. The King Charles spaniel yapped. From the controls the 2222 director screamed at the floor manager over the talk-back, "For Christshit's sake will you cue the goddam fuckin' nuns!"

Twelve pure and demure nuns were hustled onto the set by the floor manager where they formed a pure and reverent circle for God to shoot down the dirty, rotten Guff amorals. The powerhouse picked up the stool, with GoFer teetering on it. She was forced to throw her arms around his neck, and she giggled. Then he carried it to God's mark in the center of the circle, put it down with GoFer still on it, spread her astonished knees, and proceeded to horrify GoFer, the studio, and the entire Glacial Army into a gasping silence with an enormity while the cameramen (no fools they) dollied in and out on the glowing skin tones. The only sound was the yapping of the King Charles spaniel and the director.

* * *

The Therpool was new, astonishing, miraculous; the latest novelty and entertainment of the lunatic Guff. It was filled with a freak bond of hydrogen and oxygen into H_2O^n, which meant that the hybrid water could actually be breathed. It was typical of the Guff that this metabolic miracle should first be used for amusement. The pool was dazzled with a laser symphony and you swam in a consortium of *son et lumière*. You paid the equivalent of a hundred gold pieces for the luxury.

She could easily afford it, and she needed the therapy of the thermal null-G relaxation very badly. She had two dozen advertising accounts, all of them demanding and exasperating, and yet paying such exorbitant fees that she could never bring herself to dump any one of them. So instead she dumped herself into the liquid light and drifted and dreamed, drifted and dreamed.

She was alone in the Therpool (she'd paid a high

premium for the privilege), but he came out of the
depths to her like a languorous saffron shark and
courted her as gently and quaintly and gracefully as
only sea-creatures can. She was enchanted and responded, and their floating *pas de deux* was lovely.
But then he took possession of her nude body with the
savage urgency which the females of the species endure with a mixture of drifting and dreaming, pleasure
and pain, fulfillment and rage.

* * *

"I do not advantage myself with the insolence of
office to visit you in your apartment unannounced,
madame," Subadar Ind'dni said, "but rather depend
upon the *simpatico* between us. And you, too, Dr.
Shima."

"You're very kind, Subadar," Gretchen smiled.

"And very devious," Shima smiled.

"As are we, all three," Ind'dni smiled. "And that is
the basic of our understanding. We know where we
stand and unstand with each other. And on one issue
we collaborate in fear and hatred."

"The Golem."

"So you call it, madame. I think of it as the
Hundred-Hander, the mad thing that stinks of cruelty
and takes a hundred forms to execute."

"The Subadar knows something we don't, Gretch."

"More outrages, Mr. Ind'dni?"

"I will answer that question when I know why it is
asked, Miz Nunn." He was quoting her reply to the
PloFather.

Gretchen shot a look at Ind'dni who returned it
quizzically. "Oh yes. I know all about your visit to the
P.L.O. oasis. I did tell you that I do not lack resources." He turned to Shima. "And the visit to
Salem Burne. I am most admiring of your efforts to
conceal and protect. My confidence in you both is
much compounded."

"He wants something from us, Gretchen."

"Only to tell you that, yes, there have been new outrages, atrocious acts which can assuredly be attributed to the Hundred-Hander."

"What acts?"

"Tortures and Lethals. And we have some strange witness-verbal descriptions of the forms the Hundred-Hander took whilst perpetrating." Here Ind'dni paused, then continued smoothly. "Perhaps most interesting was the description of a vicious attacker in the new Therpool."

"Yes?"

"It was of Dr. Shima."

"What!"

"It was you, Dr. Shima."

"I don't believe it."

"Alas, you must. The victim's description of the criminal assaulter was unmistakable. To make certain, she was shown lineup faxes in the round. She picked yours without the slightest doubting hesitation."

"This is a damnable ploy, Ind'dni."

"No, assuredly. She described you."

"But that's impossible! Criminal assault! I've never been near the Therpool. I wouldn't know how to find it. What's the date of the attack? I can prove that I—"

"Cool it, Blaise," Gretchen cut in. "Easy, man, until we know exactly how it stands. Subadar, this was one hell of a mess to start with, and it seems to be getting worse. Now play fair with us. Give us a full report of these new horrors. All of them."

"They are not yet of public record."

"Can that matter? If Dr. Shima is in some way connected with the Hundred-Hander, as I'm sure you suspect, then you'll be telling him nothing that he doesn't already know."

Ind'dni gave her the fencer's salute, acknowledging a hit. "And Dr. Shima called *me* devious. I bow, madame. Here is what has happened."

When the Subadar had finished his detailed report there was a long silence while they digested the data.

Then Shima whispered, "Dear God," and at last found his voice. "Gretchen, I think it's time for us to—"

"Clam it!" she snapped. Ind'ni's painful account had first shocked her, then electrified her, and now she was assured and driving. "Subadar, I'm almost positive that you have the key to the Golem[100]. You don't know it. Blaise might fit it together when he comes out of shock. I know now, not because I'm smarter than you two; simply because I have access to personality and persona profiles which you don't. The psytech instinct. I believe I see the construct."

Ind'dni gave her another quizzical look. "Do you, madame? And?"

"It's based on Freud's primary psychic process." Her words came like blows. "Instinct eruption! Energy thrust! Erotic libido and death libido. Eros! Thanatos!"

"Yes, our professions require a familiarity with psychiatry. And?"

"First I must know Dr. Shima's status. Is he to be charged and arrested on that victim's I.D.?"

"He claims innocence."

"I do, God help me!" Shima burst out.

"Then what did Miz Nunn stop you from telling me? Too late now. Do you believe him, madame?"

"I do."

"Then you object to his arrest?"

"Most certainly."

"On what grounds? Personal?"

"No, professional. I'll need his help."

"You are most difficult collab-person colleague, Miz Nunn." Ind'dni smiled ruefully while he considered. Then, "Dr. Shima is charged in your category, with Felony-Five. He is placed under Guffarrest."

"Thank you."

"And now I will thank you to return the courtesy. How is he to help you?"

"Don't ask *me*," Shima muttered. "I'm wiped out.

A cipher. Criminal assault! Rape! Dear Christ help me . . ."

"How do you intend to act, Miz Nunn? What is this key which you alone know?"

Gretchen shook her head. "As subtle and sophisticated as you are, Subadar, you would never understand the psychodynamics of intuition."

"Please to try me, nevertheless."

"You would never believe."

"The Hindu culture is capable of fantastic beliefs."

"And 'The Murder Mavin of the Guff' could never approve."

Ind'dni winced. "Most unkind of you to use that label, Miz Nunn," he said reproachfully. "Do you intend to act illegal?"

"That would depend on your definition of illegality, Subadar. Let me put it this way: we're forbidden to leave the Guff precinct without your knowledge and consent. Yes?"

"My *hukm*. Yes. That is the constraint of the invented Felony-Five category."

"But what if we were to leave without leaving?"

"That is paradox."

"No. It can be done."

"Leave? Without leaving? Surely you do not mean departure through suicidal self-ending?"

"No."

"Then a departure how and to where?"

"To a reality that no culture has ever recognized or even acknowledged. To a world that is the invisible eight-ninths of human history's iceberg; a Subworld, a *Sous-monde, ein Unterwelt,* an Infraworld, à Phasmaworld . . ."

"Ah yes. From the Greek, *phainein,* to make appear. You mystify me in several languages, madame."

"And I'll mystify you even more." Gretchen was trembling with excitement. "I think this submerged, hidden Phasmaworld has finally broken through to the top of the iceberg and made an appearance."

"And now you want to return the visit? That is your departure?"

"Yes."

"How depart?"

"With a Promethium passport."

"Ah yes, the radioactive salt discovered in those bones resulting from . . . your 'contract' weapon?" Ind'dni turned to Shima before Gretchen could respond to the irony. "My forensic staff was most impressed by your expertise, doctor." He had never seemed more softly dangerous.

"If you want more expertise," Shima said wearily, "it's $^{145}Pm_2O_3$ with a half-life of thirty years."

"Thank you." Ind'dni smiled, nodded, and returned to Gretchen. "And I am requested to collaborate in this nebulous venture with you?"

"No. Only to give us your *hukm*."

"Will there be danger?"

"Possibly."

"To whom?"

"Us alone. No one else."

"Then why try to levant to this mystic Phasmaworld of your imaginings, Miz Nunn? What do you hope to gain by the delay?"

"So you don't believe me, Subadar?"

"Sadly and most firmly, no."

"Then you won't believe this either. I'm convinced that's where the Golem-Hundred-Hander lives."

12

Gretchen looked at the stunned cipher with amused pity. "My place is no place for you," she said. "I'm schlepping you back to your own saloon. You'll regroup better there."

"*Le pauvre petit*," Shima muttered.

"Maybe, but you've got to cope now, baby. We're involved in something tremendous. So let's move it."

In Shima's penthouse, she stripped him and shoved him into the mirrored Roman tub. She ran the water as hot as her elbow could stand.

"Courtesy of CCC clout," she said. "It's jaunty-jolly to be loved by the Establishment."

"You getting in too, please?" he asked.

"No time for funny business. I'm going to slug you with my coffee-cognac prescription which it could win the Nobel Peace Prize if I'd reveal the secret formula."

"After what Ind'dni made me swallow I don't know if I can get anything else down."

"Wait until I give you my Golem scam. You'll wish you were in a brain-damage slammer."

"Are you trying to scare me more?"

"Just trying to prepare you. Soak. Enjoy. Relax. Back soon."

When she returned with the slugged coffee, she knew he was recovering because he was sitting up in the tub with a washcloth covering his crotch. Shima, who was completely uninhibited in bed, was curiously modest out of it.

"French. Jap. Irish," she thought. "They all caught the fig-leaf hang-up from Eve. Funny the old Bible doesn't mention a bra." Aloud she said, "Drink this."

"Your secret formula?"

"Accept no substitutes."

"It'll ruin me for the lab."

"You won't be doing any smelling around. I won't be doing any work either. We've got to tackle one hell of a hassle."

She sat down on the loo facing him. "Can you listen?"

He nodded and sipped.

"And understand? This is going to be a mind-stretcher of fact and Freud."

"I heard of him."

"And did you hear me tell the Subadar that the key to the Hundred-Hander-Golem thing lay in the primary psychic process?"

"Yes, but I didn't understand."

"From the way he gave it a smooth slough I don't think he did either. Now pay attention, Blaise. It's one of Freud's fundamental concepts. He called it the Psi-system. Short form, P-system."

"Psi? You mean ESP?"

"No. The twentieth-century cats took over Psi for extrasensory perception. They probably never heard of Father Freud's nomenclature. Anyway, the Old Man laid it down that the P-system, the primary psychic process, was at the bottom of every human being and it aimed at only one thing, the free outflow of the quantities of excitation."

"Jeez!"

"Yeah."

"You could explain a little."

"Look at it this way. We all have the erotic excitation, the libido. That's the P-system and it's the source of all creation; literature, love, the arts, you name it."

"Science?"

"Of course, science too. It's a powerhouse of driving energy and it's always trying to collect life together into larger unities. That's the way a shrink describes the creative process. Boy meets girl and they collect to create love and a family. Scientist like you collects chemicals to create perfumes. I collect data to create solutions. All this is libido . . . psychic energy in action. Tremendous! Now dig this, man: the bee-ladies pool their energies to create a larger entity, a collection of the hive libido, the Golem[100]."

"How?"

"How? Well . . . think of it like . . . Yes, like a pastry bag for icing. You mix all the ingredients, beat and cook 'em, transfer to the forcing bag and squeeze. The icing comes out of the spout end. Well, mix the ladies' libidos, beat and cook, transfer to the ritual forcing bag, and squeeze. Out comes the Golem."

"But I—Wait. Is the Golem real or just a shadow projection?"

"What's real? If a tree falls in a forest and no one's around to hear it, does it make a real sound? In other words, must reality be reciprocal?"

"Damn if I know."

"Nobody does."

"But look, Gretchen, the Golem made those ghastly attacks. That makes it real. Only it was a different thing each time. That makes it unreal."

"Only in our terms."

"Then which is it?"

"Both. It's a quasi-reality; Adam in the second hour of creation; shapeless and without a soul. We need a brand-new vocabulary to describe it. It's a protean that can assume any shape it wants."

"Then what makes it want a particular shape?"

"Ah! I was hoping you'd get around to that. Now

we get down to the nitty-gritty which has to be described in terms of personality and persona profiles. You know the difference?"

"I think so. Personality is what you really *are* inside. Persona is how you show yourself to the world."

"Right on. Persona is the mask we wear. Like this." She snatched up the washcloth cover and dropped it back before Shima could holler. As he adjusted it, he grumbled, "Women! Let them get intimate with you, and they lose all sense of decency."

"No, we just drop the persona mask, is all. If you're strong enough to beef, you must be feeling better. Let's get down to the facts. I'll take the horrors in sequence."

"No details, I beg. Once is enough for a sissy."

"No details; just personality profiles; what was inside the victims. That girl in the stock exchange and the Golem computer mechanic . . ."

"The girl who wanted to be infected with genius?"

"Yes. Who was she?"

"How should I know? Ind'dni didn't give names. He didn't even give descriptions."

"But in personality she was a look-alike for another girl. Can you think who?"

"Well . . . She was dumb and didn't want to be."

"Exactly. And who'd I tell you about that was dumb and didn't want to be?"

"Who'd you tell me that . . . ?" Shima thought hard and at last twigged. "My God! The hive. Yes. That blonde dancer with her hair like a helmet."

"Mary Mixup. Right."

"Was the victim actually Mary? The one you met?"

"No, just the same type. Nobody's really unique; we all have personality dupes and/or physical look-alikes. Now, the second outrage in the Theaterthon with the Golem actor?"

Shima recognized the pattern she was shaping. "Of course. Sarah Heartburn, the actress *manqué*."

146

"The girl who took sanctuary in the Church of Saint Jude?"

"That well-bred one who objects to five-letter words. Miss Pot, is it?"

"No, Miss Priss, as in prisspot. The *distinguée* hostess in the Freeport Restaurant?"

"Queen Regina, of course. And the girl at the rallye assaulted by the Golem lesbian. She was the Yenta Calienta type. But who was the GoFer in Studio 2222?"

"Nellie Gwyn."

"Ildefonsa? Impossible? Ildy's a looker; you said so yourself. That GoFer was a crow."

"But the same personality."

"How d'you know?"

"Wait for it. Wait for it. Last of all, that career-type in the Therpool?"

"The one Ind'dni thinks I assaulted?"

"Yes, because she's the one who identified you."

"I can't understand how she made such a mistake."

"It wasn't any mistake. The Golem did look like you."

"How could it?"

"Because the career gal was me."

"You!"

"Me, personalitywise. That's what opened it up for me." Gretchen nodded with assurance, then leaned forward intently. "Now try to grasp this, Blaise. It'll be tough because we're past facts and into the psychic process of the Phasmaworld."

"Your Subworld. I'll try."

"Given: a plastic, protean creature making appearances in different human shapes. Given: seven of its victims, each a personality match for one of the beeladies."

"So far you've got the left-hand side of an equation. What comes after the equals sign?"

"Each of the victims was attacked by a creature

147

created by the outflow of a bee-lady's libido and shaped by that libido."

"Oh Jesus!"

"Oh yes."

"You're asking me to buy your phasma fantasy."

"I'm not selling you anything. Just look at the facts. Mary Mixup yearns for a man who'll make her smart. Sarah Heartburn—a dynamic artist-type. Miss Priss —a holy, well-bred lover. Regina—Lord Nelson. Nellie Gwyn—a King Charles the Second stud. That's how I knew the GoFer was Ildefonsa; the Golem was carrying a King Charles spaniel. Yenta—a butch bulldyke. Me—you. Q.E.D."

"What about those twins with the Russian names? Why were they left out?"

"Maybe they weren't. Maybe the report hasn't reached. Ind'dni—or the outrages went unnoticed, like hundreds more in this lunatic Guff which takes horrors for granted."

"But—"

But there was no interrupting Gretchen. "You know about the id, the deep reservoir of libido energy in every man, a hellhole of primal drives. Sure you do. Maybe you can remember that line from Hamlet? *Bloody, bawdy villain! Remorseless, treacherous, lecherous, kindless villain!* That's the id buried in the basement of the human animal; you, me, all of us."

"We can't all be monsters," Shima protested.

"Deep down inside, in our Underworld, we are. Up here, at the top of the iceberg, we censor and control it; but what happens when that brute beast in us escapes control, breaks out of the cage, and runs wild? Then you have Golem[100]."

"How does it break out of the cage?"

"Sharpen a wit, baby. The bee-ladies get together in Regina's hive. They play witchcraft games. Of course they never succeed in raising the Devil because he doesn't exist. That's just folklore."

Shima nodded.

148

"But their ids combine to generate a different demon. There isn't any inferno, but there is an Infraworld, and our remorseless, treacherous, lecherous, kindless ids live down there. The ladies' libidos merge down there, and that's the genesis of the Golem. It takes the shape of any one or all of some of their unconscious savageries and appears in our conscious world to ravish and slaughter without sense or reason . . . just savage pleasure. Erotic libido and death libido."

"You're claiming that the bottom line with the bee-ladies is the Golem[100]?"

"Yes. It's the gut-reality. Energy eruption."

"Why the bee-ladies in particular? Why don't we all generate Golems down there?"

"Three little words. Catalyst."

"Holy Saints! The Promethium."

"It's a hell of a thing to cope with, Blaise, but until that radioactive Pm got into the act the world has never been confronted with the gut eight-ninths of the iceberg."

Shima sighed. "What a rotten thing to happen to a beautiful legend," he said sadly. "Prometheus, the Fire-Bringer, teacher of the arts of life, friend and benefactor of Man. And now look at the foul fire he's generating in those filthy women!"

"They're still nice ladies, Blaise."

"No. How can they be?"

"They don't know what they're doing."

"There has to be a conscious clue."

"They don't even know their gut-drives."

"We all know that we have them in this day and age."

"The fact, but not the hideous details. Our conscious can't bring itself to examine the primal ferocity. That's why people have to suffer through psychoanalysis for years before they can come face to face with their bottom line."

"Have you come face to face with yours?"

"I doubt it. I know you haven't."

"Me?"

"You. Do you know what primal passion drives you into the personality of Mr. Wish?"

Shima was stunned.

"But you are driven, aren't you? And yet you're a nice guy . . . As nice as the bee-ladies."

"Oh Jesus! Christ Jesus! Then Ind'dni is right. I *am* a Golem."

"Easy, baby. You're not alone. Most of us are Golems, one way or another. The rare exceptions get sainted. So cool it and I'll whip up another slug of the secret formula, prized by the *cognoscenti,* and famed in song and story."

She went into the galley which was so rarely used that it was almost as sterile as Shima's laboratory at CCC. Gretchen's secret formula was the extravagant equivalent of two weeks in a spa: coffee, butter, sugar, egg yolks, cream, cognac. While she was heating and churning the hellbrew in a double boiler, her sight began to fade.

"Hey! Open your eyes," she called cheerfully. "I'm going blind."

He didn't answer. Her primary vision failed altogether, and she was left with the secondary kaleidoscope. "Damn. He's fallen asleep." She felt her way out of the galley to the bath. "Blaise! Wake up!"

No answer. She groped around the tub. It was empty. She felt the tile floor with her palms. It was wet. "He's getting dressed. Mr. Modesty!" She went into the bedroom. "Blaise?" No answer. In the lounge she called, "Blaise Shima! Come out, come out, wherever you are!" Nothing. And nothing from the terrace except the Guff's distant pandemonium.

"Damn the man. He's funked out and gone to hide in his lab. Patience, Gretchen. Patience." She allowed an impatient half hour for traveltime and called CCC. No, Dr. Shima's laboratory did not answer. No, Dr. Shima was not to be found in the CCC complex. She called the Organic Nursery. No, Dr. Shima was not dining there. Anyway, Dr. Shima always had his meals delivered.

She called the stock exchange, Theaterthon, the Church of St. Jude, the Freeport Restaurant, Station WGA, the Sheep Meadow racetrack, the Therpool. No one answering to the name or description of Blaise Shima. Now genuinely alarmed she thought of contacting Salem Burne or the P.L.O.; instead she settled for the Guff Precinct Complex and asked for Subadar Ind'dni.

"And are you calling from your mystic Subworld, Miz Nunn?" he inquired. "You did not give me to understand that it had communication with reality."

"Mr. Ind'dni, I'm in trouble."

"The identical same, madame, or more so?"

"More so. Dr. Shima has disappeared."

"Has he indeed? Best to describe event."

After Gretchen had finished a carefully edited account, Ind'dni sighed. "Yes. To be understood. Most probably Dr. Shima found your fantastic conclusions about Hundred-Hander situation as difficult to stomach as did I. He is in hiding from you and has my sympathy. But he must not leave the Guff in his flight. An A.P.B. must be broadcast."

"Not an A.P.B., Subadar!"

"Alas, what else can I do? However, I promise this: every effort will be made to keep taint of scandal from media. Code Nemo will be used."

"What? Code Nemo?"

"So. You have never heard of Code Nemo?" She could sense Ind'dni's internal smile. "I did tell you that I do not lack resources, Miz Nunn."

After contact was broken, Gretchen muttered, "To hell with his A.P.B. and Code Nemo. My staff can lick his staff anytime."

She managed her way out of the penthouse, safed it, and got down to the street, where full sight returned. When she arrived at her apartment, it was in time for a dramatic tableau. Her staff was assembled, gathered around Shima, staring at him and restraining him. Shima was stark naked and struggling politely.

"Blaise!" she exclaimed.

"The name is Wish, my dear. You may call me Mr. Wish." He gave her the glassy smile.

She shook her head like an animal trying to dislodge an infuriating fly.

"He just crunched in, Miz Nunn. Security downstairs says he asked for you by name."

"By name? He asked for Gretchen Nunn?"

"No, Miz. Just 'Gretch.' He said that Gretch from the Guff lived here and knew Mr. Wish. Security thought it was one of our codes and let him up."

"You may release me," Mr. Wish smiled. "I have nothing to grant any of you."

She understood. "No, none of us. You can let him go. He's harmless."

"Miz Nunn, why does he call himself Mr. Wish? We know he's—"

"He isn't anybody you ever saw or heard of. Mr. Wish was never here. Understood? Thank heaven I can trust you. Now out, all of you."

When the study was cleared she closed the door and stood contemplating the courteous Mr. Wish. "No, none of us. You poor schnook, you've been backtracking on your own death-wish trail. It's really hit you hard, hasn't it? Went right over the brink into the deeps."

"I remember you, Gretch," Mr. Wish smiled. "I tried to help you once. Do you remember me?"

"You're the one that's got to be helped, Blaise," Gretchen murmured. "There's an A.P.B. out, and if you're picked up in this character . . . Like down will come baby, cradle, and all." She got a giant bath towel and tossed it across his lap. "Here, wrap this around." Then she sat and breathed deep. "Now how the hell am I going to bring you out of it? Fake a suicide for Mr. Wish? What good would that do? Chem-shots? I wouldn't know what to prescribe. What you need is a psychic shock, and it's got to be homeopathic, but what, what, what?"

Mr. Wish adjusted his toga and said, "I don't think I could help the one I was following anyway."

"Not unless you catch up with him."

"It's not that. I can't find my aids. I don't seem to have them with me."

Gretchen's smile was exasperated. "Did you try your pockets?"

"I must have left them somewhere. Locked up, of course. Can't be too careful with lethal modules. I wonder where."

"Happy to say I can't help, Mr. Wish."

"It doesn't matter, my dear. I'd have to find the key first."

"Oh sure. The key first, of course, and then the lethal modules which—" Gretchen broke off abruptly. It took her a full five seconds to acknowledge her appalling idea. She began to tremble and rock, shaking her head. "I can't. I won't. There'd be no enduring that." And all the while she knew that she could, would, and have to endure. It took long minutes to compose herself. She went into her bedroom, got something from the night table, and clutched it in her palm. Then, smiling almost as glassily as Mr. Wish, she called Ildefonsa Lafferty.

"Nellie? BB calling. No, not from the hive; my own place. Nell, I've got a *crise psychologique* and I—No, love, it's not more intellect; just French for something heavy. My problem's here now, and I don't want him to know what I'm talking about. Yes, it's a he. I can't handle him. I think you can because it's one of your specialties. Can you come over right away? No, love, no hints. You'll see for yourself when you get here. Thanks, Nell." She broke the connection. "All right, Blaise. I'm going to unlock that drawer."

This was Gretchen Nunn's professional protocol. She greeted distinguished clients at the entrance to her Oasis. She met the fringe celebrities at the impressive door of her apartment with her staff in attendance. The bread-and-butter customers were ushered into her workshop where she was seated, working while she waited. (Mills Copeland, chairman of CCC, would have been deeply offended, had he known.) Gretchen met Ildefonsa Lafferty at the door of her study and ushered her in.

"Thanks for coming to the rescue, Nell. This one's a bummer."

Ildefonsa was blazing in lettuce sequins. "Who could resist the tease, BB? Of course it was a tease. I've got your number. No matter what you do, you've always got a second intention."

"I protest, Nell."

"Why deny it? That's the grabby part of your tease. I ask myself what she's up to now, and I have to find out."

"I swear it's a straight rescue."

"Like I'm supposed to believe you? Is that thing your *crise psychologique?*" She indicated the glassy Mr. Wish with a hip.

"That's it."

"You said 'he.' You didn't say a null in a toga."

"He's in shock and he's got to be stung out of it . . . Back to normal."

"What's so hot about normal? Why not let him enjoy?"

"I need his evidence-verbal for a case."

"Why call me?"

"Because you know something I don't know."

"What, in particular?"

"How to sting men."

"Well, I never yanced a zombie, but there always has to be a first."

Gretchen smiled with thin lips. "If that's the way it has to be, feel free."

"Is there any other way?" Ildefonsa strolled to Mr. Wish, inspected him casually, then bent suddenly and looked hard. "My God! I can't believe it. This is Hero."

"Hero? It's Dr. Blaise Shima. What hero?"

"Hero, short for Hiroshima. Chase him into bed, BB, and you'll find out why."

Gretchen kept her mouth shut.

"So that was your second intention," Ildefonsa said. "What happened to him?"

"I don't know. That's why I can't handle him."

Ildefonsa prowled around Shima. "Well, well, Hero. Long time no connect. Miss me, stud?"

"The name is Wish, my dear. You may call me Mr. Wish."

"God knows, you were a maiden's wish come true, stud." Over her shoulder, Ildefonsa threw, "He doesn't know me?"

"He doesn't know anyone."

"Including himself?"

"He thinks he's some character he invented named Wish."

"So you want to get rid of that character?"

"That's the op. Bring him back to himself."

"Any ideas?"

"You were my only idea. I thought, 'Nell is the one to make him conscious.' "

"Thanks, but my usual op is knocking them unconscious. I don't know about the retro ploy. Might be interesting. You want him to remember he's Shima?"

"That's the scam."

"Hmmm . . ." Ildefonsa meditated while Mr. Wish beamed up at her, looking like a pleasant Roman senator. Then, "Hey, Hero, remember this?" She began to sing in her peanut-whistle voice:

> My mother said I never should
> Prance with a yanceman in the wood.
> If I did, she would say,
> You naughty girl to disobey.
> Disobey.
> Disobey.
> On your husband's holiday.

Ildefonsa giggled. "You always dug that, Hero. Remember? You used to make me sing and dance it."

"The name is Wish, my dear. Mr. Wish."

"He's really spaced, BB. That number could always hustle him into the water gap. Hero believed I was the pure type singing smut I didn't understand."

"Way out."

"Just typical. He never knew the score. You think I should try the dance bit? It's a strip."

"Why not? Wait. Wear this."

Ildefonsa looked at the cabochon in Gretchen's palm. "What is it?"

Gretchen felt a little better. "It's an uncut diamond."

"You want me to wear it?"

"Please."

"What on? I'll be stripped."

"Wear it in your navel."

"For God's—There? How?"

"It's mounted on skinstick."

"Why do I wear it?"

"It's the key to a locked drawer."

"Whose?"

"His."

"Sounds like he's acquired some kinky kicks since I knew him."

"He has. No, Nell, don't let him see you put it in place; it's got to be flashed on him suddenly. Use my bedroom."

Ildefonsa nodded and went through the door that Gretchen opened for her. She came out in a few moments, making sure that the door remained open. "Groovy bed," she commented approvingly. "It could turn therapy into a thrill. Those mirrors! All countdown now."

"Should I leave you alone together?"

"Why? Maybe you'll learn something useful."

"There's always room for improvement," Gretchen agreed through her teeth.

156

Ildefonsa took position before Mr. Wish and began to sing and dance rather clumsily. ("Rotten coordination in the vertical.") The lettuce-sequin *apparat* was designed to break apart in convenient sections ("But not designed with dancing in mind.") which Ildefonsa cast aside any which way until she was stripped down to her glowing blush skin for the final flash. She turned slowly, displaying every thrust of her plummy body, flashed and held the pose before Mr. Wish. Gretchen choked back a growl.

The diamond was close and level with his eyes. Mr. Wish stared at it. Then his eyes dropped to the mons veneris, lifted to the breasts, and at last to Ildefonsa's face. He turned pale.

"But . . . but you're Ildy," he faltered. His eyes dropped to the cabochon. "Why . . . What are . . . Why are you wearing Gretchen's diamond?" He arose slowly and looked around in bewilderment. "I've lost connection."

Ildefonsa held out her plummy arms to him. "Come on, stud. We'll reconnect."

"But it . . . I . . . It's not then. It's now. Now." His voice strengthened. "God almighty, what am I doing with you, Ildy? Here? You like this. Wearing Gretchen's diamond. Giving me that old Ipanema gig. Christ! I put you away a year ago."

"I took her out of the drawer, Blaise," Gretchen said quietly.

He shook his head slowly. "You? Did this? To me?"

"I had to bring you back."

"But . . . But the diamond?"

"I asked her to wear it."

"Why?"

"That was the key."

"What did you bring me back from?"

"Mr. Wish."

"Oh Jesus! Jesus God!"

"It's all right, Hero," Ildefonsa said soothingly. She

157

ran her hands under the toga. "Everything's all right now. You're back. I'm back. We're both back where we started. Come on, stud." She coaxed him toward the bedroom.

Shima looked into her face. Her eyes were melting. He looked at Gretchen. Her eyes were steady. He looked from one to the other again, then turned Ildefonsa gently and started her toward the bedroom. He seemed to be following but it was only to step out of the toga which he draped around her shoulders. "Farewells should be forever," he said.

Ildefonsa turned in astonishment. Shima crossed to Gretchen. "What now?" he asked.

"Thanks for the coronation."

"It was no contest."

"It was for me."

"What now?" he repeated.

"Now? Your lab for a Pm trip. We've got to visit the Phasmaworld." She called over his shoulder to the amazed Ildefonsa. "Your count was short, Nellie. With me you have to watch out for a third intention. You can keep the diamond."

13

.!–,:''?.../;

"Here, Gretchen."

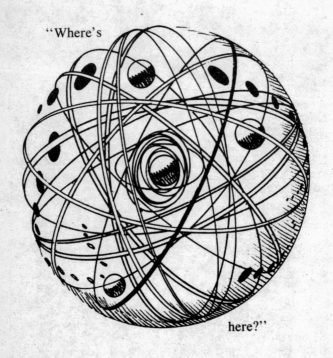

"Where's

here?"

"Your Subworld.
We mainlined P-M
        in the lab.
              A
         milligram
            each
             in
           normal
          saline."

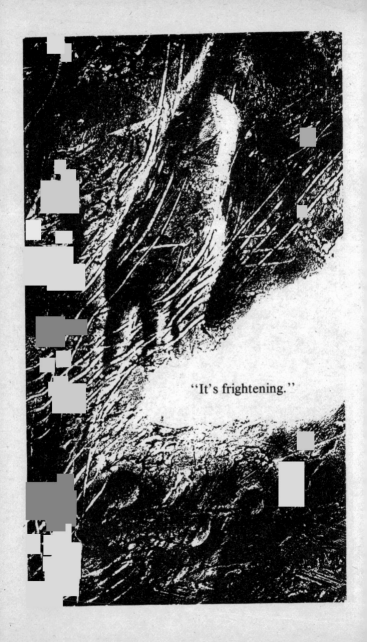

"It's frightening."

"It's fascinating. I never really
bought your Infraworld
concept, Gretchen.
I was wrong."

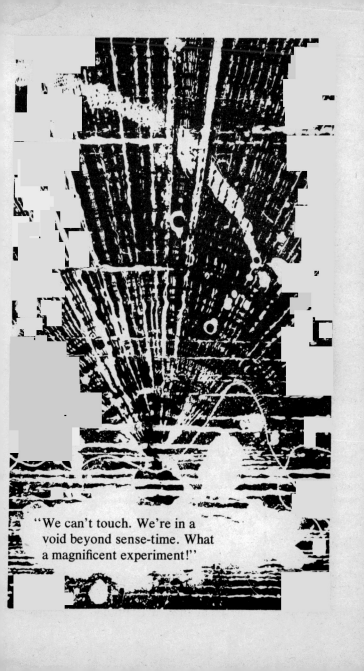

"We can't touch. We're in a
void beyond sense-time. What
a magnificent experiment!"

"Maybe for a scientist, but not
for me. Blaise, I'm terrified.
I'm seeing the craziest things."

"Me too. What are you seeing now?"

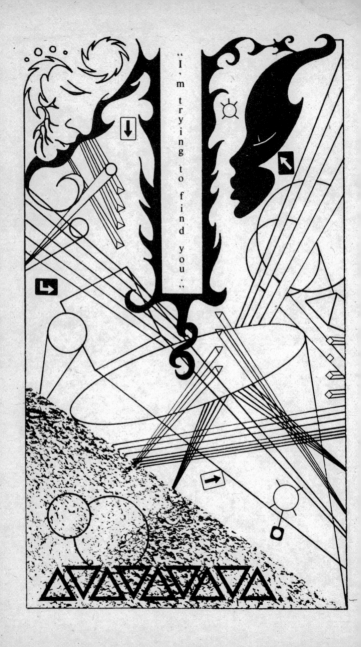

"I'm trying to find you..."

"Any luck?"

"I thought for a second—but not really. You?"

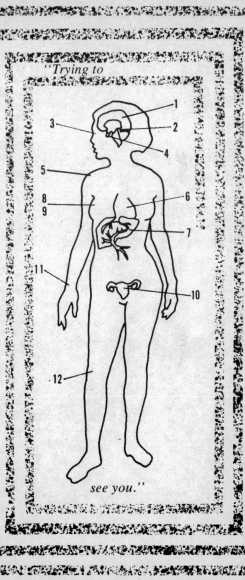

"Trying to

see you."

"Like what you see?"

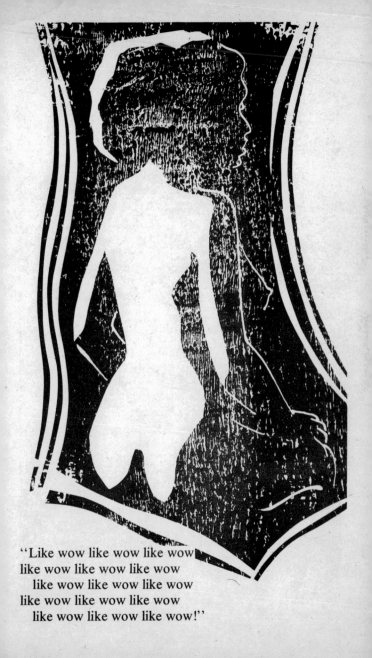

"Like wow like wow like wow
like wow like wow like wow
like wow like wow like wow
like wow like wow like wow
like wow like wow like wow!''

"Kiss me, my clown."

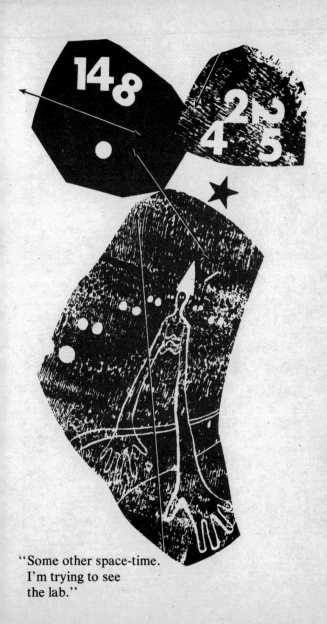

"Some other space-time.
I'm trying to see
the lab."

"Sight anything that makes sense, Blaise? I can't and it's spooking me!"

"No. Now don't panic, Gretchen. We can't really see anything yet This is our vision-sense clinging to jumbled memories, like nerve echoes after amputation. I think all our senses are doing that."

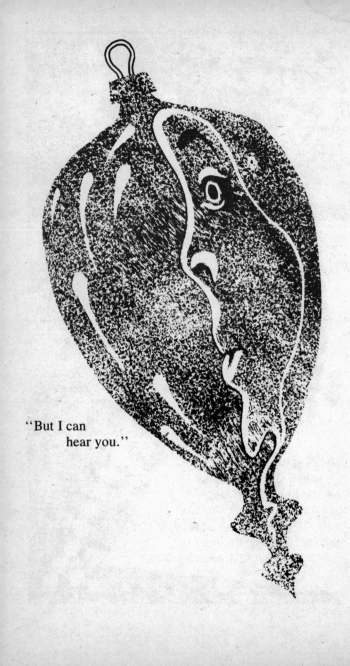

"But I can
hear you."

"I doubt it, Gretchen. I don't think we're using words."

"We're communicating on the sublevel and translating ideas into remembered sound patterns."

"Will we ever encounter this idworld as it really is?"

"When our senses kick the comfort and quit clinging to the familiar. They hate confrontation with the unknown, but they must adapt. Take five, Gretchen. Tell your nerves to accept the unknown as an adventure."

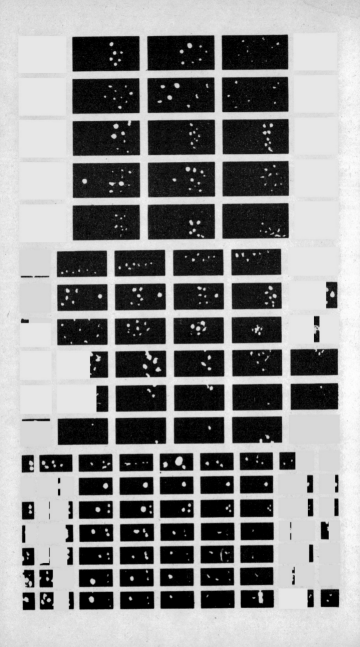

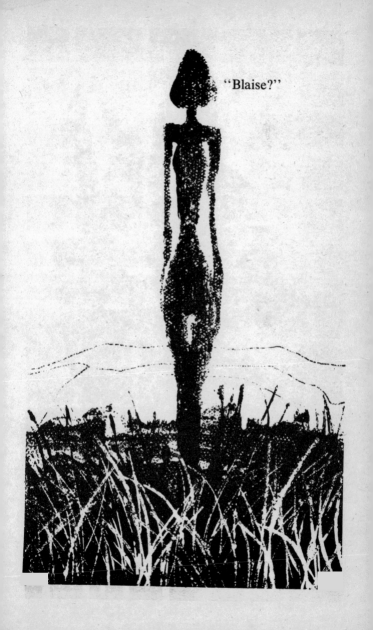

"Still here."

"Nothing for me. Anything for you?"

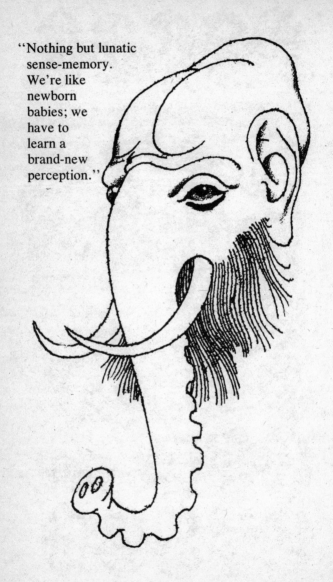

"Nothing but lunatic sense-memory. We're like newborn babies; we have to learn a brand-new perception."

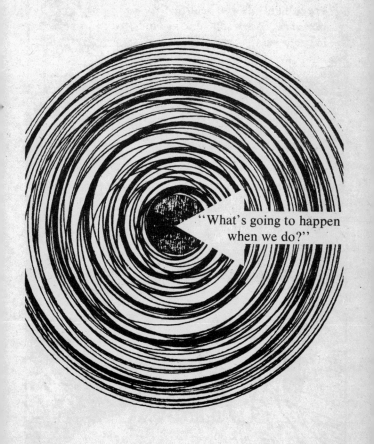

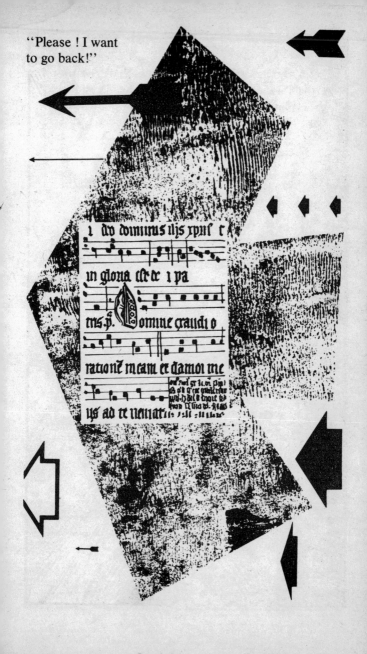

'Lost my courage. I'm in a panic.''

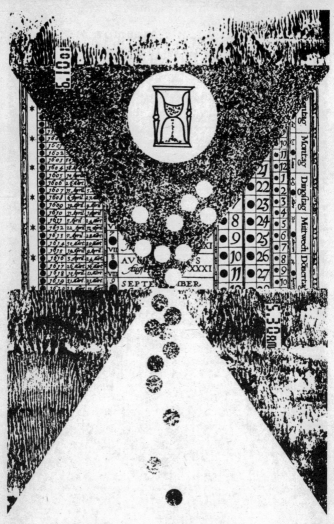

"A milligram can't last long,
only there's no long or short
in Null-space. There's no time.
There's only—

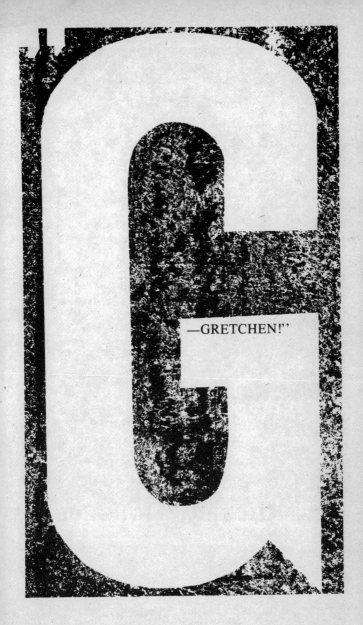
—GRETCHEN!"

"Don't frighten me. Blaise.
I'm scared enough as it is."

"I think my sense-memory
is letting go. Yours?"

"I don't know."

"Still seeing color?"

"No."

"Receiving any images?"

"No."

"Good. Now if the P-M trip
lasts, we may be able to sense
the Phasmaworld as it really is."

"BLAISE! BLAISE! THE GOLEM!"

14

Subadar Ind'dni entered Interrogation Room One. It was warm and dark. Dr. Blaise Shima glowed faintly in the soft plastic womb, narcotized, naked, curled in the fetal position. There was soothing music incorporating a gentle heartbeat. The examining officers were not shouting questions at him; rather, their maternal voices came quietly out of the dark, blending with the comfort.

"We love you, baby."

"The whole world loves you."

"You're nice and warm and safe."

"So you can tell us."

"You can tell mommie."

"What have you got against the Intra National Cartel Association?"

"And why were you looking for a virgin?"

"What girl would admit it anyway?"

"Tell us."

"Tell mommie."

"Where did you get the firecrackers?"

"Did you make them yourself?"

"Tell us, baby."

"That kite fight must have been fun."

"Did you talk to those people?"

"Tell us what you said."

"Tell mommie everything."

"Didn't you remember we sold the Statue of Liberty for scrap years ago?"

"We sold Bedloe's Island, too."

"What were you really doing?"

"Tell mommie."

"Did you actually want a skin-join?"

"With ink?"

"What did you really want?"

"Of course you know what naked girls look like."

"Everybody does."

"So what did you really want from that dead one?"

"Tell us."

"Is it because you like girls?"

"Then why try to paint them black?"

"And do you hate your job that much?"

"Or do you hate CCC?"

"Maybe you hate science. Tell us, baby."

"Maybe he hates himself."

"Is that why you tried to take off into space, baby?"

"Tell mommie. You don't have to be afraid. You won't be punished for anything."

"That was a fun musical show you put on."

"But you're not only color-blind, baby, you're tone-deaf."

"Mommie's proud of you anyway."

"So tell us why you did it."

"Baby, you really shouldn't try to bang a broad in a supermarket."

"Everybody loves you, but not that much."

"Or was it a secret message?"

"Tell us."

"And how could an elephant get into your Oasis?"

"Let alone your bed."

"Silly baby!"

"You didn't really think you could push that rain tank over all by yourself, did you?"

"Of course not."

"So what were you really trying to do? Was it a signal to the P.L.O.?"

"Tell us, baby."

"Tell mommie."

"Tell us."

Shima never responded. He floated in the womb with his head between his knees and his arms wrapped around himself, never moving a muscle. Subadar Ind'dni sighed, turned, and left as quietly as he had entered. He visited Interrogation Room Two. It was identical to Room One with the exception of the paternal voices and the occupant of the plastic womb, Gretchen Nunn.

"We love you, baby."

"The whole world loves you."

"So you're nice and warm and safe."

"And you can tell us."

"You can tell daddy."

"You know we love toys, don't you?"

"And they love us."

"So what were you really trying to do in that toy store?"

"Is there a squeam scam we don't know about?"

"Tell us, baby."

"Tell daddy."

"You were naughty in the art museum."

"Daddy's told you a hundred times not to touch things that don't belong to you."

"Why did you do it?"

"Little girl, you know you're the wrong color for a tattoo."

"So what were you really after? Is that man a pusher?"

"And you ought to know that you can't give the hots to a poster."

"It didn't need it anyway."

"So why try?"

"Or was it an undercover signal to some person or persons unknown?"

"Tell daddy."

"What made you think you could star in that opera?"

"Or are you sore at the Glacial Army?"

"And you ought to know we need all the perfume we can get these days."

"So why crunch the source?"

"Or are you sore at CCC? Tell us why."

"That was our good, sweet little girl to spray Christmas all over the launch pad."

"But Christmas colors aren't red and green anymore."

"They're black and white. What have you got against black, baby?"

"You're black yourself. Are you ashamed?"

"Why didn't you let that funny man catch up with you in the supermarket?"

"You let him catch up with you before."

"Why not this time? Tell us."

"Tell daddy."

"Tell us what you have against star sapphires."

"Is it because you hate all stars?"

"Or is it a code?"

"Tell us."

"And wherever did you learn dirty Latin?"

"Or was that code, too?"

"Tell us, baby."

"Tell daddy."

"Tell us."

No response from Gretchen Nunn. Subadar Ind'dni sighed again, turned, left, and sauntered to his office in the Precinct Complex.

It was hardly the conventional business office of a high-level executive. Ind'dni had withdrawn from the fevers of the Guff nightmare into Japanese simplicity; uncovered polished teak floor, neutral screens, unobtrusive ebony furniture. There was no conventional conference table; instead there was a tile charcoal firepit in the center of the office. Around this Ind'dni and his conferees sat on the rim with their legs dangling down in the warmth. Quite naturally, the Subadar's staff loved even the most abrasive sessions with their chief.

Perhaps the most remarkable aspect of the Japanese mystique was the single decoration standing before the screened windows; a four-foot weathered, gnarled and twisted cedar trunk. Its ivory-smooth surface was almost hypnotic. Even Ind'dni could not resist the impulsion to stroke it, which he was doing now.

At last he spoke. "And so, please? Response, if any?"

His office was empty but a disembodied voice answered, "None, sir."

"Not even customary denials?"

"No, sir."

"Then what, if anything?"

"Nothing, sir. A complete blank. Both seem to be spacing out."

"Most strange. You have pursued standard operational procedure in questioning?"

"We've not limited it to that, Subadar. We've tried every innovation we could invent."

"And still negative time-lapse?"

"Sorry, sir."

"No, no, not to regret. Most interesting and unusual challenge compounding excruciating perplexity of Hundred-Hander beast. Please to dress—Do I hear laughter?"

"Sorry, sir. I was remembering their appearance here at the precinct."

"Yes. To be agreed. Most unexpected and amusing advent. To some. So. Please to dress them, restore to contemporary consciousness, and bring to me."

Blaise and Gretchen weren't tottering when they entered Ind'dni's office but they weren't exactly jaunty-jolly. They displayed the confusion of someone who has awakened in an alien room without the vaguest recall of who, what, when, where, why.

"Most welcome," Ind'dni said. "You have led the wicked sheriff a merry chase through the forest of Mr. Sherwood. So kind of you to drop in on me at eventual last."

They stared at him.

Ind'dni indicated the tiled firepit. "Shall we seat and warm ourselves and confer?"

"Listen—" Shima began.

"Or would refreshment be preferred first? You have both had a busy night."

"Listen—" Shima tried again, but this time Gretchen cut him off.

"Busy night, Subadar?" she asked. "It isn't even night yet. It can't be later than five or six in the afternoon."

"You think so, madame?"

"I know so."

"And this is your construct of situation?"

"Of course."

"Listen," Shima began for the third time. "I want to know how in hell we got from my lab to the Guff precinct and why. Is this another Ind'dni ploy?"

"Or brutality of police?" Ind'dni smiled. "Most interesting state of confusion. Come, sit down in warmth and tell me why it can't be later than five or six o'clock post meridian."

"Because we went to Blaise's lab not more than an hour ago."

"Ah yes. At CCC complex. It is permitted to ask where you located Dr. Shima, madame? You will recall that you reported his disappearance to me."

"I did. Just a few hours ago. And you broadcast an A.P.B. on your quote secret unquote Code Nemo, over my protest."

"What else could I do? Yet you found him before my staff did. Where?"

205

"In my apartment."

"Safe and of sound mind?"

"Why ask that?" Gretchen snapped.

"Is it not conventional condition in which missing persons are hoped to be found?" Again Ind'dni sounded smoothly dangerous. "Safe and sound. No?"

"Safe and sound. Yes."

"But you did not report discovery to me despite your prior agitation. Why, madame?"

"Because I—Because we had something far more urgent to do."

"Precise nature of same?"

"A Promethium trip."

"Ah yes. Hoping to visit the Infraworld of your fanciful imagination."

"I didn't believe her either," Shima broke in. "I was just being polite. But it's not imaginary, Ind'dni, it's fact, goddam cold fact. Maybe I should call it hot news because it was out of sight! Wild!"

"And all this when?"

"Not more than an hour ago." Shima was feverish in his excitement. "It's a discovery that'll make history when I can get it documented and publish. They'll call it the Shima Syndrome or maybe the Nunn Effect. We mainlined a milligram of Pm each in my lab. We shot ourselves in matching veins to make sure the effect would hit us at approximately the same time, and the Pm must have taken over within minutes. The effect was fantastic, Subadar. Unbelievable! There *is* a goddam Phasmaworld. There might even be an entire goddam Phasmaculture buried deep under externals, for all I know. We weren't wherever we were long enough to do much exploring."

"You really believe this, Dr. Shima?"

"Believe? Damn it, Ind'dni, I *know*."

"You were in madame's Subworld together?"

"Together, yes; but not in the Ourworld sense."

"And how long did the visit last?"

"That's hard to say. Our space-time orientation was

wiped out. All our normal everyday senses were wiped. But a milly of Pm couldn't have lasted very long. I'd say twenty minutes. You, Gretchen?''

''Closer to a half hour.''

''And during all this, where were you in . . . what did you call it, doctor . . . in the Ourworld?''

''In my lab at CCC.''

''That is, our bods were,'' Gretchen explained. ''I told you that we'd leave the Guff without leaving, Subadar, and so we did.''

''You did not,'' Ind'dni said quite distinctly.

Gretchen took a breath. Then, ''You think we're lying?''

''No.'' Ind'dni was quietly emphatic. ''No. I think you're mad, both of you . . . Promethium mad. Evidently the chemical is extremely dangerous.''

''What? Why? How do you—''

''Please to listen. Five o'clock in the afternoon was yesterday. It is past six o'clock in the morning of today. Your half hour lasted twelve hours.''

''But—That's impossible!''

''And I can account for some of them. There was that A.P.B. and an alert on Code Nemo. There was a watch and the reports came in from all points on your insane careering through the Guff.''

''But we weren't out in the Guff,'' Gretchen protested. ''We never left Blaise's lab, physically.''

''But you did, both of you.''

''This *is* a damned ploy, Ind'dni.''

''On my honor I assure you not, doctor.''

They both knew he was a man of honor and were flabbergasted. They could only stare silent questions.

''Shall I tell you the story of your missing twelve hours?''

Neither could answer.

The story (Ind'dni continued) cannot give accurate times and sequences. It is probable that events have been omitted because staff had great difficulty tracking your madly unpredictable adventures. One, who is precinct chess champion, reported that you both leaped about like the knight's move in torus chess.

We start at five o'clock yesterday afternoon. Following took place: Madame invaded premises of F.A.O. Noir toy emporium and tried to incite toys to riot against children. She was heard exhorting a stuffed ostrich: "Kill, baby, kill! Kill the kids."

Meanwhile, the doctor was in the complex of Intra National Cartel Association searching for a virgin. After much perplexity, I realized that the initials of the company form noun, INCA. Apparently Dr. Shima wished to sacrifice to Aztec gods by cutting out the heart of a virgin. His sacrificial knife was a ruler. Metric.

Item: Dr. Shima was discovered in bowels of the Hudson Hell Gate dam with avowed intent of blowing up entire structure which—his quoted words—was a rapacious rape of coastal ecology. His explosive was a ten-foot string of Chinese firecrackers which he ignited and escaped in consequent confusion.

Miz Nunn next manifested in the Guff Art Museum, where she astonished many serious students and scholars by running from statue to statue, grasping the male genitals, and complaining that they were cold. She escaped apprehension by flinging a fig leaf in a guard's face.

In Central Park Dr. Shima tried to destroy the kites of children and adults by flying a killer kite. Fortunately its tail was not armed with cutting blades, as is the custom, but merely a cordless shaver. He next appeared on Bedloe's Island resolved to climb to the top of nonexistent Statue of Liberty and relight the lady's torch. The island, you know, was sold to the Anti-Vivisection League and is maintained as an animal refuge. The league did not take kindly to the flaming combustibles that Dr. Shima was carrying. Neither did the animals.

Together you invaded premises of a respectable tattoo practitioner and demanded that he marry you by tattooing you two into one. When he tried to explain that he was not licensed to marry anyone by any means whatever, you threw him down and tried to tattoo the letters F.I.N.K. on his already completely ornamented body, meanwhile singing, "*Walter, Walter, lead me to the altar, and I'll show you where I'm tattooed.*"

Dr. Shima then appeared in the Guff morgue where he engaged in a bitter altercation with a celebrated necrophiliac over the body of a dead girl. It seems that Dr. Shima wished to inspect her internal organs by means of dissection, a discipline which he regretted never having studied at Princeton, M.I.T., or Dhow Chemical. The gentleman had other designs on the body, for which he had already paid. A most unfortunate confrontation.

Staff next reported you, madame, pressing your pelvis in most lascivious manner against a three-sheet 3-D poster. It was an advertisement for "UpMan," a cantharis, featuring "before" and "after" depictions of a nude man. Your attentions were devoted to the "after" gentleman, who was highly colored and considerably larger-than-lifesize.

Dr. Shima was also rather erotic at this time. He was dashing about, ripping garments off passing ladies and spraying them black, chanting the words, "Black is bangable! Bang is blackable!" Most odd because the ladies were already naturally black.

It has not been reported where you obtained cosmetics, Miz Nunn, but you appeared in studios of Glacial Army's Station WGA in full clown makeup and attempted to brazen your way into their broadcast of *Pagliacci* as revised by Scriabin Finkel to demonstrate that jealousy is contrary to God's will. You kept sounding your high C as proof of your artistry, which same inspired many stray dogs to howling.

Staff located you both together, after another knight's leap, at CCC complex. You had wrecked Dr. Shima's laboratory in process of mixing all chemicals and reagents in a gigantic top hat stolen from a peanut advertisement. Resultant odor was most unpleasant. On one wall you had finger-painted in potassium permanganate ($KMnO_4$) the slogan: KILSTENCH—THE STINKING MAN'S SCENTARETTE!

At Staten Island Dr. Shima tied himself to the nose of a Saturn launch vehicle and urged Miz Nunn to light a match, fire the rocket and launch him into outer space, but she was too busy spraying the concrete pad with Christmas red and green decorations, affirming that the alien inhabitants of distant stars would comprehend *Luke, ii, 14* far more readily than $E = Mc^2$ or even $1 + 1 = 2$.

Our A.P.B. watch next sighted the co-conspirators —staff's words—intruding on a fully authorized gathering of the Black Ku Klux Klan, where you extinguished their sacred flaming mandala in a most scatological manner and improvised a performance of the classic *Porgy and Bess* opera which unbiased witnesses describe as merely pathetic.

Still together in unholy alliance—my words—you were observed in a markethon where Dr. Shima pursued the screaming and laughing Miz Nunn with patently carnal intent. You pelted the lady with phallic objects, doctor; asparagus, celery, bananas, mushrooms, and sausages. To make certain that your intent would be understood by all, you had embellished the objects with crude but specific details.

There was some sort of gap here in your knight's moves, but apparently you split up again. Madame was pursued in the Strøget where she was smashing star-sapphire displays and denouncing conspicuous consumption, proclaiming, "Vanity of vanities; all is vanity." Dr. Shima invaded the Equal Rights maternity hospital and disrupted and endangered several crucial deliveries shouting that he had been impregnated by an elephant and needed an emergency abortion.

You took refuge in the Church of All Atheists, Miz

Nunn, where you shocked those few unbelievers who understood Latin by chanting in a loud voice as follows: "*O tua lingula, usque perniciter vibrans et vipera. O tuae mammulae, mammae molliculae, dulciter turgidae, gemina poma.*" For shame, madame.

And you, Dr. Shima, mounted to the roof of an oasis adjoining the P.L.O. headquarters and tried to topple their two-ton rain tank onto the pinnacle of the P.L.O. pyramid with your bare hands. You were heard howling, "She may enter you but never vice versa." Really, doctor!

Final act of madness: The two of you burst into this H.Q., sought me out, and tried to stone me to death for being—your words—the wicked sorcerer who had conjured up the Golem[100]. Fortunately, you were armed only with magical toadstones, which ancient sorcerers believed resided in the heads of toads and could destroy all evil. They are not lethal. But most unfortunately you had neglected to remove the stones from the toads.

Subadar Ind'dni stopped, smiled, drew a deep breath, and crossed to the tree trunk, which he stroked absently. There was silence.

Then Shima croaked, "We did those insane things?"

"And perhaps more," Ind'dni murmured.

"For twelve hours?"

"A most provocative drug, your Promethium, doctor. Incidentally, may I suggest that you and Miz Nunn submit to a physical examination in near future. Promethium *is* radioactive, although no reports were received of your glowing in the dark."

"I know," Shima muttered. "It was a calculated risk."

Gretchen said, "I don't know whether to laugh or cry."

"Neither will help, madame. More important is to learn how and why you did what you did."

"Then you believe we have no knowledge or recollection, Mr. Ind'dni?"

ing. Yes, I do. Now, are you willing to discuss an impasse with me?" Ind'dni returned to the charcoal pit and seated himself on the rim. "Before you answer, permit me to assure you that I make no official threats. Your absurd acts were mischief, merely, which may easily be healed by fair payments to victims which I know you will do. The precinct will not advise Legal to prosecute. In any event you could not be immediately punished because tomorrow is the first Opsday of Ops Week. No, my entire concern is the Hundred-Hander beast and I am convinced that you are deeply and secretly involved with that obscene creature. Do you insist on keeping your secret? It is your privilege, and that is the impasse."

At length Gretchen said, "I think we'll have to open up, Blaise."

"I wanted to before but you stopped me."

"The timing was wrong then. Now is the moment of trust."

"Reserving what?"

"Nothing."

"Your phony weapon? My Mr. Wish?"

"Both."

"There go our careers."

"Not if the Subadar can be trusted."

Ind'dni called quietly, "You are taping?"

The disembodied voice answered, "Yes, sir."

"No longer, please. This consultation is now for my ears only, on my sole responsiblity. You will end record on these words."

"Yes, sir. Ten-four."

Gretchen gave Ind'dni a grateful look. "Yours the grace, Subadar."

"Mine the honor, madame. Now then . . . ?"

And they told him everything. Ind'dni gave them the courtesy of unmasking his face as he listened; he registered surprise, exasperation, anger, incredulity, and even occasional amusement, but not once did he express sympathy. In fact, when they had finished the long recital, he spoke with the severity of a father. "For two distinguished persons, educated and expert, among the elite of the Guff, you have behaved like silly children playing—what was that antique game? —playing Cops and Robbers."

"We were only trying to meet a strange problem with a strange solution," Shima muttered.

"No." Ind'dni was emphatic. "You were trying to answer strength from weakness. If I am to believe your analysis, madame, I—"

"Do you?" Gretchen cut in.

"I am strongly tempted for a reason you have given me quite unaware. Perhaps I will manifest it later. According to your analysis, this Golem monstrosity knows none of the logic of human behavior. It is undiluted passion. It is savagery. Then how meet it with rational reasoning? Can we anthropomorphize a cyclone? And this maleficent is a cyclone tearing apart the Guff. You say you saw it in your Subworld?"

"We think so."

"Describe same. No, not yet. First describe the subterranean continent as you saw it."

"We didn't see it at first," Shima said. "Our senses were merely echoing."

"Then describe echoes."

"But it was just silly nonsense, not worth repeating."

"You think so? But I have reason to ask. Do not underestimate my cerebral intelligence, I beg. Please to answer."

Ind'dni listened intently to the description of their fantastic sensory flashes during the Promethium trip. When they were finished he nodded with satisfaction.

"And now the lunacy of your twelve-hour peregrinations is explained," he said. "Can you not link up parallels between the real world—the Ourworld, Dr. Shima calls it—and your Phasma adventure?"

Shima seemed angered by the Subadar's grasping something he had missed. "You tell us," he growled.

Ind'dni's face flickered; he had noted Shima's annoyance. "No need for exhaustive detail," he said smoothly. "I am sure you will construct all for yourselves after I have given a few clues . . . signposts to guide you. Did you not, doctor, appear to Miz Nunn as an Aztec god? And your search for a virgin at Intra National Cartel Association?

"At another point, attempting to perceive Miz Nunn, you saw figure of a nude woman with internal organs displayed. Does this not tie in with your event at the Guff morgue? Madame, attempting to see you, saw a tattooed Japanese samurai. And what of the happening in the real tattoo parlor?

"You saw yourself, doctor, as a grotesque man with an elephant head. No connection with your invasion of E.R. maternity hospital claiming to have been impregnated by an elephant?

"You saw yourself as a Christmas ornament, madame, and meanwhile in physical life you were covering Staten Island launch pad with Christmas red and green, insisting that aliens on distant stars would understand *Luke ii,* 'On earth peace, good will toward men.' Enough signposts? Need I continue?"

Shima whistled. "By God, he's right! Everything ties in. When I saw you as a beautiful black nude . . . that must have been when I was spraying women black."

"Yes. And when I saw myself dancing with you, that's when I was seducing the poster."

"But why didn't we realize it?"

"You had not time for reflection," Ind'dni interposed. "Do not feel chagrin. From your last lunacy here in the Center, you went directly into narcotic examination."

"And we told you what?"

"Nothing, doctor. You have no memory of those twelve hours. You were completely spaced out and timed out because apparently you were functioning entirely as somatic entities . . . naughty animals, prankish but not—Yes, madame?"

"I want to apologize, Subadar. I *did* underestimate you; not your intelligence, your instincts. I felt contemptuous because you seemed to brush off my analysis of the Golem[100] too lightly. Now I know why you did. I'd ignored the soma factor, and your instinct told you that. Mine did not. I'm sorry. I do apologize."

"Most courteous and generous, Miz Nunn, although I confess I do not yet understand."

"Me neither," Shima grunted.

"My gut understands. The trouble is, our bods are on speaking terms with our minds, but not the other way around. It's a one-way street."

"What the hell are you talking about, Gretch?"

"About my mistake, which the Subadar sensed. I was so obsessed with exploring the Phasmaworld concept that I ignored the reality of the human physical world. I'm a traitor to psychodynamics. But let's drop the psytech jive and talk plain housekeeping, shall we?"

"A pleasure, lady."

"We've got a mind and body. Are they separate?"

"No, they're one."

"Who's in charge?"

"Both."

"Can you have a living bod without a mind?"

"Yes, a vegetable."

"Can you have a living mind without a bod?"

"No, unless you believe in ghosts."

"So the mind, the psyche, has got to have a home, and the soma is the house for the psyche. The bod's the lodging house; the pysche's the tenant. Agreed?"

"Agreed."

"And whatever the psyche produces—art, music, science, logic, ideas, love, hatred—is really a product of the whole house."

"I'll concede that."

"You better concede it. The Golem is a quasi-living entity. It must be the product of a house."

"You said it's the product of the bee-ladies."

"And their hive is its house. That's my point. The hive is the hearth and home of the Golem." Gretchen turned to Ind'dni. "Am I making sense, Subadar?"

Ind'dni smiled. "You omit the soul, madame."

"No, I merely omit mention. The soul is the tonus of the soma. It's metabolic music."

"The hell it is," Shima broke in. "Not that I buy the concept of a soul. But if there is one, it belongs to the mind . . . to the psyche. It's the thinking part of us."

"Not to me, Blaise. I believe it's a resonance of the soma, the flowering of a million years of evolution, the cultural unconscious in all animals."

"Animals! *All* animals?"

"All," Gretchen said firmly. "Do you think a tiger has a soul?"

"A lot of religions say no."

"Saint Francis of Assisi didn't. The tiger has a soul. It can't compute. It doesn't pray. You never hear a tiger say, 'What did the Polack do when he got lost in the jungle?' His soma and psyche are purely reflexive, dedicated to survival and satisfaction, but I say the tiger has a soul, all the same, and I rest my case."

"Yes, but what is your case, counselor?" Shima was in deadly earnest.

"That the ladies' hive is the body and soul of the Golem, its house. Do you agree, Subadar?"

"Most unusual construct, as is your wont, Miz Nunn. But does not the Golem have a body of its own . . . a hundred bodies? Most unhappily I do not know whereabouts of its soul, if any. Shall I issue an A.P.B.?"

Gretchen laughed. "Using Code Nemo?"

"Perhaps a Code Credo would be more *à propos*."

"Damn it! If you two are going to start clowning—!" Shima burst out.

"Cool it, baby. Just relieving the tension, is all," Gretchen soothed. To Ind'dni, "It's a quasi-body, Subadar; a projection, along with its primal drives, of the hive. That's why it's polymorphic. Think of water in free fall. Without gravity the water can be shaped into anything. The Golem has no real form of its own. The hive is its generator and shapes it *ad lib*."

Shima demanded, "Then you mean destroy all the bee-ladies to zap the Golem? I can just see our good friend here standing by and permitting that."

"Hardly likely," Ind'dni murmured. "I permit no destruction whatever."

"I don't mean destroy the women," Gretchen explained. "It's a collective act, remember? Break up the colony and you destroy the Golem's home."

"Scatter them?"

"Yes."

"How?"

"I'm not sure."

"Why not?"

"Because I'm not sure whether the beehive parallel goes that far."

"Let's suppose it does."

"Then it's still iffy. The life of an insect colony can go on whether there's a queen or not. Only the beehive must have a queen."

"You mean what's-her-name . . . Winifred Ashley?"

"And that's the big 'if.' Is she really a queen in the bee sense, holding the colony together? Is she the prime factor in the generation of the Golem? Damn it, I don't know, and I don't know how to find out."

"There's an obvious solution, another Pm trip."

"But I'm afraid of that, Blaise. We can't trust our senses because they panic and short-circuit. And certainly we can't trust our somas when the rest of us vacate."

"If I may make a suggestion?" Ind'dni spoke from the cedar trunk.

217

"Please."

"The next Promethium trip may be made under controlled environment. The bodies can be restrained."

"That's true, Subadar, but it doesn't solve the problem of our unreliable senses."

"Not Dr. Shima's, perhaps, but yours alone, madame?"

"Mine? Alone?"

"I have begged not to be underestimated. Yes, I knew all about your seeing at second hand before your confession. You are a *lusus naturae*. You did sense this Hundred-Hander?"

"I think I did."

"Appearance, please."

"An unformed, man."

"Actions?"

"None."

"You perceived the beast with your own senses or through Dr. Shima's?"

Gretchen was thunderstruck. "My God! I never thought—I honestly don't know."

"Do you know whether its behavior in your Phasmaworld might reveal its prime source?"

"It might. Maybe. Does this mean you believe me now?"

"Maybe. Your word. But does it not occur to you that your second-handery will enable you to visit the Phasmaworld with virgin senses and perceive what truly transpires?"

"By God!" Shima exclaimed.

"The expedition can come only after planning and careful preparation. Now you must go and rest. You both need it." Ind'dni was firmly in control. "Next, doctor, you will test madame's senses. We know about her sight, but sound must also be examined. That, too, may be crucial."

"What about the other three; smell, taste, and touch?"

"But I already know from confession of true events. *That* was your unaware reason for my belief, madame, which I told you I would manifest later."

"What did she confess that tells you so much?"

"Touch, doctor? Did she not feel sensation of cold when the creature invaded?"

"She did, by God!"

"Wait," Gretchen said. "I might have gotten that secondhand from the Golem itself."

"How, madame? Does the creature have senses in human terms? And would it be aware of the cold it exuded? No. That sense was your very own."

"He's right, Gretch. But smell and taste, Ind'dni? They're linked, of course."

"Ah! That was clincher, as Legal would say. Miz Nunn, of herself, with her own senses, smelled the typical odor the Hundred-Hander emits, the *bouquet de malades*, the aroma of the mad. I have smelled it myself and that was what convinced my belief. The Bombazine mind is most often enforced by subtleties."

"This smartass skog really is something, Gretchen," Shima growled, again angered.

Ind'dni's face flickered in response to the pejorative. "Please not to delay testing, doctor. There is time urgency. 'The Assyrian came down like the wolf on the fold.' For 'Assyrian' read the Hundred-Hander Golem. Of course you will make redress to victims of your escapades. My staff will assist."

"How?" Shima demanded. "With money?"

"With knowledge." Ind'dni arose to escort them out. "What then, doctor? You are unacquainted with scandal of Mount Everest ski lift?"

"Certainly I'm acquainted. It collapsed."

"Plunging fifty misfortunates to injury and death. That was not the scandal I refer to. When rescuers arrived at scene of disaster there were not fifty, there were one hundred and five victims, in quotes, writhing

219

in the snow crying for medical *and* legal. That was the scandal and it must not happen to you."

Ind'dni opened the door, smiled them out with a soft, "Opbless," and closed the door. He pressed a button and called to no one, "Please to resume recording and send in Mr. Droney Lafferty."

15

Ah yes, the first wild Opsday of Ops Week, traditional Opalia (the Women's Movement counter to Saturnalia) dedicated to reckless entertainment . . . as if the Guff needed any additional excuse for madness. Ops, wife of Saturn, Earth Goddess of Plenty (she gave her name to "opulent") in whose honor one touched earth instead of wood for luck, gave earthenware gifts, and fraternized regardless of rank or clout.

No schools, no disciplines, no punishments, no status dress or speech or courtesies; just free-for-all fun, and the best way to begin the carnival was to entertain a woman with her butt firmly pressed against earth, as Blaise Shima had just done.

"Opbless," Gretchen gasped.

"Opbless, love."

"But this gravel is killing my back."

"Gravel? For shame, Gretchen. It's earth, imported all the way from *la belle France*. We grudge no expense."

"Then French-type love is too pebbly. You might at least have sifted it through a screen or something."

"But I did, through a *passoire*, French for a colander. Our loving made it lumpy again."

"And I thank you for that. Opbless. Make me a mattress, please."

"Climb on top."

"Ah! That's better. Thank you again, sir."

Two minutes, or perhaps twenty, slid by while they drifted and murmured on the terrace.

"You have the nicest bumps, love . . ."

"Yours is the greatest . . ."

"Not no more."

"He'll be back . . . That boy's got strent."

"The only thing about me that has . . ."

"Don't put yourself down."

"Just facing up to *le pauvre petit*. I wish I had your strength, Gretchen."

"I'm no stronger than you."

"Ten times as."

"Never."

"Five times as?"

"No."

"Two and a half?"

"You've got your own kind of power, Blaise."

"Not me. I feel as soft as Ind'dni."

"Don't underestimate him. There's iron in that man. I can feel it."

"So long as you don't feel *him* . . ."

"Blaise! You can't possibly be jealous?"

"Well . . . Sometimes I catch you looking at him kind of funny-like."

"Just sizing him up . . . Feeling for his design. He's got controlled violence in him, Blaise. If he ever loses control—Look out!"

"That bearded Hindu skog? Never!"

"Funny you should say that, because you're like Ind'dni."

"Me!"

"Oh yes. There's violence in you . . . Only yours is attack-escape."

"You're putting me on."

"No way. Either you're *le pauvre petit,* hiding from

tough situations in your lab, or you attempt to escape from a *crise* by attacking it. And when you do—Look out for Mr. Wish!''

"I couldn't agree less. I've never wanted to hurt anybody or anything. There must be another explanation for the Wish lunacy.''

"Maybe you're right. I'm too happy to argue. Let's just go on drifting. . . .''

"Too comfy, you mean.''

"And sleepy. Do we have to do anything today except enjoy Ops?''

"Pay off for our pranks. The Subadar gave me a list of legit claims.''

"Oh . . . Yes . . . We'll split it up.'' Gretchen's yawn tickled his ear. "That shouldn't take long. My place afterward?''

"Not long for you, maybe. Me, I've got another something else to do.''

"My! Aren't we busy, busy, busy . . .''

"I've got to find a location where I can check out your senses.''

"Oh that. Can't you do it in a lab?''

"No. It's got to be a locale completely insulated from all externals.''

"Like empty outer space?''

"Space is far from empty, but that's the idea. Some place deep and isolated with a power source . . . It won't be easy to find. . . .''

"For a genius-type like you? Go on!''

"Opthanks, lady. Would you mind getting off'n me?''

"But I'm so comfy . . .''

"Off . . . Off . . . Off . . .''

Gretchen got to her feet, grudgingly, and looked around through Shima's eyes. "I'll sweep the terrace.''

"Leave it for the end of Ops Week. We've too much to do today. What are you going to wear?''

"Plain white coveralls. Nothing fancy. You?''

"Coveralls, too, only blue work-denim."

"So . . . Luck, man, and Opbless."

"Luck, lady, and Opbless."

* * *

The giant boardroom of CCC was jam-packed with freeloaders in tattered clothes, all shouting, singing, drinking, guzzling. A long trestle stretched the fifty-foot length of one wall. It was heaped with food, drink, and squeams, and behind it stood the eleven distinguished directors of CCC, wearing stained chefs' costumes, and cheerfully serving all comers. Opsday.

Shima squirmed through the mob and reached the trestle at last. "Opbless, senator, I—"

"It's Jimmy J. today, Blaise. Opbless. What can I serve you?"

"I'm looking for the chairman, Jimmy J."

"You mean Mills? I think he's handling the Squeamwich department. Down the road apiece."

Shima fought down the trestle. "Opbless, general."

"It's Georgie, Blaise baby. Opbless. Say, I've got some ninety-caliber squeams and morwiches. What'll it be? White? Rye? Fiber? Glass? Poly?"

"I thought the chairman was handling this concession."

"Millsie? Not now, baby. He's shifted over to the rotgut counter."

Shima struggled again. "Opbless, governor."

"It's Nelly today, Blaise. Good old reliable Nelly. Say, I got something for you, son. Just what the doctor ordered. That's a joke, son. It's my own invention, The Earache. It sends, fella, it sends."

"How, govern—Nelly?"

The governor pointed to half a dozen grinning supines jumbled in a corner. "All sent by Nelly's elixir, The Earache."

"What's so special about it?"

"You don't drink it, son. You drop it. In your ear

and you have ignition. Now here's a dropperful and—''

"Not just now, sir—I mean Nelly. I'm really looking for the chairman. I was told he was here."

"Mills? Oh. No, Millypooh's taken over soup."

In his bedraggled chef's costume the chairman was ranting like a sideshow pitchman. "HURRY! HURRY! HURRY!" In one hand he held a soup tureen, in the other an enema bag. "HURRY! HURRY! HURRY! COME ONE! COME ALL! MEET THE BELLYWHOPPER! IT MEETS IN THE MIDDLE! THE ONLY SOUP THAT TASTES FROM THE INSIDE OUT! Hi, Blaise. Opbless."

"Opbless, Mr. Chairm—Mills: Sir, I—Excuse me. Millie, I came to square the account for my ruined lab."

"Forget it, Blaise. THE BELLYWHOPPER! THE BELLYWHOPPER! This is the first of Ops Week. All forgiven, and we'll set your lab up for you again. MEET THE BELLYWHOPPER! BOTH ENDS AGAINST THE MIDDLE! We can afford it. God knows, CCC's made enough money out of you."

"Thank you, Mills."

"Opbless, Blaise."

"Sir—Millie, something else. I need a very special environment for a very special test I've got to run as soon as possible. Does CCC own a deep mine with a power source I could use? I need a place where the subject can be completely isolated."

"Mine? Mine? My God, we've got a dozen exhausted mines all over the world, but not one you could use in a hurrry, Blaise."

"Why not, Mills?"

"In the first place, all wiring and utilities were ripped out for scrap ages ago. In the second place, they've been taken over by squatters. Thousands of them. Would take at least a year to evict them, kicking and screaming. HURRY! HURRY! HURRY! THE BELLYWHOPPER!"

* * *

Gretchen couldn't assay the mob surrounding the art museum because lifestyle was abandoned by the entire Corridor during Ops Week. Those who didn't dress badly, faked it. Those who didn't speak or behave without style, faked it. But she was sure of one thing: most of them had to be art lovers.

Because the museum followed a hallowed Neapolitan New Year's custom. The Neapolitans save up all their unwanted household furnishings and decorations and on New Year's Day they throw them out of their windows with hilarious celebrations, and if you're walking the street, you'd better be on the alert for falling furniture.

The museum, always plagued by storage problems, followed this custom on the first Opsday. Whatever clutter they had occupying precious space, judged unworthy and proven unsalable (for a decent price) was tossed out the top-floor windows.

So down came paintings, prints, etchings, posters, statues, objets d'art and vertu, empty frames, pieces of armor, period costumes, papyrus, Baroque instruments, mummified cats, battered pistols, crumbling pewter.

There were shrieks of laughter from the windows as the mob fought hysterically to catch and possess in fee simple absolute each falling object, and Gretchen knew that getting rid of the museum's worthless clutter was only half its enjoyment. Although she was out on the fringe of the mob, she found herself surprisingly and massively jostled by a large human object.

"Sorry. Opbless," she muttered, shifting aside.

"Opbless," said a clear, cultivated voice with no attempt at faking Ops Week commonality.

Gretchen turned curiously. It was the Queen Bee, Winifred Ashley.

"Regina!"

"What? BB? Is it really you, my dear? How unexpected and how very nice. What are you doing here? Touching earth for something?"

"Not really, Regina. I was hoping to apologize and make up for a disturbance I created the other day, but I see it's quite impossible. And you?"

"Ah! I'm hoping for a secret treasure."

"Can you tell me?"

"But of course, dear. After all, you *are* one of us." Regina lowered her voice. "They have a player-piano gathering dust in a corner. Every year I hope they'll tire of it and throw it out."

"But you already have a player-piano in your beautiful Communist apartment, Regina."

"Yes, BB, but I don't want the museum's old pianola. I want what's in it. I'm the only one who knows. The first pianola roll of the 'Internationale' by Pottier and Degeyter, 1871. It will make the focal point of my decor. Can't you hear it?" Regina sang as mellifluously as she spoke, *"Arise, ye prisoners of starvation . . ."* She laughed. "Perhaps only a dream, but still I touch earth. We'll see you at my place this evening, of course, dear BB? A lahvely Opsparty to entertain our men. Opbless."

* * *

It was free baths for all in the spillway of the Hudson Hell Gate dam. Fresh water, hot from the breeder cooling system. Slightly radioactive, to be sure, but what the hell, Opsday. Live a little, touch earth, and to hell with the rest. The four-acre spillway was seething with naked bodies, glowing from the heat, foaming with soap, submerging, surging up like porpoises, laughing, shouting, choking, coughing rhapsodically.

"Sooner or later one of them has to drown," the man alongside Shima murmured. "Maybe on her own or maybe with a little help. I keep hoping. Opbless."

"Opbless," Shima answered and inspected the stranger. He was startling; tall, Lincolnesque in face and figure, and markedly piebald. The hair was albino, the beard black, the eyes red, the skin blotched with random black-and-white patches.

227

"I'm a haploid," the stranger said casually, almost mechanically, as though he had responded to Shima's surprised take a thousand times before. "Chromosomes from one parent only."

"But you *are* a kind of albino, aren't you?" Shima asked, much interested.

"Haploid albino," the stranger said wearily. "Let it go at that, doctor. Don't try any dissection on me."

"What! What? You call me 'doctor'? Are you the —?"

"Yes. Yes indeed. And apparently you have no memory. May I ask what squeam you were shooting?"

"Promethium. The hydride. PmH_2."

"Never heard of it. I must remember to try it. Now this time, doctor, if one of them drowns, with or without help from me, kindly do not interfere. No rescue. No resuscitation. If there's any mouth-to-mouth, I will apply it in my own fashion."

"My God! You're sick!"

"Don't knock it if you haven't tried it."

"Christ! I'd rather die first."

"Sorry. I don't dig boys."

Shima took a deep breath. "No. I'm sorry. Really sorry. I apologize for losing my head. I'm not here to argue or hassle with anybody, and certainly I'm in no position to pass moral judgments. I beg you to forgive me."

"Nicely put."

"So if you'll excuse me . . ."

"Where are you off to?"

"I'm trying to get an interview with the dam director."

"Oh, are you really, now?"

"Yes. Would you know where I might locate him or her, please?"

"Do I owe you favors?"

"No. I owe you."

"Nicely put. The dam director is a Mr. Lafferty."

"Thank you. And where might I find him?"

"Here. I'm Lafferty."

Again Shima lost his poise. He gawked and stammered, "But—But—But—"

"But how?" Lafferty smiled. "Simple. Brilliance. Hard work. And the fact that I inherited fifty-one percent of the Hudson Hell Gate stock."

"Ildefonsa would," Shima said under his breath.

"Must you bring her up at the beginning of the *fête,* doctor?"

"Sorry again. Apologies again. I'm an ass today."

"Accepted without reserve."

"Mr. Lafferty, I—"

"Opsday. Droney."

"Droney. Thank you. Opbless. I . . . I came to ask a favor of the HHG director . . ."

"Ask it."

"I need a very special environment for a very special sensory test. It must be completely isolated from all sight and sound. I was hoping that the dam depths might—"

"No way," Lafferty interupted. "If you hadn't been so busy with your silly firecrackers down there, you'd have noticed that the depths are filled with rumblings and water-wooshings. Speaking of which, there goes a charming young girl under for the third time. She needs tender care. Excuse me."

Shima could not reply.

The celebrated necrophiliac gave him a benign smile. "We will discuss your landing Subadar Ind'dni on my back another time." As he plunged into the spillway, Lafferty declaimed, "Strong as an eagle! Swift as a vulture! Go! Go! Go! Go! Necro culture!"

* * *

Gianni Jiki's tattoo parlor was by no means a hole in the wall. It was virtually a hospital with a central reception hall hung with display charts and a dozen side clinics with a dozen assistants working on the assembly-line principle. If, say, a Guff buck desired the prized (and rather expensive) cobra tattoo, the snake was first outlined around his waist in one surgery, detailed in the next, colored in a third, and the fanged head finalized in a fourth after a most respectful and tactfully induced erection. The lady who desired her *labia majora* converted into the lids of a roguish eye received the same respectful and tactful assembly line attention.

But on this first Opsday it was not business as usual, it was the mendicants' carnival. In addition to decorative and erotic tattooing, Gianni Jiki also contrived magnificent injuries; bruises, contusions, livid scars, fresh wounds, and malignant skin eruptions for the larcenous accident "victims," the blackmailing beggars, the deadbeats of the Guff. Consequently, his hospital was the informal clubhouse of the Guff's professional panhandlers.

A joyous prosthetic dance was in progress in the main hall when Gretchen Nunn arrived. Synthesizers screamed. The professional cripples had removed their prosthetic arms, legs, hands, feet, and even half a neck and a shoulder. They were sitting in a circle, laughing and keying their tiny hand controls, while their detached prosthetic parts danced and cavorted in response to the radio commands. Lone legs kicked or tapped or soft-shoed. Single arms entwined with others in a prosthetic square dance. And some manipulators were clever enough to turn the fingers of their detached hands into chorus lines.

A jolly man, four-by-four-fat, stark naked, tattooed from head to toe, came up to Gretchen, beamed and greeted her. *"Buon giorno.* Opbless. Never, I thought, *mai,* never would you return."

"Opbless," Gretchen answered. "You—You're Mr. Jiki, of course?"

"Si. Gianni. You were *pazza* the other night, eh? Too much wine?"

"I've come to apologize and make it up to you, Gianni."

"To apology? *Grazie.* Most *gentile. Grazie.* But to make up? What? A joke only, eh? *Molto cattiva,* but yet only the joke. You have come, and my Opsday is made. That is enough."

"But I must do something for you."

"You must, eh? So." Gianni considered, then beamed even broader. *"Bene!* You will dance with us."

Gretchen stared at him. He met her look and nodded toward the floor. "Pick your partner, *gentile signora.*"

She was not the one to cavil or hesitate. Gretchen stepped onto the main floor, cased the cavorting prosthetics, and at last tapped the shoulder of a shoulder-and-arm.

"Sigfried," Gianni called to three-quarters of a beggar. *"La signora* will waltz with you."

Gretchen danced. Gianni Jiki sang, *"Gualtiero! Gualtiero! Condurre mi per altare . . ."*

* * *

They had this wretched hull of a Mississippi paddle wheeler for a barge and were holding their KKK Bar-B-Q on it. Shima found the celebration impossible to believe. There was a bed of glowing coals. There was a gigantic rotisserie revolving over it. And on the massive steel spit roasted a trussed form that was unmistakably humanoid.

"Dear God!" Shima whispered. "A cannibal barbecue."

A seven-foot Watusi king, carrying all the accouterments of African royalty, greeted Shima. "Opbless, Dr. Shima, and welcome to our Honkfeast."

"Opbless," Shima replied faintly. "So you remember me?"

"Who could forget your rendition of that quaint *Porgy and Bess* with Miz Nunn? It is to be treasured."

"I'm here to make amends for that. I'd like very

231

much to square it with you; courtesywise, moneywise, anywise. You name it."

"On Opsday? Impossible. Forget it, doctor. *We* have. Now come and join the feast. Dinner is about to be served."

"I'd really like to do something for you," Shima persisted, "because I want something from you."

"Oh? What?"

"An estimate."

"Yes? Of what?"

"I must conduct a sensory test which requires absolute isolation of the subject. I was considering some sort of small, thick concrete bunker."

"Yes. And?"

"You people have a lock on the construction industry. How quickly could you put a bunker together and for how much? Can you give me a time and cost estimate?"

The Watusi king shook his head sadly. "Alas, impossible to gratify you, Dr. Shima. We are out on strike protesting management's use of P.L.O. guards for security. They are not genuinely black, despite all P.L.O. claims. It will probably last another three months, and we are preparing for bloodshed. So sorry. Now come and join our feast."

Shima waved queasily. "So sorry, but I have no appetite for long pig today."

The Watusi lowered his voice conspiratorially. "Please do not disillusion our other guests, doctor, but we would not demean the KKK by roasting a mere Honk. We're celebrating with a delicacy far more rare and expensive."

"Than a man? My God! What?"

"A gorilla."

* * *

Opsday! Opsday! Opsday! And in the Church of All Atheists they were crowning Christ "King of Fools"

232

while the organ thundered sardonically. It was live, not a recording, Gretchen noted with surprise. There was a raving maniac on the organ bench, feet pounding the pedal bass, hands mangling the four keyboard manuals, and he was singing, groaning and growling a running continuo to his Satanic music.

She couldn't appraise his class or status from his Ops rags, but he seemed to be an Iroquois Indian from his face and head. Swarthy complexion. Jutting nose. Wide, thin lips. Heavy ears. And a shaven skull, with the exception of a stiff black crest running from brow to nape.

"All he needs is a war bonnet," she thought as she stole into the loft for a closer look.

Evidently he had wide side-vision. "What the hell are you doing here? Opbless."

"Opbless," Gretchen called over the roar of the organ. "I came to cool a scandal I created in the church the other day."

"Oh. R. Like wow. You're the bije babe who sang Orff's *Catulli Carmina*. Forget it. The church has. Got a credit line of your own?"

"Credit?"

"Stay with it, babe. Credit. I.D. Name."

"Oh. Gretchen Nunn. You?"

"Manitou-Win-Na-Mis-Ma-Bago."

"Wh-what?"

"In your language means, He-Who-Charms-Manitou-Out-of-Sky."

"You're an Indian?"

"Most of me."

"Like Opbless and wow and what do I call you? Mannie? Mr. Bago?"

"Hell no. That don't go down. Call me Finkel."

"Finkel!"

"R on. Scriabin Finkel."

* * *

"The Right to Life" ballet of unborn children was being danced by twenty naked midgets in the Equal Rights maternity hospital. Each of them was connected to the tip of a phallic maypole by an umbilical cord, and all were mewing a fetal chorus to the muted orchestral accompaniment conducted by a savage Cossack who snarled at Shima in B-flat minor, "Get the hell out of the act, dude. Opbless."

"Opbless. Sorry. Don't mean to intrude. I'm just looking for someone in charge."

"I'm in charge."

"I want to apologize for the fuss I kicked up the other day, and square it."

"Oh. R. You're the joker that said he got banged by the elephant?"

"Yes."

"Got a name?"

"Shima. Blaise Shima. Yours?"

"Aurora."

"What?"

"Yeah. I was named after the battleship that backed the Red Revolution. R. Apology accepted. No hard feelings and Opbless. Now get the hell out, Shima. We've got to transpose, and these clowns can't hack it."

"Guff thanks, Mr. . . . What do I call you? Aurora? Orry?"

"Hell no. It's Finkel. Scriabin Finkel."

"What? Then *you* wrote that great Glacial Army anthem, '*Where You Beez* . . .' I'm impressed."

"We all did, turkey—A-MINOR, YOU GODDAM BUMS! A-MINOR! The whole Finkel stable."

* * *

They call the fine debris of jewelry manufacture "findings." Workshop floors absorb a dusting of precious stone and precious metal residues in the course

234

of a year, and on Opsday the Strøget throws open its workshops to an eager multitude equipped with brooms, dustpans-and-brushes, and containers. To this date of writing it is not yet known whether any of the scavengers has ever profited by his recovery of "findings" dust.

It was inevitable that as Gretchen walked the Strøget, apologizing to and punching checks for the proprietors whose displays she had smashed—the luxury trade is never in the forgiving business—it was inevitable that she should recognize a familiar bod in the mob of panting, sweeping scavengers; Yenta Calienta, armed with a battery vacuum cleaner. Yenta was spending as much time protecting the machine from resentful broom-wielders as she was sucking up dust.

* * *

Damn if half of them weren't in peanut drag, complete with monocle and top hat. The advertising manager was in costume, too, but that didn't prevent him from accepting Shima's apology and check. Then he conducted Shima to an enormous transparent top hat filled with a magenta hellbrew. It was three times the size of the bronze hat which Blaise and Gretchen had stolen. The advertising manager pointed proudly.

"A square yard of Demerara rum. Fifty gallons of grenadine. Juice of one hundred reconstituted lemons. Fifty pounds of confetti sugar. One thousand maraschino cherries. Planter's Punch. Help yourself, doctor. Enjoy. Opbless."

He waddled off. Shima looked at the awesome top hat doubtfully, then shrugged and mounted the scaffolding leading to the ten-foot-high brim. He received a frosted earthenware mug and was told to take it home as a gift. He took his place on line and spoke to the tall, vivid young woman ahead of him. She held a stained mug in her hand.

235

"Opbless. I see you've tried this punch before. How is it?"

She turned and raked him with clever eyes. "Opbless. This is my fifth time around."

"Is it that good?"

"It doesn't matter. This firm is one of my clients. It's my job to flatter them."

She scooped up a mugful of punch and made way for Shima. As he bent over the rim to fill his mug, he was suddenly seized by the ankles and upended.

"You son of a bitch! This'll pay you back for the Therpool!"

He was plunged, head foremost, into the Planter's Punch, joining rum, grenadine, lemon juice, sugar, and a thousand cherries. She held her grip on his ankles while he thrashed and strangled. Just as he was on the verge of losing consciousness, his ankles were released. He managed to flip and upend. There she was at the hatbrim, glaring down at him while she struggled with the advertising manager.

"Wasn't me in the Therpool, lady," Shima gasped.

"The hell it wasn't! I'd know you anywhere."

"But Guff thanks anyway, lady. You've solved my insulation problem. Opbless."

* * *

When the exhausted Gretchen at last got back to her apartment, she found a few of her staff there, holding the fort. Their Ops Week clothes were so stylishly bedraggled that she had to smile. Shima? No sign of him. "Has anything happened?" she wondered. "Has he gone on the attack-escape again?" But a messenger just delivered this tape from Shima. "From his penthouse?" No, from the Precinct Complex. "Oh God! The idiot *is* in trouble." But her fingers did not tremble as she switched on.

* * *

I'm taping this to you, Gretchen love, because I'm completely wiped. I can't face another human being; not even you.

I encountered an event, a Golem coda, when I was squaring it for that stolen top hat, which clued me into the modus operandi for your sensory tests. A bathysphere. It's already equipped with communications, life-support systems and power—which were some of the problems of complete insulation—and at ocean depths nothing external can penetrate except maybe some slight radiation from the earth's mantle, and maybe a stray neutrino or two.

So I went over to the Oceanography Center to beg the loan of a bathysphere from Lucy Leuz, an old buddy from M.I.T. That's Friedrich Humboldt Leuz, Ph.D. and DODO, in caps. Not the extinct bird; Director of Drogh Operations. I know he has a baby bathysphere.

They were celebrating the advent of Ops Week with a raw fish festival, using their aquarium surplus for the feast. Gretchen, you haven't known guilt until you've had an Alaska king crab look you in the eye while you're breaking off one of its legs. Anyway, Lucy gave me an Opbless and the go-ahead, so we're all set for tomorrow—and we'd better be—because I know now that Ind'dni is right. Time *is* of the essence. I think you'll agree by the time I'm finished.

Then I went to the Glacial Army H.Q., thinking you might be there cooling your *Pagliacci* rap. You weren't so I settled up for you, and those saints are real greedy. They were mounting a hysterical revival to counter the Ops Week debut—Naturally the Army hates the false goddess Ops and her dirty, rotten, sinful Opalia.

There must have been a thousand there, led by another clown from the Scriabin Finkel stable, a crazed Cockney calling herself Sabrina Finkel. They were howling "Where You Beez . . ." and spasming with the jerks, smashing things, rolling over and fainting in ecstasies. The fervor was terrifying; they acted like a lynch mob. A girl took refuge behind me and I couldn't blame her for being frightened. I was, too.

"You look like a gent, even in that filthy coverall," she said. (I was blotched with Planter's Punch, which I'll explain another time.) "Will you for Jesus sake get me the hell out of here. This is sick."

"Where's the geek what brung you?"

"Don't Op-talk me. I know you're a gent. He's fainted dead away with his head through a throne."

So we left the *fête choréatique,* grabbed transport, and set out for my Oasis. She sat in her corner and I sat in mine. Neither of us said anything. She was sulky; I was pooped. But when we got to the Oasis, I had to go through the motions of the gent. I offered her the choice of keeping the transport and going on to wherever it was, me paying, or coming up to the penthouse for a drink.

"Baby, do I ever need a drink," she said. "That damn Army is desert dry. R. But no hots."

"For Christ's sake!" I was disgusted. "Who d'you think I am, Casanova? So come on. I'm freezing."

We went up to the penthouse. I started a fire in the lounge and she watched me fussing with the kindling.

"You've got cherries sticking inside your collar," she said. "Did you know?"

"I should have guessed. I had a run-in with a bowl of Planter's Punch."

She wandered around, exploring. "Gee, I've never been in a high-class place like this before. You sure got class. I knew it, even in that dirty coverall with those crazy cherries sticking to your neck."

"I'm a walking whisky sour," I said. "So come have your drink, and we'll figure out how to get you home-free through the Guff."

We sat at the fire and drank. She was a redhead with exquisite skin but was no looker by any stretch of charity. She talked, but not about getting home. She had a kind of naïve, prattling charm. She worked for the Glacial Army, job unspecified, but it sounded like running errands. She enjoyed reporting the secret sins of their saints.

Suddenly she said, "I've got to call Philly."

"Philly who?"

"Philadelphia. It's where I live with my folks."

"You don't have to call. The pneumo'll shoot you there in twenty minutes."

"I know that. I have to tell them I'm not coming home tonight."

Which was all I needed. "The phone's out of order," I said.

"Don't guff," she said. "What kind of rip do you think I am? I wouldn't lay a call on you."

"You really should go home, Miz—" I still didn't know her name.

"I'm staying. Don't worry, it won't hurt. This is first Opsday, and I'm going to start your Ops Week for you, touch earth."

"The phone's in the bedroom."

"I know, and it works. I tried it. I'll call from the public CB down in the lobby. I don't want to take anything off you, dude, except your clothes. Maybe you don't know there are girls like me. Maybe you'll find out, touch earth."

She left. I sat at the fire, trying to figure out how I'd gotten into this *tsimmis* and how in hell I was going to get out of it without hurting feelings. No attack-escape; I just prayed. There was a knock on the door.

"It's open," I called.

The door opened. It was Ind'dni. My prayers were answered. There *is* a God.

"Bless you, Subadar," I said.

"Alas, I have no pleasant greeting for you, Dr. Shima."

"Is it a bust, I hope?"

"Please to come downstairs, doctor."

"I'll go quietly, but I—"

"Come, please."

So I come please. Ind'dni was silent and despairing. I was completely bewildered. In the lobby, the hommy squad stood around the glass CB booth. There were spectators staring; some vomiting. The glass door was shut tight. A body'd been jammed into the booth, head down, the veins torn open, and she'd drowned in her own blood to begin my carnival for me.

16

They were out at sea aboard the nuclear trawler, *Drogh III*, far beyond the sight of land and the stench of the Corridor. The derrick boom was swung to starboard, and the winch was slowly releasing the heavy multi-cable as the bathysphere containing Gretchen Nunn descended. Inside, she was entwined and embroidered with electrode contacts.

Doctors Blaise (Shim) Shima and Friedrich Humboldt (Lucy) Leuz were in the control cabin which resembled the flight deck of a spacecraft; four walls of illuminated readout panels, dials, and projection screens.

Lucy Leuz was power gone to fat. Not tall, enormously bulky, with arms and legs as big around as a girl's waist. A bathtub could barely contain him plus five gallons of water. Oddly enough, his voice was completely out of character with the menace of his bulk; soft and sweet, the vowels curiously inflected with umlauts. "True" was "Trew." "Moon" was "Mewn."

"She deep enough, Lucy?" Shima asked.

Leuz was concentrating on the depth dial. "Almost. Patience, Shim baby.. Patience. Got your sensory program set?"

"Uh-huh. All five ready and counting."

"Five? Five senses? I thought you said that Subadar Ind'dni told you—"

"To hell with what he said. I'm testing everything; sight, sound, touch, taste, smell. They learned us to take nothing for granted at Tech. Remember?"

"Painfully. Are her electrode contacts secure, but I mean really?"

"She'll never shake 'em off."

"And she knows the scam? She won't panic when you jolt her?"

"She's been briefed. She knows. Don't worry . . . Gretchen's got a cool that could start another ice age."

"R." Leuz pressed a stud. "We stop the descent here. Two hundred fathoms."

"Thank heaven it's a calm sea."

"Down two hundred fathoms your girl wouldn't know if a typhoon was blowing upstairs."

"The fun you DODO dudes have."

"You want to signal her that you're starting, Shim?"

"No, that's not in the program. She's on her own, down in the deep blue yonder."

"It's the deep black yonder, where she is. The girl is about as insulated as she'll ever be."

Shima nodded, threw a switch, and Gretchen's total State of the Body flashed onto a projection screen.

_+	H	C	N	U	Ü	E	3	A	G	HH
P		B	B	D	A	B	B C	E	A	A
V	Ä		A	C	C	B	B	B	O	B³
D	A	8	A B	A	A	C	D	C	A	
B	M	M	M		B	A	A	A	A	A
C	M	M	M	M		A	E	C	A	O
II	M	M	7	D	A?		O	P	A	Ä
M	B	B	A	B⁴	O	O		O	D	D
F	E	D	A	A	C	C	A		E	G
LL	A	A	C	C	Ä	D	D	D		O
S	D	A	A	A	A	A	B	A	AB	+
O	C	C	C	C	C	C	C	C		D
Q	A	6	O	A	A Ä	A	B		B	A
5	E	E	E	E	E	E		E	E	8
N	N	N	N	N	N		4	6	E	O
8	D	E	D	E		3	5	7	E	O
R	A	A	B		5	7	4	6	E	O

A·5 B·10 C·15 D·20 E·30 M·100

"Whatever in the cockeyed world is that, Shim?"

"Metabolic readout, Lucy. Pulse. Temperature. Respiration. Tension. Tone. Etcetera. Etcetera."

"In decimal? *Decimal!* Talk about old-fashioned!"

"Yeah. It's an antique program I pulled out of the software library at CCC. It was the easiest and quickest to convert to these tests. Any self-respecting computer will translate the decimal into modern binary, if I need it."

"Was the old original a sensory test program? Like how and why customers smell CCC perfumes?"

"Hell, no! It was probabilities for *n*-tuplets worked out for Sales. But you write a classy program, Lucy, and its algorithms can be adapted to anything. You know that. Snips and snails and puppydog tails, and such are computers made of."

"The fun you science mavins have."

"Oh, a science, am I? And what are you, pray, Doctor Friedrich Humboldt Leuz?"

"I, sir, whatever your name is, am an *Untersee Forschungsreisende* . . . And what's more, I can spell it."

"And a hearty *Sieg Heil* to you. I'm going to hit her with sound now. Got to find out if her hearing is secondhand, too. Ind'dni said that might be important. He didn't say why . . ."

Shima examined the readout of Gretchen's sound-responses with perplexity. At last Leuz inquired, "Got a problem?"

"It's the damnedest thing," Shima said slowly. "She can hear all right, but she has a very low quantity threshold. In other words, she can hear, say, distant thunder, but not thunder cracking overhead. She can hear a canary whisper, but not a bull sea-lion roar. That's a complete switch on your run-of-the-mill deafness."

"Fascinating. You know, Shim, Miz Nunn might be a new evolutionary quantum jump."

"Oh?"

"The crux of survival for a species is adaptability. What knocked off the extincts? Inability to roll with the punches of change."

"No argument."

"Our environment has been changing drastically," Leuz continued. "One of them is the battering of our senses by sights and sounds beyond endurance, which is why we have so many crazies in Bedlam-Rx. Thousands and thousands who've rejected an impossible reality." Leuz meditated. "Maybe they're the sanes and we're the crazies to put up with it."

"And Gretchen? Is she rejecting?"

"No, she's adapting. Mother Nature is always pushing species toward the primal pinnacle, and that includes Man. Regrettably, you and I are far below that pinnacle."

"Careful with your slander, Lucy. I'm taping everything that goes on here."

"Mother Nature, with her glorious improvisation, is trying to generate an advanced species of Man through a freaky adaptation to our changing environment. Another push toward the primal pinnacle . . . and that's your girl, Gretchen Nunn. She's rolling with the punches of degenerating sights and sounds."

"Hmmm . . . The primal pinnacle . . . You may be right, Lucy. Certainly you're right about my being nowhere near it. But Gretchen? I don't know. I do know that, near or far, she's unique."

"All of that. The only question is whether it's a genuine mutation and inheritable. Are you doing anything to investigate that?"

"The pill is her option," Shima smiled. "R. No more rapping; we mustn't keep the lady waiting. I'll check taste and smell now."

"Man! What a peak! Ind'dni was right. The little lady sure can smell and taste."

"What'd you hit her with, Shim?"

"H_2S. Hydrogen sulphide."

"What? Rotten eggs?"

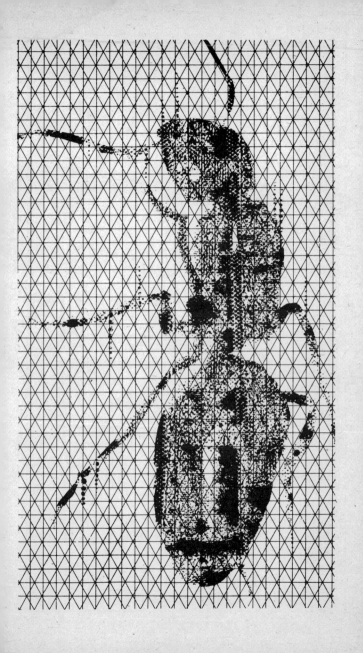

"Uh-huh."

"That, sir, is cruel and unusual punishment, expressly forbidden by the Constitution of the United States."

"She was programmed to expect the worst."

"So now what fiendery?" Leuz chuckled.

"Now the poor kid gets bombed with a dirty, rotten universal hang-up."

"Money?"

Shima laughed. "You know, Lucy, you *Forschungsreisendes* can be real profound at times. No, not money, acarophobia."

"What?"

"Formication."

"What?"

"The Cocaine Bug." Shima looked at Leuz' blank face. "You still don't understand?"

"No, and I don't think I want to."

"Maybe it's just as well. You'd shoot me, and no jury would convict. Here we go, Gretch. Sorry, but I've got to test your sense of touch."

"Look at her bod shrieking! I'm sorry, love. I'm sorry. It's all over now. At least I know you can really feel." Shima turned a pale face to Leuz. "And I'm feeling it too, by empathy."

"What was she feeling? What's this Cocaine Bug bit?"

"Insects crawling all over the skin. Psychiatric cant for C and skag symptoms."

"Ugh! Likewise eeyuch! You were right. No jury would convict."

"I told you it was universal, Lucy. Look at your arms; you're all gooseflesh."

Leuz rubbed his arms vigorously. "Sometimes I have my doubts about entomologists . . . Or do I mean etymologists?"

"Try it *auf Deutsch*."

"*Wortableitung?* No. I must mean *Insektenkundefachmanns*."

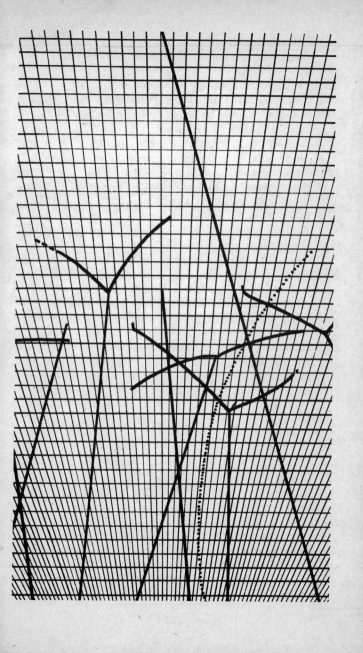

"Try *entomologie professeur*."

"Thanks a huge bunch. So now what?"

"Now sight."

"But you already know it's secondhand."

"Sure, but only for the normal visual spectrum. Quaery: can she see beyond? In the ultraviolet or infrared? Here we go."

Shima let out a low whistle, then muttered, "Closer and closer to your primal pinnacle, doctor. This girl *is* a giant quantum jump ahead."

"What? How?" Leuz was confused.

"Gretchen's blind, isn't she?"

"You said in the visual spectrum."

"Well she's halfway between seeing and sensing in the ultraviolet."

"Seeing? In the UV? Impossible!"

"Lucy, she's reacting, she's sensing UV radiation. There's no single word for her response. Gretchen probably thinks she's just got flashes and lights in her eyes . . . phosphenes . . . but she's actually—Oh, hell! Let's invent a word. She's . . . She's . . . She's seesensing high-energy particles that—"

"No. Reverse it, Shim. Senseeing works better."

"R. She's senseeing the particle barrage shooting up from the earth's radioactive mantle below her . . . Through a sort of somatic cloud chamber."

"My God! Fantastic! A seventh sense?"

"Exactly."

"But how can you be sure it's cloud-chamber sensight?"

"We had a piece of freak luck."

"Such as?"

"She peaked off the scale like an eruption at one point. Just once, and it was one in a million."

"Consisting of?"

"She was senseeing a neutrino encounter."

"No!"

"Yes."

252

"But the neutrino's a neutral particle with zero rest mass. It reacts with hardly anything," Leuz objected.

"Gretchen 'saw' it and it had to be a neutrino. Nothing else from space could penetrate twelve hundred feet of water. It streaked down, through the Van Allen belts, through the atmosphere, through two hundred fathoms of water, through her, and her somatic cloud chamber 'saw' it. By now it's through the earth to the other side and on its way to wherever."

"I'll be damned."

"And you're absolutely right, Lucy. Gretchen's a fantastic mutation, a quantum jump toward the primal pinnacle. And if I believed in God, I'd pray that this genetic change is favorable and inheritable."

"Amen."

"And so say we all. Now let's bring the New Primal Man up."

* * *

Seated gracefully cross-legged in the padded cell, Subadar Ind'dni switched off Shima's taped recording of the *Drogh III* tests and regarded Gretchen Nunn with an expression that was close to worship.

"You are truly remarkable phenomenon, madame. Even inspirational. *Lusus naturae* does not do you justice. Dr. Leuz was quite correct. You are a fantastic quantum jump beyond us."

"The quote New Primal Man unquote?" Gretchen actually blushed.

The corners of Ind'dni's mouth quirked under his jet beard; a blushing Negro is an adorable sight. "Even that is inadequate descriptive. Legend alleges that the gods, in human guise, sometimes visit their poor relations down here on earth. Which are you? Sarasvati, divine protectress of poetry? Uma, goddess of light? I prefer to believe you are most probably Gauri, the brilliant."

Gretchen, even more embarrassed, laughed and

253

waved a hand. "Thank you, Subadar. If I'm to be a god in human disguise, it would most probably be the Mundingoe bugbear, Mumbo Jumbo, who terrified the African women."

"I hate to throw a cold douche on the holy sacrament," Shima said sourly, "but I had an unholy experience with the Golem[100] last night. Remember? I'd like to get on with our business."

"I have not forgotten, doctor," Ind'dni answered. "Perhaps, even, I remember more poignantly than yourself. Do you not recall that after you departed from Precinct Complex, I was left with the pathetic victim? That was no Ops party."

"The party!" Gretchen exclaimed. "Regina's Ops party for the men. The whole bee colony was there. That's what brought the Golem back again."

Ind'dni nodded. "Cause and effect. It has been demonstrated. But now I am concerned about the effect on yourself of a second venture into the Phasmaworld . . . this time alone, without comfort of Dr. Shima as fellow traveler."

"Why the heavy concern?" Shima demanded. "She came through the first unscathed, at least in her head. So far as the physical pranks of her bod go . . . Well, here we are, locked in a padded cell."

"Agreed, doctor. Bedlam-Rx was most cooperative, and this cell is reasonably safe. At worst, Miz Nunn can only attack quilted walls. At best, she will accost you, as she did that 'before and after' poster." Ind'dni smiled. "I promise to close my eyes."

This time Gretchen actually giggled. "We're all in this together, Subadar. We should have no secrets."

"Many thanks for confidence in my discretion, madame, but is it not possible that I may have secrets of my own wishful to conceal? However. Here is point of my concern; prime thrusts of the Id are pleasure and survival. What if your visit prompts this savage subworld to use you for its brute satisfaction?"

"But of course I expect that, Subadar," Gretchen said, "and I'm prepared to protect myself."

"Prepared to protect yourself against the unknown? How, madame?"

"My lord! Haven't I lived and worked in the real world of the Guff for close to thirty years? And what d'you think the Guff has done except try to use me for its pleasure and survival? The only difference is that I make the Guff pay. I'm armored by experience to withstand any and all psychic pressures."

Ind'dni looked from Gretchen to Shima. "And you, doctor? Are you, too, armored, no matter what Miz Nunn experiences in the infernal subworld and no matter how her somatic self behaves in this cell?"

Gretchen answered before Shima could open his mouth. "No he's not. So if *le pauvre petit* withdraws into sulks, you'll have to understand. I'll soothe the baby when I come out."

"I do not sulk," Shima growled. "I am not a baby."

Ind'dni sighed. "But perhaps I am, doctor. Sad to confess I also am not armored against possible outcome of this extraordinary venture of Miz Nunn, but . . . so be it. Let us launch her on her lonely trip into the unknown. The Promethium injection . . .?"

* * *

"STOP IT! STOP IT! STOP IT!" Gretchen screamed. "For God's sake, what are you doing?" She lurched out of the quilted corner where she had recovered consciousness, stumbled across the padded cell-floor, and tried to separate the two men. Shima had his hands around Ind'dni's throat and was trying to throttle him and batter his head against the wall. The Subadar was gripping Shima's wrists. Gretchen flung her arms around Shima's neck and let her dead weight tear him away from Ind'dni.

"You bitch!" Shima was panting like a tiger on the

255

attack. "You black bitch's bastard! And this skog's your yancyman!"

"For God's sake, Blaise!"

"God damn you. Damn the day I ever met you."

"What are you talking about?"

Ind'dni massaged his throat. "Evidently Dr. Shima is less than unarmored, madame; he is vulnerable. All of his educated responses betrayed him, and he attacked when he should have withdrawn."

"From what? What happened?"

"Describing event delicately, Miz Nunn, it became apparent that it would be Dr. Shima who would be required to close his eyes."

"What?"

"Your unconscious body accosted the wrong man."

"You mean I—? You—?"

"Yes, you, him," Shima shouted. "And for how long?"

"Blaise! Never!"

"Yeah. Sure. In physical fact, never . . . Maybe . . . But how long have you been wanting, eh?"

"No, Blaise. Never."

"Have you patience for friendly counseling, doctor?" Ind'dni said gently.

"You God-damned yancy skog, smiling and sneaking—"

"Shima!" the Subadar's voice was not raised, but it had the piercing thrust of cold iron. "Do not ever use that word 'skog' to me again."

Shima was frightened into silence.

"Your rage bases itself on your assumed knowledge of Miz Nunn's manner of acting, yes?" Ind'dni's tone was gentle again. "She feels first and then proves it. I have sometimes heard you tease madame for thinking with her gut. Yes?"

"Yes," Shima muttered.

"Then how could you take this naughty prank of her unconscious body seriously, when internally she has known all along that I am homosexual?"

"Wh-what?"

"But of course," Ind'dni smiled. "I neither conceal nor parade it, yet Madame has felt the truth since first we met. At best, she merely accosted another wrong poster. At worst, her body was guilty of another childish practical joke, since it knew that her challenge could not and would not be accepted."

Shima was aghast. "Oh Jesus! Christ Jesus! What a damned idiot I've been. Suspecting. Watching how she looks at you. I'm a clown!" He burst into hysterical laughter, began to cry, then turned and buried his shamed face in a quilted wall.

Gretchen looked hard at Ind'dni. He lifted a brow and smiled at her. She shook her head emphatically. His smile never altered.

Shima turned abruptly. "I want to apologize."

"Not necessary, doctor."

"Damn it, I've got to apologize."

"And you have already."

"So cool it, baby," Gretchen soothed. "You've reached the bottom of your barrel. There's no lower to go. You can start climbing up, now."

"Most mixed metaphor, but most apt nevertheless." Ind'dni laughed. "The worst is over, and there is no cause for guilt or shame. We must not permit the insanity of the internal inferno to bleed into our civilized lives. We will leave this unpleasant scene and visit a more grateful atmosphere . . . my own apartment. You will find it healing and restorative. And we must hear madame's account of her expedition into the Phasmaworld while it is still fresh in her memory."

As they filed out of the padded cell, Gretchen silently mouthed to Ind'dni, "You. Are. A. Great. Good. Man."

17

There were elegances in Subadar Ind'dni's apartment
appealing only to the elite. Illumination was by clear,
filament light bulbs. "Ah yes. For enormous bribe I
will make known identity of modern Thomas Alva
Edison who crafts them for me." A two-foot world
globe was so ancient that there were blank regions
labeled *terra incognita*. A green fly had died on lati-
tude 47°N. Only close examination revealed that the
corpse was composed of jade, jet, and lacy gold.
"Brutal blackmail required to force me to disclose
modern Fabergé who fashioned same for me. And
now, if you are both quite restored and comfortable,
let us begin."

"First, how long was I gone?" Gretchen asked.

"Twenty minutes," Shima answered. "I reduced
your Pm shot to a quarter of what we'd taken the first
time around. That skag's wild. It's got to be handled
with care."

"And you didn't reduce it a quarter too much,
Blaise. The Phasma scene was a shivery Rorschach
world for my crazy primal senses . . . all murky ink
blots, or maybe I should call them id blots. I still can't
understand half of them. First I went to black . . .

"That would be madame without the advantage of reading your senses, doctor."

"R."

"Miz Nunn, as you recall experience, could you possibly sketch perceptions for us? Here is pad and pencil."

"I'm no artist but I'll try, Subadar."

"Many thanks. Will be most helpful for interpretation."

"Then the dead black became sparkled with stars and lines and whorls and silly symbols. Should I try to draw that? It was complicated . . ."

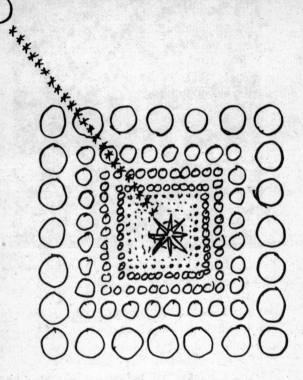

"No need, Gretch. That's simply the way you think you're seeing your cloud chamber perception of high-energy particles."

"Then I went to white and some kind of Black Hole that was either a bird in flight, or a helmet, or a *Folies Bergere* wig by Toulouse-Lautrec. It looked something like this . . . And it was looking at me . . .

It got bigger and sort of turned into an urn or maybe a soup tureen . . .

. . . But would you believe a tureen with eyes?

Then a vase . . .   At least that's how I saw it;
but I'm sure that each in-
dividual would see a different image in the Rorschach
id blots . . .

But now, thinking about it, I'm reminded of the Tarot
card *Le Pendu*, "The Hanging Man," and I'm frightened . . .

And began to condense and break up into—into
I don't know what, but it was damned ugly.
Look at it . . .

Then it became a crown or butterfly over a heart, or spade, or plumb bob, like this . . .

But always there seemed to be two eyes watching me constantly . . .

Then suddenly I was seeing a snow goose in
flight or a stinging bee attacking . . .

Only the Phasmaworld is a nightmare of transfor-
mations and I was seeing id blots without identity. The wings of the goose or the bee turned
into an African devil mask, a witch-doctor mask,
a voodoo mask, but at the same time it looked
like the head of a key to something . . .

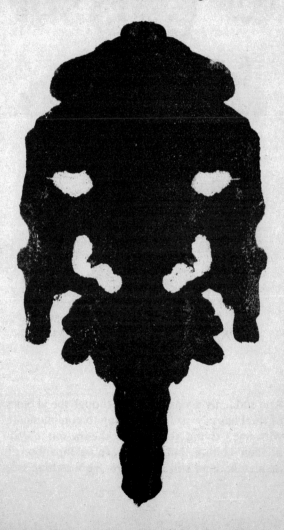

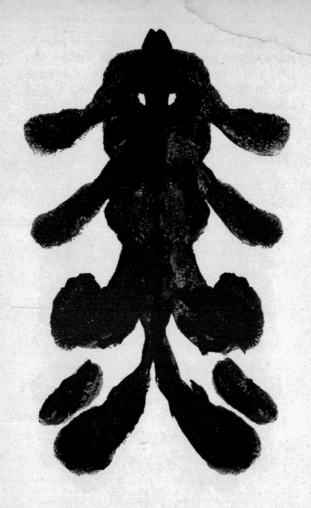

And suddenly it was almost as though the id blots of the Phasmaworld were trying to communicate with me, trying to explain the *raison d'être* of their culture, but in Chinese or Japanese or Spacetalk. And still the eyes were watching me.

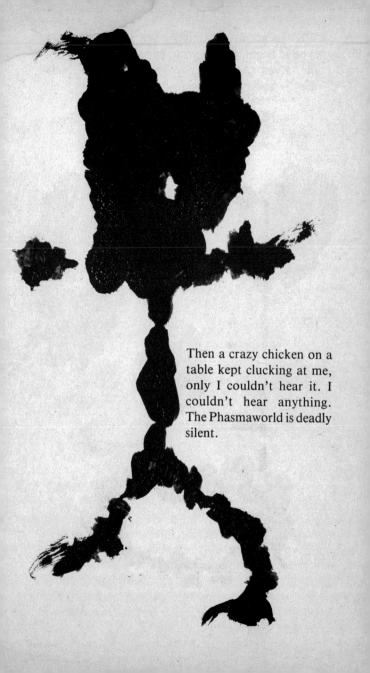

Then a crazy chicken on a
table kept clucking at me,
only I couldn't hear it. I
couldn't hear anything.
The Phasmaworld is deadly
silent.

Who so surprised as me when a pretty female-type id began flirting with me and making eyes at me. Eyes. Always eyes. Ink blots or id blots, they're still eyes. Like so . . .

And some empty stick-figure man began making advances. You're right, Subadar; pleasure and satisfaction are prime motives . . .

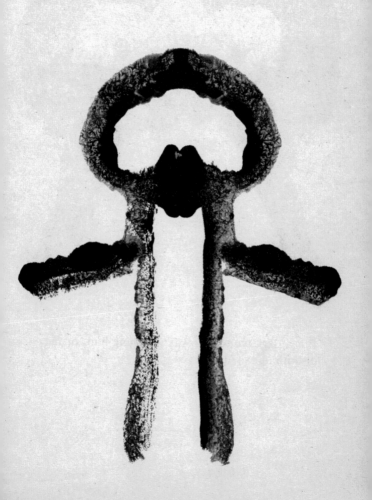

But a dark woman-id was watching him, or me, or both of us. Again eyes . . .

And her face turned into another
devil mask.

Then a Negro stick-figure made
its move at me . . .

And transformed into Death in
a cloak clutching at me . . .

I think, perhaps, that I tried to escape, and a form appeared that—I don't know—that seemed to be an open trap set for me. Like this. Could inanimate objects also have ids . . . ?

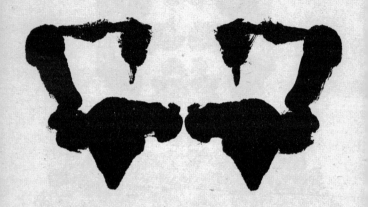

And it melted into or was replaced by this. I don't know what it was. Maybe kissing Siamese twins?

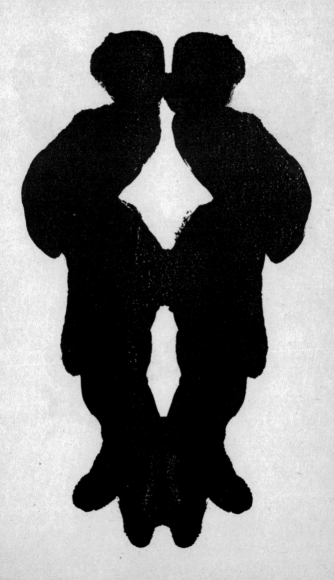

The pretty one came back, flirting again. There is
a strange sort of continuity and persistence in the
Phasma civilization . . .

And that vague thing I thought might be an
open trap turned itself into a coronet. It's a slid-
ing, misty, fluid world, the gelatin reality of
people . . .

And then it enlarged into an
imperial crown . . .

And then the imperial crown on a devil, witch-doctor mask. Very much like this . . .

The Siamese twins returned, this time back-to-back and apparently not on speaking terms; or maybe I was seeing a pair of dancing cobras. Look at them . . .

Then, out of nowhere, appeared
a fat letter double-U . . .

Which turned into a pair of upraised arms with
enormous biceps; something like this . . .

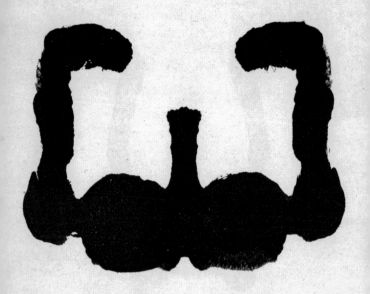

And then transformed itself into
a ludicrous, droopy fat ass . . .

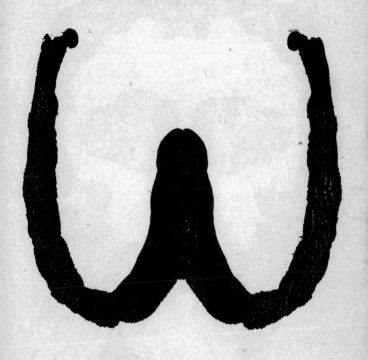

And there was a sunflower explosion
into infinity, and—

"—and then I came back to the cell."

Gretchen tried to catch her breath; she'd been pouring out her report and sketching for half an hour. Both men were so deeply absorbed that they ignored her. Despite the painful shocks she had suffered, Gretchen was forced to chuckle. Shima was focused on the jade fly dead on 47°N. Ind'dni was studying her sketch notes with the concentration of a connoisseur of id blots.

At last Gretchen said, "So?"

"That explosion," Shima asked the Fabergé fly. "The explosion into infinity. . . ?"

"Was your attack-escape against me," Ind'dni murmured. "In all likelihood it was cause of Miz Nunn's abrupt return." He looked up from the sketches. "I think you may agree, doctor, that it reveals most curious and unexpected relationship."

"Between Gretchen and me? There's nothing unex—"

"No, no. Between soma and psyche." Ind'dni turned to Gretchen. "You are always a source of inspiration, madame."

"Thank you, Subadar."

"I devoutly wish I had you on my staff." Back to Shima. "Now, doctor, have you drawn any astute conclusions from Miz Nunn's exploratory?"

"I have; that I was right. It isn't the Golem^{100} alone. There *is* an id population."

"Yes. And?"

"That there's an entire Phasmaculture."

"And?"

"And that there *is* a link between Realworld individuals and Phasmaworld iddividuals."

"*Id*-dividuals? Well put, doctor. I like 'iddividuals' very much. Anything else?"

Shima grimaced. "A rotten conclusion. Given my analysis of the scene: we'd have to know Ourworld individuals intimately before we could establish their links with Phasmaworld iddividuals, and vice versa.

288

Summa: it'll take ages to discover the source of the Golem.''

"Bravo, doctor!" Ind'dni beamed. "I agree in entire, with exception of your estimate of time required."

"You don't think it'll take time? Why?"

"I come last, doctor. Now it is madame's turn. If you have recovered stamina, Miz Nunn, please to give us your conclusions."

"Well . . ." Gretchen began slowly, "as I said when I was reporting, Subadar, you were right to be concerned. The Infraworld is motivated by pleasure and satisfaction on the basic brute sublevel. But . . . But that's what confuses me because I sensed so much danger and death."

"Why the confusion, madame?" Ind'dni was faintly surprised. "Selfish pleasure may often endanger others. For the cruel carnivores is there not pleasure in slow killing? Have you never seen a cat delay final demise of a mouse?"

"That's true."

"Then with confusion resolved, what did you construct of dissolving images, the id blots that drifted and replaced and transformed? Are you able to interpret?"

"But I gave you my interpretations as I reported them, Subadar."

Ind'dni shook his head ruefully. "Alas, there we have dilemma of laboratory experiment. The subject is too engrossed in the test to give objective estimate of experience."

Shima broke in. "If you've come to different conclusions, Ind'dni, let's have 'em, for God's sake. Don't play cat-and-mouse with us!"

"Such was never my intent, doctor; I am no cruel carnivore. I *have* been able to interpret a few of madame's primal perceptions . . . her senseeing, Dr. Leuz called it . . . and should like to submit same for your judgment."

"Time estimate first," Shima insisted. "Why'd you disagree with mine?"

"Because Miz Nunn has, I believe, achieved the goal of her Promethium trip. She has unconsciously disclosed true source of the Hundred-Hander-Golem beast."

"What?" Gretchen exclaimed. "I did? When? How?"

"Who?" Shima shot.

"Your suspicions were correct; Winifred Ashley, Queen Bee of the hive."

"How did you come to that interpretation of the id blots, Subadar?" Gretchen was bewildered.

"First I must point out that many of your perceptions were through your cloud-chamber-seventh-sense which Dr. Shima so brilliantly discovered. (Patience, I beg. The chain of induction is delicate and must be taken link by link.) In fine, madame, you were often sensing living energy auras which can be as powerful as subatomic particles."

"Yes, and . . . ?"

"The eyes watching you constantly: for the physical eye of sight substitute the psychological 'I' of ego. You were seeing yourself reflected in the Phasma-entities and, no doubt, they were seeing themselves reflected in you. The Phasmaculture is a world of mutual masturbation."

"My God!" Shima exclaimed. "What a concept!"

"Now I come to most delicate link of all," Ind'dni continued. "The dark woman-id watching you, Miz Nunn, who transformed into a devil mask . . . Examine your memory objectively . . . Look at your sketch again . . . Could the mask not have been the letter 'R' attached to its mirror image?"

"What? I never—"

"And supported by your Siamese-twin impressions?"

"It never occurred to—"

"The open trap which transformed into a coronet,

then an imperial crown, then a crowned devil mask? Look at your sketch. Is not the mask the letter 'R' attached to its mirror image? What does a crowned 'R' suggest to you?"

"It can't be mistaken . . . now! The Queen Bee. Regina." Gretchen turned to Shima. "He was right, Blaise. I *was* too engrossed in the Pm trip to form any constructs."

"Another delicate link," Ind'dni went on. "The flying snow goose *or* the stinging bee?"

Shima nodded with conviction. "Regina, the Queen Bee. It has to be."

"Indeed yes. We have established the prime source of the Hundred-Hander. It is generated by the colony, the hive of bee-ladies, but the colony is held together by its queen. The queen is the source."

"So the queen is the house that must be destroyed," Gretchen whispered.

"But what baffles me," Ind'dni said slowly, "is the letter 'double-U' which turned into strong arms and then large buttocks. Why did it inspire the appearance of death?"

"Death appeared to me before that, Subadar."

"Yes, in response to 'R.' Why subsequently in response to 'double-U'?"

"Obvious," Shima said. "For 'double-U' as in Winifred."

"A little too obvious for me, doctor." Ind'dni sighed. "Perhaps it is a flaw in the Bombazine attitude to reject the immediate obvious, yet I don't like it. There must be a deeper, perhaps double implication in Death hovering over that letter, the robust arms, the buttocks . . ."

"Aren't you creating unnecessary complications, Subadar?" Gretchen asked.

"Perhaps." Ind'dni took a deep breath and smiled. "Or perhaps, to paraphrase Dr. Shima's dictum, I am trying to meet the unknown with the unknown." He took another deep breath. "At any rate we know

where we stand *vis-à-vis* Golem[100]. It is an iddentity
—thank you for the coinage, doctor—linked firmly to
the psyche of Miz Winifred Ashley through the colony
which she controls. If she can be deposed, the colony
will be scattered and the Golem will have no home."

"That'll be a job for me," Gretchen said firmly.
"I'm in the hive. I'll have to figure out a way to under-
mine Her Majesty."

"Boring from within?" Ind'dni smiled. "A pardon-
able treachery in this fantastic situation. However, I
suggest that the planning wait until tomorrow. This is
not the time for sustained discussion. We're all very
tired and require rest."

"He's right," Shima yawned. "I'm wiped. Come
on, Miz Lig. Leave us go to bed, and no funny business."

"It's *Jig*, Mr. Jap. Can't you ever remember?"
Gretchen led the way to the door. "We'll see about
the funny business when we get to your place. There's
still earth on the terrace. Good night and Opbless,
Subadar."

Ind'dni made no response and no move to see them
out. He sat and watched the Jig and the Jap leave with
a horrified expression of enlightenment and incredulity.

18

"This is the original medieval mass from which the song was adapted," Gretchen said, "or copied or stolen. I had it faxed for you, Regina, because I thought it would fit into your lovely Communist decor. Naturally, I used a modern piano score when I played it for you."

Regina's eyes were brimming. "This is the sweetest, most thoughtful gift I've ever received, BB. I'm overcome. Truly. Opbless, dear, and a thousand thanks."

"Well, I knew you didn't get that pianola roll," Gretchen smiled from the piano, "so I dug out the music. That was the least I could do for you, Regina."

"And played so beautifully! Didn't she, ladies?"

"All heart." Ildefonsa applauded. "All heart, hammer and sickle."

"AYE! Mock BB if you will, Nell," Sarah Heartburn burst out, "but the PROLETARIAT were inspired by that SACRED ANTHEM to give their lives in the battle to wrest ☛ DEMOCRATIC ☚ art, science and freedom from the greedy grasp of capitalist, imperialist *BOSSES!*"

In the stunned silence that followed the outburst, Gretchen said, "I didn't know you were a party member."

"Oh, Sarah isn't," Ildefonsa said. "She played *The Rebel Girl, a Precious Pearl* who made the labor exploiters tremble with terror. I caught the show. That was her big Act One curtain speech. Pfui!"

"Now, now, Nellie," Regina chided. "We mustn't tease Sarah about that performance. Surely an actor can't be held responsible for old-fashioned speeches in historical romances. Sarah was truly dedicated to *The Rebel Girl* and can't be blamed for the silly words the author put into her mouth."

"Who wrote it?"

"An Old Wave dramatist named Szechuan Finkel." Sarah mused. "D'you know, I think they may really have talked like that back in the Red Flag days."

"When was that?" Mary Mixup asked.

"Ages ago. I'm not sure. I think it was when some saint named Joe Stalin drove the bosses out of the temple—or vice versa."

"But what was a boss?"

"A sort of Bigfoot with fangs."

"It doesn't matter, Mary," Regina interposed. "All

that's ancient history now. BB dear, please play it again and we'll sing it with you. We've been rehearsing in foreign languages, hoping I'd get the original pianola roll. We were going to play an underground Bolshevik International. Now we can, thanks to you, dear, so let's organize, organize. Pi-girl! Make sure the vodka is iced.''

"Only frozen bathwater, Miz Winifred."

"Quite all right, child. You don't put the ice *in* the drinks; you ice the bottles. Now, BB . . . ?"

"Once more, with solidarity, comrade," Ildefonsa laughed.

"Oh, do be serious, Nellie. Our theme is 'The Red Front Forever,' and we must be sincere. We must believe in the coming revolution.''

Regina began to sing to Gretchen's accompaniment:

> Arise, ye pris'ners of starvation!
> Arise, ye wretched of the earth.
> For justice thunders condemnation,
> A better world's in birth.
> No more tradition's chains shall bind us.
> Arise, ye slaves, no more in thrall!
> The earth shall rise on new foundations.
> We have been naught, we shall be all!

Regina bowed graciously to the applause. "Thank you, comrades, thank you. Solidarity forever, and Pi-girl where is our vodka? Next we have tovarisch Mary Mixup, our French mavin, to sound the tocsin of the despotic ruling class. Mary?" The Queen made way for Mary Mixup who took her place alongside the piano.

Gretchen pointed to the music as though coaching her. "When you sing, mean it!" she whispered. "Regina never takes you seriously. Nellie Gwyn is always making fun of you. Don't be in thrall. Assert yourself.''

Mary stared, then turned and began to sing:

Debout, les damnés de la terre,
Debout, les forçats de la faim!
La raison tonne en son cratère:
C'est l'éruption de la fin.
Du passé faisons table rase,
Foules d'esclaves, debout, debout!
Le monde va changer de base:
Nous ne sommes rien, soyons tout!

Through the applause Gretchen whispered, "*Debout! Debout! You* should be all!"

"And now," Regina announced, "our own Yenta Calienta. The Jews of the world have always been in the forefront of the fight for freedom and the liberation of ethnic minorities."

"But I couldn't do it without my rabbi," Yenta said as she took Mary's place alongside the piano."

"What are you doing with Regina and her goyish friends?" Gretchen whispered. "They're all dreck! Mary can never get a bargain straight. Nellie has no respect for money. Regina's too rich to care. When you sing about liberation, mean it for yourself!"

Yenta cocked an eye at Gretchen, then turned and sang:

Sheit oif ir ale wer nor shklafen
Was hunger leiden mus in noit.
Der geist er kocht un ruft tzu wafen,
In shlacht uns firen is es greit.
Di welt fun gwaldtaten un leiden
Tzushteren welen mir, un dan
Fun freiheit gleichheit a geneiden
Bashafen wet der arbetsman!

"*Freiheit! Freiheit!*" Gretchen whispered. "*Sheit oif! Sheit oif* with your rabbi!"

"Next, our 'Rebel Girl, a Precious Pearl' will favor us with the 'Internationale,' as sung for the finale of the play of the same name."

"But not, I say, NOT in drab English. In the only VERO language of BELLEZZA ARTI!"

☆☆☆☆   ●●●●

"What does Regina know about beautiful art? She's just a rich reactionary. What do any of them know? Yenta is commercial. Mary's too dumb. Nell's insincere."

> Compagni avanti! Il gran partito
> Noi siam dei lavoratore.
> Rosso un fior c'è in petto fiorito;
> Una fede c'è nata in cor!
> Noi non siamo piu nell'officina,
> Entro terra, nei campi, in mar,
> La plebe sempre all'opera china
> Senza Ideal in cui sperar.

"*Avanti,* Sarah! *Avanti!* Leave these superficial UNCREATIVE women. They're beneath you."

"Miss Priss has chosen the precise tongue of Karl Marx and Friedrich Engels," Regina said. "They are the godfathers of our glorious Bolshevik Epiphany, and she perhaps may become the godmother."

"Regina's always putting you down," Gretchen hissed. "She's rich and vulgar. They're all vulgar and common. The twins are marital perverts. Nell Gwyn is worse than a whore."

> Wacht auf, Verdammte dieser Erde,
> Die stets man noch zum Hungern zwingt!
> Das Recht, wie Glut im Kraterherde,
> Nun mit Macht zum Durchbruch dringt.
> Reinen Tisch macht mit den Bedrängern:
> Heer der Sklaven, wache auf!
> Ein Nichts zu sein, tragt es nicht länger—
> Alles zu werden strömt zuhauf!

"*Wacht auf,* Priss! *Wacht auf!* Wake up. Get out of here. You're too nice and decent for these rotten women who're completely without cultivated manners."

"It's no secret that our beloved Nell Gwyn is the color of our beloved Revolutionary Red Flag," Regina smiled, "but I do have a secret to reveal. She is of Spanish descent, and that *rara avis,* a titian Castilian."

"And she's a bile-green turkey, Nell. Green with envy. She knows you ought to be holding the meetings in your beautiful apartment and running them in your high style. She's jealous of you. They all are."

> Arriba los pobres del mundo
> En pié los esclavos sin pan
> Y alcémon todos al grito de
> Viva la Internacionál!
> Rompamos al punto las trabas
> Que impiden el triunfo del bien
> Cambiemos el mundo de fase,
> Hundiendo el imperio burgués!

"*Triunfo,* Nell! *Triunfo! Viva la Internacionál!* Believe what you sing. You know damned well that *you* should be the queen."

* * *

As the depressed Gretchen strolled the Strøget, chewing over her failure to arouse the bee-ladies to a hive revolution against Queen Regina, she was astonished and delighted to see Blaise Shima bearing down on her like the Flying Dutchman, full-sail and silent. She ran to meet him, seized his arm, and before they could exchange greetings was pouring out an account of the psalm-singing for the coming of the glorious Bolshevik epiphany.

". . . And then the twins, *Oodgedye* and *Udgedye,* sang it in Russian and I handed them the same number —You two are the only really liberated women here, and all the rest hate you for it; Regina, Priss, Sarah, Yenta . . . Why don't you get lost from this dull

298

scene? Why don't you take the song to heart? Same result. Nothing . . .

"My God, I'm glad we ran into each other, Blaise. I'm heartsick. I couldn't start a palace revolution in the colony, even with malice, jealousies, rivalries, anything. Regina binds them together, and she's too strong. The Queen Bee has got to be removed if we hope to scatter the hive and wipe the Golem. But how?

"Don't bother to answer, Blaise. It was a rhetorical question. I know the answer and it sickens me, but it's the only way out for us and the rest of the Guff. I'm going to the P.L.O. and buy a contract on Winifred Ashley with the PloFather. She can and will wipe her. It's horrible—neither of us is a deliberate destroyer— but there's no other way. What do you think, Blaise? Will you go along with it? God knows what Ind'dni will do when he finds out—that cat finds out everything—but are *you* with me? What do you think?"

"uoy kcuf lliw I kniht I"

"What?"

"uoy kcuf lliw I kniht I"

"Blaise!"

"uoy kcuf lliw I kniht I"

"For God's sake! What's this gibberish?"

"uoy kcuf lliw I kniht I"

"You've gone out of your mind!"

Gretchen tore herself away from Shima's clutch, gave him one stupefied look, then dashed out of the Strøget. She careered around a corner, another, and came face to face with Salem Burne, smooth, slender, polished. The psychomancer smiled and held out his arms, grasping and clawing.

"uoy kcuf won llahs I"

"What!"

"uoy kcuf won llahs I"

"Are you insane?"

"uoy kcuf won llahs I"

"You're mad, Burne. The whole Guff's gone mad and gibbering!"

"uoy kcuf won llahs I"

She ran again, panting, trembling, and rammed into Dr. F. H. Leuz. The Drogh Director caught and enveloped her massively as she staggered.

"kcuf lamirP"

"For God's sake, Leuz! Not you!"

"kcuf lamirP"

"First Blaise? Then Burne? Now you? No! No!"

"kcuf lamirP"

"This is a nightmare. It has to be. This garble! I'm asleep somewhere. Why can't I wake up?"

She fought free of Leuz and reeled back into a doorway. She hid in the darkness in a panic. She was suddenly swept into the arms of the "UpMan" poster's Mr. "After" who spun her around, beamed, and bruised her crotch with battering ram blows of his larger-than-lifesize.

"kcuF kcuF kcuF kcuF kcuF kcuF"

"Christ almighty! Dear God almighty!"

She stumbled out of the doorway, ran blind, ran hot, ran broken, sobbing, flinching and flailing, and

there was		holding out
the		her
Statue	*F*	arms
of		and
Liberty		flaming torch.

And as the ponderous metal arms crushed around her, Gretchen fainted.

* * *

"No, you have not gone mad, Miz Nunn," Ind'dni assured her. "What you have experienced was not hallucination. It was a nightmare of quasi-reality; the

300

reality of the polymorphic Golem beast in many guises: Dr. Shima; Salem Burne, the psychomancer; Dr. Leuz, the much-respected Director of Drogh Operations; the 'UpMan' poster come to life; the long-ago-scrapped Statue of Liberty."

"And the gibberish it spoke?"

"Feeble attempts at spoken communication, which it got backwards. The creature is not of intelligence and has no grasp of our reality. It is merely brute passion using what it dredges up from your memory as decoys. I'm surprised that the Hundred-Handed animal did not appear as a computer or transport or anything else in your experience. I have no doubt that it is too primitive to understand that machines cannot speak."

"And you rescued me, Subadar?"

"Staff was only too happy to oblige."

"Your staff just happened to be passing by?"

"Not quite, Miz Nunn. After the ominous revelation of last night, I had you followed."

"What ominous revelation?"

"You and Dr. Shima have private and intimate nicknames for each other, yes? Archaic pejoratives?"

"The Jig and the Jap. Yes."

"And it never occurred to you that your final perception in the Phasmaworld—the letter 'double-U' which transformed into upraised muscular arms and then buttocks, bringing on the threat of death—it never occurred to you that this image was composed of two letters, 'J,' facing each other? Jig and Jap. J and J."

Gretchen was thunderstruck. "And *that's* the double implication you were trying to find last night, Subadar?"

"Indeed yes. Your exploration made you aware of the Golem, but it also made the Golem aware of you and your potential menace. I said that the motives of id-creatures are satisfaction and survival. The Golem must survive, so it is now attacking the danger; not

Miz Winifred Ashley, no, you. I suspected the possibility and gave instructions, which is why staff was following you to protect."

"Just me alone or Blaise, too?"

"I anticipated for both, and particularly for Dr. Shima. Please not to resent plain speaking, Miz Nunn, but where you have much strength, the doctor has weakness. You are the New Primal Man. Dr. Shima, despite all brilliance, may be one of the expendables. We cannot know Nature's standards for her pinnacle."

"Ummm." Gretchen thought that over. "Maybe. No matter. He *is* protected?"

Ind'dni sighed. "Alas, staff has lost him."

"Lost him? How? Where?"

"I need not point out the finesses of our mutual profession, Miz Nunn. You do know that whilst tailing a subject half the art lies in recognition of customary behavior patterns so that one is never at total loss."

"Yes, I know that. And?"

"Dr. Shima abruptly broke usual, familiar patterns, and staff was at total loss."

"How did Blaise break his usual patterns?"

"I am saddened to suggest that he has probably gone into fugue again."

"Mr. Wish?"

Ind'dni nodded.

"Did the Golem bring it on?"

Ind'dni shrugged helplessly.

"Who's Mr. Wish following?"

Ind'dni shrugged again.

"My God! My God! It's all falling apart. Those damned bee-ladies . . . Everything's falling apart."

"We must not despair, madame."

"No. No, you're right. We've got to act." Gretchen took a deep breath of resolution. "Yes. Act hard and fast."

"Staff is doubling energies."

"Thank you, Subadar, but I mean me."

"Ah? What do you contemplate?"

"Is this being taped?"

"Recording can be ended immediately if you so desire."

"No. I'm going to do something rotten brutal and I want to go on record."

"Yours the honor, Miz Nunn."

Gretchen firmed her lips. "I'm going to the P.L.O. pyramid for a meeting with the PloFather. I'm going to negotiate a contract on Winifred Ashley, the Queen Bee who's holding the hive together and providing the Golem with a home. I'll be accessory to murder."

"Say, rather, an instigator?"

"Then both, and I'll take what's coming to me—with honor, at least. The only way to destroy that damn horror is destroy the Queen and her hive."

Ind'dni sighed again. "You know, of course, that I cannot permit."

"I know, but you cannot stop. By the time you and Legal have me gagged in the slammer, the contract will be signed and nobody can stop the P.L.O. soldiers. Christ Jesus, Subadar!" Gretchen shouted. "The wolf on the fold. Your words. The wolf! The wolf!"

She was headlong out of the office before he could answer.

* * *

"The name is Wish, dear lady. You may call me Mr. Wish."

Regina inspected Mr. Wish. "You seem to be a harmless young man, and quite attractive. May I ask why you're foolish enough to follow me?"

"But I'm not following you, dear lady. I'm following something else, something extraordinary, and our paths happen to coincide."

"What are you following?"

"Ah!" Under his glassy exterior Mr. Wish was excited. "You seem to be a harmless lady and quite attractive, so I'll confide in you. I'm drawn by something new. I play a private game, a fun sort of paper chase or treasure hunt, and suddenly I find myself drawn by a novel trail of clues. They magick me. They beckon me. They hypnotize me.''

"What are these mysterious magic clues?"

"Double death; given and received."

"Good heavens, Mr. Wish!"

"Merely poesy, dear lady."

"Oh, you're a poet, are you?"

"A poet of destruction. A singer of the re-establishment.''

"The Establishment? I find that a contradiction in terms, Mr. Wish. No poet of any merit was ever reconciled to the Establishment."

"You misheard me, dear lady. I am a poet of the RE-establishment. I am a singer of the thanatatic."

"And what, pray, is the thanatatic?"

"It is the deep, basic human urge to re-establish the state of the universe as it was before it was disrupted by the emergence of life."

"Disrupted? You are anti-life?"

"I am the enemy of disruption, of anything that mars the pristine logic of nature, and whenever life attempts to end its intrusion on the perfection by destroying itself, I'm drawn to help. That is my treasure hunt.''

"You must be an unusual poet, Mr. Wish, and I should like to hear your verse. Will you read for me? Here is my card. I receive Thursday afternoons. There will be other guests and, to be sure, refreshments. Now, *au revoir*. I must be getting along. I have an appointment.''

"So have I, and it seems in the same direction. Shall we?"

They continued together through the malignant streets and alleys of the Guff, casually detouring around rubbish, trash, and rotting forms that once were alive. All this they accepted as, indeed, did everyone. This was the advanced twenty-second century and a price must be paid for progress. Regina chatted graciously about poesy and the decorative arts, but seemed almost as excited as Mr. Wish.

"You've confided in me, sir," she said at last, "and I will reciprocate by confiding in you. I'm reaching the end of a treasure hunt, too. A friend, or rather the husband of a friend, attended a party at my place on the first Opsday. He is a collector of oddments and he revealed something that thrilled me. He owns a treasure I've yearned for, an original pianola roll of the 'Internationale' by Pottier and Degeyter. He was generous enough to offer it as a gift, and I accepted. The gentleman lives here. Goodbye again, sir."

Regina turned into a magnificent Oasis and Mr. Wish followed. She regarded him. He smiled. "My trail ends here, too, dear lady. Another odd coincidence."

She was flustered as she was passed through by Security, but not too badly. Yet she was rattled enough not to notice that Mr. Wish had been passed under her aegis. They entered the express elevator together and were shot skyward.

"I'm for thirty-one," Regina said.

"So am I, but not to be alarmed, dear lady. There are four apartments to the floor. Coincidence once more, and I shall compose an epic on the coincidence of Thanatos for your next Thursday afternoon."

But when Droney Lafferty opened the door for Regina, he stared and exclaimed, "What? You too, doctor?"

Mr. Wish smiled into the piebald face. "The name is Wish, sir. You may call me Mr. Wish. I've come to help you."

He glided past them into the apartment. Lafferty lifted an arm to block him, suddenly smiled raffishly and permitted him to pass. Mr. Wish gazed glassily at the illuminated vitrines displaying Lafferty's curious collections; sundials, ear trumpets, walking sticks, matchbook porn, lurid French letters, and death masks of Lucrezia Borgia, Eleanor Gwyn, Catherine II, Pauline Borghese, Emma Hamilton, Lola Montez, Elizabeth I, and Elizabeth III.

"Now don't let's have another awkward scene, doctor. Sit down and behave. An audience may add something extra."

"The name is Wish, sir. You may call me Mr. Wish," Shima said and sat down obligingly, his eyes fixed on infinity.

"Do come in, Miz Ashley," Droney said. "And be welcome. I didn't know you were acquainted with Dr. Shima, but then I know very little about either of you."

"But he says his name is Wish." Regina was bewildered. "A poet named Wish."

"Yes, I've experienced Dr. Shima's fantasies before. It's not one of his more attractive attributes. Now let me parade my collections before I give you your pianola roll."

Mr. Wish unobtrusively removed a hangman's noose from his pocket and set it on the floor alongside his chair.

"I adore my death masks of these divine ladies of Easy Virtue. Now you may object that a mask was never taken from Eleanor Gwyn, say, or Pauline Borghese, or Catherine the Great, and you would be quite right. But the ingenuity of the collector can always triumph over mere reality. I assembled all existing portraits of these lascivious ladies and then commissioned a plastic surgeon to mold duplications onto the faces of bodies in the morgue. The masks were taken from them. I may add that there would have been no need to re-create Emma Hamilton if only I had known you then. You are a reincarnation of that magnificent demirep."

A laser burner and 8-mm. palm-pistol joined the noose.

"I'm extremely proud of these erotic matchbooks

which took years to assemble. The constraint of the collector's matchbook is that it must be virgin; the matches unused, the striking surface unscratched. These are from India and each displays one of the mystic love-positions from the Kama Sutra. Inspiring, don't you think, Miz Ashley?''

A pressure bulb labeled $(CN)_2$ was placed on the floor.

"I was showing this collection to a guest once and before I could stop him he pulled a match out of a book and struck it. When he saw the horror on my face he asked, 'Is anything wrong?' and I said, 'Oh no, nothing at all,' and then I fainted. Fortunately I was able to replace the matchbook with another virgin. Are you a virgin, Miz Ashley? I think so. They have a magnetic attraction, as do you.''

A scalpel glittered down to the floor.

"Now this is my collection of dog collars. Some are fascinating reflections of their times. The spiked German for giant Great Danes, reminiscent of the spiked steel ball-on-chain, *der Morgenstern,* used by mounted knights to smash the heads of foot soldiers. Here is an original Saint Bernard collar with miniature cask of brandy attached. I've never dared sample the brandy. A harness for a twentieth-century 'Seeing Eye' dog. French jeweled collars for toy terriers. That strange thing is an Eskimo husky sled harness. And this beauty is a silver curb-link choke collar.

"Choke collar?'' Regina asked.

"Why yes. It was used in the days before vets devised implanted radio controls. It restrained the animal when it was on the leash. Let me show you. Here, put it around your neck—You know, it would make a fabulous necklace, and I'm almost tempted to give it to you—That's it. Now, the leash was attached, and the collar was loose and comfortable so long as the dog accompanied its master dutifully; but if it tried to explore or wander or run away? One pull on the leash would strangle it into submission—Like this!''

Lafferty's huge fist twisted the chain until it disappeared into the skin of her neck. Regina's eyes started and she flailed as Droney maintained his grip on the silver garrote and thrust her supine on a couch with his body on top of hers. *"Kommt Hure! Herunter! Sitz! Liege! Bleib!"* His lips were on her distorted mouth. "Yes. Speak French to your mistress, Italian to your wife, English to your horse, German to your dog. *Sterb Hund!* Yes. *Sterb Hure!* The moment I met you I knew you would die passionately and give passion to me. Yes. I knew—Ah!"

As Regina shuddered into death spasms, he penetrated her while gazing expectantly at Mr. Wish. Then he screamed into the orgasm which her last contractions produced, and slowly collapsed.

At length he arose from the dead body and disentangled the buried chain, meanwhile regarding his audience wistfully.

"No response, Mr. Wish? No reaction? Shock? Horror? Disgust? Fear? Nothing? No, nothing. Too bad. I'd hoped for your extra added fillip, Mr. Wish. This was no better than the necrolovelies in the morgue."

"The name is Shima," Mr. Wish said. "Blaise Shima."

He reached down, picked up the laser, and burned Droney Lafferty through the head.

19

Subadar Ind'dni appeared absorbed in Droney Lafferty's bizarre collections while the Ghoul Squad hauled out the wrapped bodies, the Molecular Squad hypo'd their print readouts and left, the Telly Squad left, the Media Team left, and the *Polizei* and Hommie Squad left, carrying with them the noose, laser, pistol, scalpel and $(CN)_2$ bulb, all eternalized in plastic. When they were at last alone, Ind'dni turned from the vitrines and spoke to the stunned Wish-Shima.

"Merely going through motions for Legal," Ind'dni said. "Legal is obsessed with evidence factual which they add and subtract and compute. They are accountants at heart. It is my belief they are all failed IRS candidates."

"I killed him," Shima-Wish muttered.

"It will never come to trial," the Subadar continued casually, "unless I press for speedy action. Calendar at present is backlogged seventy-nine years. Judges are appointed, serve, retire, die, and never have tried a case that initiated during their term on the bench. I myself have seen in court grandchildren of accusers and accused, perpetrators and victims, standing before grandchildren of judges. You must now regain control,

Dr. Shima. Strength is required. You must strive for the beckoning primal pinnacle, and I'm sure you will achieve it along with Miz Nunn. I envy you."

"I killed him."

"So you did. It is permitted to ask: as Dr. Blaise Shima or as Mr. Wish?"

"I won't plead insanity."

"Most honorable but please to answer question. Did you burn the brain of our celebrated necrophiliac as Dr. Shima or as Mr. Wish? Can you remember?"

"As both."

"Bravo! Good news indeed. Then your moieties are on speaking terms at last. They are aware of each other and reconciled to each other. Result of witnessing shocking outrage perpetrated against Winifred Ashley, no doubt. Most fortunate disaster for you, doctor; it has welded you together. I doubt very much whether your fugues will ever again occur."

"I burned him in cold blood," Shima persisted.

"And now you want luxury of repentance? You were raised French Catholic in a place called Johnstown, yes? Tsk! Their floods have washed them back into the Medieval. This is the enlightened twenty-second century after Christ, doctor. If Johnstown cannot think in modern terms, Jesus surely would if He returned to the Guff. The spirit of that sage is always in touch with the times."

"I killed him in cold blood."

"And you need no longer feel guilty about Mr. Wish. He was instrumental in destroying the Queen Bee and the hive-home of the Golem. Discontinue your *pauvre petit* obsession, I beg."

Shima croaked.

Ind'dni spoke slowly and distinctly. "Doctor, you killed Lafferty in self-defense."

Shima stared. Ind'dni nodded. "That is my version for Legal. You saw him strangle Winifred Ashley with the choke collar. He arose from her body with chain in hand. You feared you would be next to be murdered by this insane creature, and rightly so, for you were sole witness. So you killed him in self-defense. Homicide found corpse with chain in hand. *Quod erat demonstrandum.*"

Shima's head wobbled dazedly. "But—But you're always so—so—such pure, unadulterated cop."

Ind'dni sighed. "Alas, the Western world can never fathom our values, which is why you have always failed in India." His tone turned brisk. "Now come, doctor. There is Miz Nunn to consider. Last bulletin informs that she is en route to P.L.O. pyramid to negotiate a contract on Miz Ashley. I have had death of latter much publicized through Media to forestall madame's involvement with the PloFather, but am informed that the pyramid admits no current news. We must go in person."

"Informed? How?"

Ind'dni clicked his tongue again. "Has not that remarkable woman told you that once she enabled a P.L.O. girl to elope with a Christian infidel?"

"No. She did?"

"She did, at great personal risk. The girl is still grateful."

"And this P.L.O. girl is your source?"

"No, her husband is. The infidel is precinct chess champion I mentioned previous. Now we must act quickly, Dr. Shima. I cannot send staff; they would never gain entrance. We may, on our own recognizances. The PloFather is a dangerous woman, and Miz Nunn may find herself webbed in disaster attempting to bargain for the murder of someone already demised."

"But wait a minute, Subadar. Doesn't the death of the Queen Bee mean the end of the Golem? Won't that solve all our problems? That was Gretchen's theory."

Ind'dni was exasperated. "Do not plague me, I beg, doctor. You have just joined the pieces of yourself

311

together at a frightful cost. And now you ask me to put all other pieces of this deadly crisis together? Instantly? And at what price? Come, please!''

* * *

When a commune loses its queen, the subjects lose all sense of order. They become distracted, irritable, aggressive, and begin to cluster in desperation. Occasional loners may join the cluster, kindled by the angry vibrations. Occasional ''false queens'' may try to take over the commune but are treated with a mixture of token respect and impatient hostility. Only a true queen can win true respect and gather the cluster into another ordered commune. But to generate a true queen, a royal home and royal food must be provided, and then she must be coaxed out to be mated by the world.

* * *

He's dead he's dead and the piebald son of a bitch never got around to changing his will like he kept threatening I'm burning a fancy number where she's taking it up the ass and he's on one knee what are you burning Yenta oh lovely she's taking it in her tits while he's standing on his head let's all go to India drink up drink up use the ear trumpets for glasses just shove your thumb over the ear end and fill up drink up he's dead the bastard black and white for Christ's sake Mary how long does it take to get a walking stick fire going never mind the gold heads let'm burn and melt just knock their noses off Sarah but save the Nell Gwyn mask for me I want to do a special number on her Pi-face what the hell are you doing here yes yes we know Regina's dead it's all over the Guff we know we know you don't know what to do drink up girl grab a container an eyecup an ear trumpet a snuffbox fill up and drink up hey Priss got a stick between your legs at last no baby it's no hobbyhorse and if you could straddle like that on a real stick you could teach India les-

312

sons hey here's a wild position where they're ouch I
burned myself how's that fire doing Mary hey Ood Ud
come into the bedroom and help me lug out that damn
coffin he made me lie in the son-of-a-bitch we're going
to burn it Christ it's heavy you're dead the black-and-
white freak said you're dead you're not breathing your
heart's stopped beating you're white as death Mary
you're a genius blowing it up like that help her Pi we'll
blow up all the French letters and have a balloon as-
cension no Ood stick the small end into the fire first
it'll fit help her swing it around Ud that goddam cedar
ought to burn like crazy Christ knows how many times
I did a burn in it while that piebald bastard told me I
was dead I wasn't breathing my heart stopped beating
and dangling his polka-dot prick in my dead face because that was the only thing that could stiffen it hey
great the coffin's caught I wish he was in it dead or
alive Jesus he was dead anyway but wouldn't admit it
but he never changed his will and I've got Regina to
thank for that when I take over like BB said we'll hold
services for Regina every week we'll play funeral and
take turns delivering the eulogy and I'm going to have
the piebald son-of-a-bitch buried at a crossroad with a
stiff prick through his heart will you look at that coffin
burn but the satin stinks Pi-girl you'll come and work
for me girl so don't worry Jesus Christ look at those
flames the ceiling's caught my God three cheers the
whole goddam freakhouse is going to go up and to hell
with it he never changed his will I can live where I
goddam please and for how much I Christly please
and let's get the hell out of here before we catch
fire not that I'm not on fire already bring the French
letter balloons and any other souvenirs you want
from his slob collections come on to Sarah's sa-
loonnnnnnnnnnnnnnnnnnnnn

'Tis BEAUTY calls and GLORY shows the WAY Alex-
ander the Great Act I Scene 3 ladies I can NOT permit
us to look like this we are be-DRAGGLED we are un-
BEAUT-i-ful we have failed our duty to our public we

must dress to the nines and my wardrobe is yours and my dresser this is darling Norah my dresser is yours and NORAH will GARB you FITT-ingly and in character starting with me of course because I am the

of the company sequins silver sequins Norah and slinky form-fitting with rhinestone straps Nellie of course will be GAFOOZALUM the harlot of Jerusalem put her in the belly-dancer drag no no Yenta don't object I've cast you in a role that will CREAM your devoted public Norah dress Yenta Calienta in the Delilah rags but put a beard on her and turn her into *Moïse* Mary Mixup does the soubrette bit playing the lady's maid of pertness and intrigue no no Pi-face you won't be a servant in service my God these sequins scratch the boozalum you become HOBO the wandering worker and darling Norah will give you the original Hollywood costume it was a place out west in the entertainment business before it fell into itself Priss is BEAUTY in the fable the Cinderella ballgown for her Norah and *Oodgedye* and *Udgedye* will play a two-headed BEAST in fright-wigs and that eight-armed drag from Scriabin's *Kackula the Monster That Ate Nizhni Novgorod* what Norah you want to join us come on then but in what role I know the BOADICEA I played in the play of the same name you can't have the chariot it's in some warehouse but you can spray yourself blue with the cobalt on my dressing table my god you're all FANTASTIC ladies mag-NIF-i-cent we're the greatest show on earth all we need is fanfares TA-DA-DA-DA-DA-DA-DA-DA-DUM-DEE-DUM   and we're going to dress up like this at every meeting I hold here and where to now great Yenta's place great great GREAT applause applause APPLAUSE curtain call curtain call curtain call bows bows BOWSSSSSSSSSSSSS

The carpenter in the nail apron making with the glue

and the pegboard is Bimmy Braham my personal private rabbi say hello *vos macht ir* to the ladies of my colony Bimbo they've all heard about you which is why I'm protective I wish you all could see Bim's kidney transplant but we didn't have a window installed I traded a first edition of *Gray's Anatomy* for it only two pages missing in the middle and the donor never noticed if he ever does and tries to repossess his kidney *mazel tov* is all try our vodka ladies we brew it ourselves Bimmy and me sure the restaurants give you their potato peelings and carrot tops and corncobs and wilted greens if you haul the junk away saves them garbage fees Bim and I *schlep* the stuff back here and ferment it and distill it and Bimbo pronounces the conjure word congener and hey presto one hundred proof redeye vodka it's the beet skins that give it the color drink up drink up you like the glasses huh Mary they're my prize collection of logo plastics you get them for free advertising you know my favorite is this number from *Mugative* that's the mouthwash you use and your breath is guaranteed to set a mugger's face on fire I don't know how they do it the miracle of modern chemistry I guess drink up drink up the redeye won't set anything on fire but your *pipiks* no there's nothing dirty or suggestive about that rug Priss it's all innocent geometric design there was a hell of a hole in the center but Bim and I rewove it I had to trade a thundermug for the wool the mug had a crack in it but the dye in the wool ran so it all came out even drink up drink up I want to try a lobster vodka from free shells but my Bimbo won't drink it because it isn't kosher Bim show the two-headed monster that movie poster of *Drekula* we got in a trade for the makeup mirror with Sarah Heartburn Bimmy hey Bimbo-baby *Roboynov shel oylom* she's smashed she's stoned we're all fractured jingle jangled *Gottenu* Bim you're exploding the glue it's going up like Roman candles doesn't mix with congeners huh out out come on come on everybody out let's buzz buzz buzz off you too

Bim be with the fellas no don't get out of your jump suit and keep the apron you'll be in drag like the rest of us in the hive and let that hammer keep hanging from your delicious delectable divine assssssssssssssssssssssssss

No mizuses this is not a pubic mardygrass it is a private celebration I don't know what the vibes are for maybe for my former miztress person which she was murdered something cruel by the man person which was married to my present new miztress person of generosity oh I don't know if you can join the vibes you'll have to ask some person in charge but I don't know whom she excuse me whom the *person* is why don't you ask my present miztress person whom is wearing the bellydancerrrrrrrrrr

Hey sure the more the merrier who the hell hey are you two suckers Emily Post Mortem yeah and Joan who what Coldslaw Jesus Christ on a raft what a name Coldslaw with or without mayo have a belt have a smack Emily-Joan and take off those brassbound bras we're too many for the Guff rape *schtik* off off and let the tits vibrate each way free we're going to the two-headed monster's pads you heard me plural with an S sure it's got two pads it's got two twibbies don't it one for every two legs one for every two tits I wish I had two for one in reverse if you dig and my yancemen had two for two what a ball it would be to take it both ways from one yanceman what a ball with brave ball-busting vibrations vibrations vibrationsssssssssssssssssss

No it's no accident we bought everything in dup
No it's no accident we bought everything in dup

licate and the apartments are dupes too no I object to
licate and the apartments are dupes too no I object to

telling you whose apartment this is I don't even remember
telling you whose apartment this is I don't even remember

myself we're in and out of both so much that I lose track
myself we're in and out of both so much that I lose track

no we're listed separately downstairs in security I'm
no we're listed separately downstairs in security I'm

Germaine Storm we made sure to hook our husbands in dup-
Lorraine Drang we made sure to hook our husbands in dup-

licate too young men in grey flannel jump suits which is
licate too young men in grey flannel jump suits which is

why they never notice the different vibes in bed buzz buzz
why they never notice the different vibes in bed buzz buzz

is all the same to them and BB was wrong when she said that
is all the same to them and BB was wrong when she said that

they knew and liked it and Larry kept his mouth shut about
they knew and liked it and Barry kept his mouth shut about

the scam about the only thing we don't dupe is the squeam
the scam about the only thing we don't dupe is the squeam

scene you hard-line a joint like this see and then you
scene you hard-line a joint like this see and then you

have ignition and liftoff and space on a far-out buzz
have ignition and liftoff and space on a far-out buzz

but we're not together on that Lorraine uses a single
but we're not together on that Germaine uses a double

line and I don't dig her style because it's too hard you've
line and I don't dig her style because it's too soft you've

got to try it my way all you ladies buzz buzz into the far
got to try it my way all you ladies buzz buzz into the far

out buzz you might as well get used to it because we'll be
out buzz you might as well get used to it because we'll be

igniting and burning and spacing every time we meet here
igniting and burning and spacing every time we meet here

buzz buzz that's the way we have countdown we have ig-
buzz buzz that's the way we have countdown we have ig-

nition we have liftoff we have far-out buzzzzzzzzzzzzz
nition we have liftoff we have far-out buzzzzzzzzzzzzz

And these are my four roomies Dixie and Nixie and Pixie we all went to school together that's funny Dixie that's one Nixie that's two Pixie that's three how did I ever get to four oh of course I'm the fourth I forgot me Mary and Dixie and Nixie and Pixie four and we have seven husbands one apiece except one has three me I think but I'm not sure I lose count and they're all so nice now let's have some more drinks and squeams the liquor is in Dixie's darkroom of course it makes sense Nell D for darkroom and D for Dixie who's our bartender Nixie keeps the squeams in her bedroom and that makes sense too Nell because a Nixie is a female water sprite and we always shoot our smack with water I wouldn't anybody sit on that couch please just now it's got our prickly needly cactus plants under it because it's their resting season and they need dark oh Yenta please don't explore that closet oh please don't open the door there see what you've done I was storing everything in that closet until we could arrange everything and now you've turned the whole lounge into a closet everything poured out like an avalanche and there's no room for us now because everything's underfoot why Pixie there's that sleep-reader we were looking for and I could have sworn it was in the tape cabinet with the Irish music don't be silly Nell I for intellect of course so drink up and squeam up everybody and let's get out before we trample all the goodies and next meeting here you'll all have to help arrange things come on everybody you too Dixie and Nixie and Pixie bring the drinkables and squeamables onward and upward to Priss no she doesn't live high up in a penthouse really Nell you're impossible her real name is Hilda Hayes H for heights which makes sense to meeeeeeeeeeeeeeeeeee

Mummy is reviving the Victorian style which is why the palm leaves over the pictures and all the tassels and all the fringes and the skirts around the piano legs no not Victoria the fourth she was wicked she was no lady the first Victoria who was married to Prince Albert who was always the perfect gentleman Mummy says that Victoria wasn't a perfect lady because she had bad table manners Mummy says there aren't many ladies left and gentlemen are hard to find I do not wish to be discourteous and would be happy to entertain you all but I don't think Mummy would like to see what you're doing when she comes home seven-letter vibrations with each other are rude even though we are all the identical ess ee ex and when you come back for the weekly meetings Mummy will be here to chaperone and make us mind our manners so perhaps it would be best to leave now and visit BB who is a genuine lady and in every sense the perfect queen that Victoria was not I'm sure that Mummy will admire BB much more than Victoria and try to find another perfect Prince Albert for her it's awful to be alone and wasted please please please Mummy will be back any moment let's go to BB's place please please please pretty pleaseeeeeeeeeeeee

Hey you Chorley-grills you're one hell of a corner combo great street trio have a smack on us have a blast Nell I think it would only be polite to make a contribution of appreciation Sure Prissy drop some change in their pessary Hey twins you dig the way big-tits cuddles her clarry-o-net in her cleavage you want to ride it hobby horse Mary how about that fat-ass on the horn Bimmy beats your hammer-hung ass any time Maybe Nelly-belly but could she try blasting it from her other end Have a bomb you suckers Have a blast Have a buzz Listen you want to trade your slide-horn for a squeezebox with only one key missing I HAVE IT I HAVE IT they ought to dress their act with CLOWN makeup where's Norah NORAH DAHL-ing did you bring my coshmetics COS-meshiks Dixie didn't we shtow a clown hit height hat in yr closet or wash it in Joaney Cabbages no she don't room with us well you make childsloug out've chabbage don't you Hey play an up-beat funeral march for the b/w bashtard Chorley-girls *Wacht auf, verdammte dieser Erde* I don't think these grills speak England my Mummy says that music is the Juneversal language Hey pessary-grills you tollerday donsk you talkatiff scowegian you spiggotty angleasy you phonio saxonnnnnnnnnnnnnnnn all they twig is B-flat so go on making music and come with wiz no *with* us to the heiths hoyts hits howls highs *heights* got it at last Shrrist I'm bombed we're all bombeddd buzzzzzz bobbed bombed bombeddddddddddddddddddd

* * *

Ind'dni and Shima located Gretchen at last. They caught a glimpse of her profile through the open window of a magnificent black brougham; she was seated on the far side of the legendary PloFather, who was making one of her rare public processions. The carriage was drawn by camels, of course, and escorted by tough P.L.O. soldiers. Sheikh Omar ben Omar was up front in the open coachman's box supervising the outing. Every so often he scattered bronze piasters to the excited crowds. An occasional scrofuletic was permitted through the cordon to be touched by the PloFather's spidery hand. In this psychosomatic century her touch cured the King's Evil as often as not.

Using every karate trick he knew, Shima twisted through the crowd to the edge of the cordon. "Gretchen!" he shouted. "Gretchen! Can you hear me? It's Blaise. We've got to go to a funeral."

"What? What?" Gretchen leaned forward and peered past the PloFather. "Is that you, Blaise?"

"Yes. Can you hear me? We have to attend Winifred Ashley's funeral."

"Who? What?"

"Winifred Ashley. She's dead. She was killed. Don't make any deals with the P.L.O. The Queen Bee's dead."

The brougham door was thrust open and Gretchen was out like a shot followed, amazingly, by the psychomancer, Salem Burne. Shima hustled her through the crowd to Ind'dni who was waiting at the fringe. Burne followed.

"Most welcome, madame," Ind'dni said. "It is permitted to inquire whether we found you in time? Have you completed contract with P.L.O.?"

"Yes," Gretchen gasped.

"Extremely odd. Why, then, did the PloFather permit your departure?"

Still too breathless to speak, Gretchen could only point to Burne.

"Good evening, Mr. Burne." Ind'dni nodded courteously. "I take it you have some influence with the PloFather?"

"Good evening, Subadar." Burne was smooth and polished as ever, despite his rough passage through the mob. "I take it this is in confidence?"

"Most certainly."

"The PloFather is my patient."

Shima was flabbergasted. "You *have* to be guffing!"

"Why so surprised, doctor?" Burne permitted his controlled face to reveal humor. "I told you that most of my patients are women."

"But—"

"And the PloFather takes my advice. I suggested— one never commands a patient—that it would be best to release Miz Nunn."

Gretchen finally caught her breath. "Now what's all this? Regina dead? Killed?"

"Alas yes, madame, by Mr. Lafferty in bizarre circumstances. Lafferty was subsequently killed by Dr. Shima . . . in self-defense."

"What? Regina? Droney?" Gretchen shook her head. "What a scam. Unbelievable! What happened? How? When? I—I've got to be filled in."

"Most assuredly, Miz Nunn, but not in this crowd. Where will you feel most receptive? My office? Dr. Shima's penthouse? My apartment?"

321

"No, mine. Let's go."

"Then I'll be taking my leave," Burne said. "Good evening to you all."

"No," Gretchen said. "That wouldn't be fair, after all you've done for us. You were in on the beginning; you should be in on the end."

Transport was impossible to find during the evening rush hour, so they were forced to walk to Gretchen's Oasis in the Guff's·"Old Town," which had once been the despised Lower East Side of Old New York. Now it was fashionable, expensive, and glamorously restored, from delicatessens to pushcarts. Gretchen's Oasis had been cut, tunneled, and excavated out of the giant masonry pier of Brooklyn Bridge.

There was an outrageous uproar pounding out of the apartment as the four approached from the elevator; cacophonous music from competing brass, piano and harpsichord, singing, screaming, shouting, buzzing; and there were competing songs: HAIL! HAIL! THE GUFF'S ALL HERE . . . THERE ONCE WAS AN INDIAN MAID . . . THAT MASTURBATIN' FORNICATIN' SON-OF-A-BITCH COLUMBO . . . SWEET VIOLETS SWEETER THAN THE ROSES . . . ROLL ME OVER IN THE CLOVER . . .

"Jesus God!" Gretchen exclaimed. "What's all this?"

"The Golem?" Shima was still on edge.

"Surely not in multiple, doctor," Ind'dni murmured.

"Hardly an atmosphere for consultation," Burne said. "Perhaps my place in Hell Gate?"

"D'you think it could be the PloFather striking back at me? She—" Then Gretchen saw one of her staff standing stricken alongside the door. "Alex! What's all this?"

"They're crazy, Miz Nunn. They broke in."

"Broke in? Through Security? How?"

"I don't know how. They broke in and threw me out. No drones in here, they said. No male animals.

This is a queen cell, they said. Then they chopped through to the Raxon apartment under us for more room and ordered up food and—"

"They? Who they?"

"Lunatics in crazy costumes. Go in, Miz. You'll see. They're waiting for you. Dozens and dozens and dozens of them." He pushed the door open.

There were indeed dozens and dozens and dozens. The Raxons, mother and three daughters, had not only surrendered their apartment downstairs, but joined the swarm. Gretchen's two girl assistants had joined. Three of the Security guards from the Oasis lobby (women) had joined, which accounted for the unprecedented break-in. The two apartments had been transformed into a giant duplex with a makeshift ladder thrust through the crater in the smashed floor. Figurantes, columbines, ballet girls, pulcinellas, soubrettes, even a belly-dancer clung to it like grape clusters, heaving, shouting, singing.

> Hi-ho, Gafoozalum,
> The Big Bang of Jerusalum.
> Hi-ho, Gafoozalum,
> The vengeance of the rabbi.
>
> With yancey glance and lustful look
> She lured him to a secret nook.
> She cracked his crotch and out she took
> The pride of all Jerusalum.
>
> Hi-ho, Gafoozalum,
> The Big Bang of Jerusalum.
> Hi-ho, Gafoozalum,
> The malice of the rabbi.
>
> But she was swinging on her kang;
> He missed her mouth and hit her bang.
> He knew it by the feel of fang
> In the fancy of Gafoozalum.

The four crowded the doorway and stood, gaping at the spectacle. Young Alex had reported correctly;

there wasn't a man present. Shima, Ind'dni and Burne didn't dare enter; only Gretchen took a few steps into her apartment.

Suddenly Shima said, "Looking at all these women, something just occurred to me, Ind'dni."

"Indeed? What is it?"

"Why doesn't the Golem ever appear as a woman?" Shima asked.

"An interesting point, doctor," Ind'dni said. They could barely hear each other over the uproar. "Perhaps our psychomancer can answer."

"Possibly Jung's construct of the 'inward face' of people," Burne said. "The Golem might be generated by the *animus*, the masculine side of the female psyche; hence it always takes the form of a man. If it were generated by men, their *anima* or female side would produce a woman."

While they were considering this, Gretchen shouted, "Will you look at the banquet these crazies have put together!"

There was indeed a royal banquet, fit for a Bee Queen. Trays and dishes and platters and tureens of food everywhere; Bee's Wing Broth, Honey-baked Hams, Mussels in Oyster Sauce, Royal Jellied Eels, Lobster tails in thyme aspic, Pollen Fritters, Hive Tack, Protein Pudding, Honey Cakes, Sucrose Sherbets, and stockpots of honey Mead and Welsh Nectar. There were trays of every sweet-scented squeam on the market. There were garlands of green, danced and trampled into the floors, emitting pungent scents of tansy, lovage, rosemary, sage, and sweet basil.

HAIL! HAIL! THE GUFF'S ALL HERE! Hey, BB! Hi, BB! Regina's dead. You know? Every person knows. My former miz-person was famous. This is her wake, BB. The queen is dead. Long live Nellie the Second Regina. *Zolstu azoy laiben!* It's Yenta the First. Who says? Bimbo, the Bold says with her Hammer of Thor. I've decided WE shall be:

324

saRah the viRgin queen

Haaaaaa! And how would Sarah like five in the pie-slot from Ood, the Terrible? We are not amused. Could I please be Pie, the First? Mummy would want me to call myself Victoria R, the Clean Queen. There's regal drag on the costume rack; how about Norah R, the Darlin' Queen? Vote like for The Pessaries, the Combo Queen. But how can R stand for queen? I thought it meant king like in R.F.D. Makes sense to her. It's Latin, dummy. All hail Mary, the Dumbo Queen! HICK! HIKE! HOKE! THE QUEEN'S ALL HERE!

"My God, Subadar, this is a disaster! I thought Regina's death would solve everything; end the colony, end the Golem, end the crisis in the Guff, and now look at this lunatic scene. What, in heaven's name, are these insane women doing?"

"That is not the crucial question, madame. We understand what they're doing."

"I don't. What are they doing?"

"Mr. Burne," Ind'dni turned to the psychomancer. "You are the expert in somatic language. Tell Miz Nunn."

"They're selecting a new queen to lead their commune. Agreed, Subadar?"

"Agreed, Mr. Burne. But the crucial question is, what is the Golem Hundred-Hander doing through all this?"

"But Subadar," Gretchen argued, "didn't we agree that it couldn't survive without the bee-ladies' collective to generate it?"

"We did, but it must exist still. It is too strong and protean merely to cease, *punkt!* And it will most probably be searching for another source to give it soul and survival."

"*Jesu!*" Shima exclaimed. "Then it might be in this mob right now, looking around."

"Not likely, doctor," Ind'dni said. "Please to listen to the chorus of the assembled swarm . . ."

> Mother, may I go out to yance?
> Yes, my darling daughter.
> Shake your hance in a grabby prance,
> But don't go near his mortar.

"Do you hear a man's voice, doctor? No. It is patent that there are only women here, and Golem[100] never manifests as a woman."

Shima nodded. "R. Then what will this ship-wrecked-to-hell creature be doing?"

"It will be swimming desperately," Burne put in. "Agreed, Subadar?"

"Emphatically agreed, Mr. Burne. I believe this plastic, soulless eidolon will be ranging up and down the spectrum of people, perceptions, terrors, compulsions; through colors, sounds, waves, particles; desperately searching for another generator, another collective soul-home to ensure its survival. We must pray that it does not."

"*No,* Subadar!" Gretchen's voice verged on hysteria.

"No, madame? You are agnostic?"

"Nothing of the sort. Blaise, is that bathysphere of Dr. Leuz still equipped with your neurosensory contacts?"

"Yes. Why? Thinking of taking another deep dive to cool the heat?"

"No, I want to use it on dry land."

"Gretch! Will you make sense!"

"I can't. I'm possessed."

"What possesses you, Miz Nunn?"

"Projection," Burne said. "The fever in these women is rubbing off on Miz Nunn. Pulse and respiration rapid. Muscle tone spasmodic."

"And I'm beset with mad ideas," Gretchen added.

"Can you specify, madame?"

"One of them is that I can't let go of the Golem

monster with just a prayer. I—I want to—I *must* be in on the kill."

"Hold it, Ind'dni," Shima said. "I think I know where she's headed." To Gretchen, "You want another Pm trip into the Phasmaworld to observe, using the bathysphere setup to report. Yes?"

"Yes, but not me. Someone better equipped. You can interface the observer with your neural contacts, Blaise, and we'll get realtime observations."

"It's an idea, Gretch . . ." Shima took fire. "By God, it's a damned good idea. Then we'll know for sure."

"But who better equipped than yourself, madame?" Ind'dni asked. "You are uniquely suited, and have had the experience before."

"May I translate what I read in my distinguished colleague, Subadar?" Burne asked.

"By all means."

"She wants an observer too subtle, too sophisticated, too firmly anchored in deep emotional resources to be overpowered as she was by the disorientation of the Phasmaworld. Strong enough to resist. Controlled enough to report dispassionately. Mystic enough to understand the transcendental."

Gretchen stared. "My soma said all that to you?"

"Not quite, Miz Nunn. You made many things clear when we were chatting on the way to this Oasis."

"But great Dyaus!" Ind'dni exclaimed. "How will we find such a paragon? Does he exist?"

"He does, Subadar."

"Where?"

Burne turned to Gretchen. "Tell him, please."

"I will," she said. She looked Ind'dni full in the face. "In you."

20

The *Drogh III* was berthed in the Sandy Hook marina of the Oceanography center. The bathysphere was cradled on the foredeck of the trawler and Ind'dni was inside, encoiled as Gretchen had been, with neural contacts. There was a significant addition, however; a sensor had been interfaced with his larynx to enable his speech to be heard . . . if he could shape any words from the Phasmaworld.

Shima injected Ind'dni with the Pm hydride, slapped his shoulder twice, and scrambled out of the bathysphere. He slammed the hatch, dogged it, and dashed to the control cabin where Gretchen was waiting. He gave her a short nod, switched on the instruments and scanned the panels. "All nominal," he muttered.

The bathysphere was less than a hundred feet away from the cabin but a good country mile via the winched cable that connected them with the Subadar. Shima picked up the microphone communicating with the bathysphere and waited. Salem Burne would have said of him, "Pulse and respiration rapid. Muscle tone spasmodic."

The same could not have been said of Ind'dni.

At last a calm voice came through the control cabin speaker. "Do you read me, doctor?"

"Loud and clear, Ind'dni."

"Miz Nunn, are you still in attendance?"

"Yes, Subadar."

"This is of intense interest. Unlike you two who went into black per your descriptions, I have gone into white. Apparently the Promethium drug does not affect all identical."

"Are you sure the white isn't a sense-echo?"

"Quite certain, doctor."

"Then its effect is on the psyche rather than the soma, Subadar," Gretchen said, "and all are different. Apparently you can maintain contact with the real-world while you're in the Phasmaworld. Blaise and I couldn't."

"I would agree, Miz Nunn. All somas are similar, more or less; otherwise medicine would still be in the medieval; but no two psyches are identical. It will be interesting, if ever they succeed in cloning people, to find whether the personalities will be as identical as the bodies."

("This dude is really cool. Gretchen.")

("That's why I wanted him sent under.")

"Still nothing but white, doctor," Ind'dni continued reporting, "but I am assured. There is a Hindu saying: 'It is certain because it is impossible.' I—Wait, please. Something is beginning to manifest . . ."

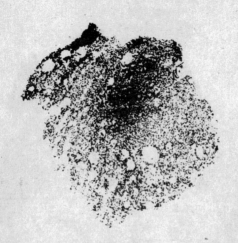

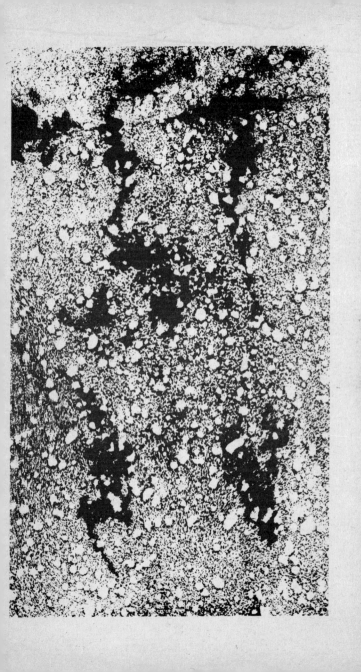

"Ah yes. Remarkable. I am sensing a particle perception in this Phasmaworld. I am also pleased to report that my guess was correct. The Hundred-Hander creature is most probably starting its search at the very top of the electromagnetic spectrum. Perhaps the Id is strongly attracted by high-energy sources . . ."

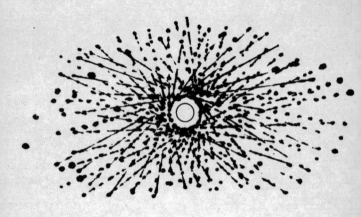

"I am perceiving the Ourworld . . . the tip of the iceberg, you called it, Miz Nunn . . . through the perceptions of the Idworld. It is bizarre, to say the least, and arresting. That line of Robert Burns: *Oh wad some power the giftie gie us to see oursels as others see us!* Apologies for most maladroit Scots pronunciation. You have given me the power, Dr. Shima and Miz Nunn, and I am intensely grateful."

("He's so goddam sophisticated!")

"Ah! Formless shapes are now being perceived in the Ourworld by the Idworld. I would guess that the Phasma sensing is descending down the spectrum to —What would it be, doctor?"

"It would still be particle bombardment, Ind'dni. Probably the gamma-ray region. Hard X-rays. Around ten to the minus eight centimeters."

"But is it the Golem's perceptions, Subadar?"

"Most likely, Miz Nunn. We are very much *en rapport* with it after earlier encounters, but I do not yet know certainly."

"You are infallible as ever, doctor. The residents of our iceberg tip are now being perceived with gamma-ray vision. . . ."

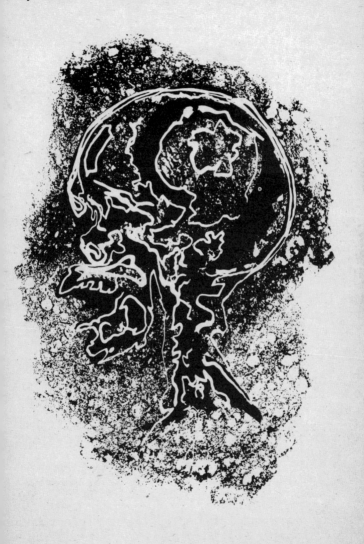

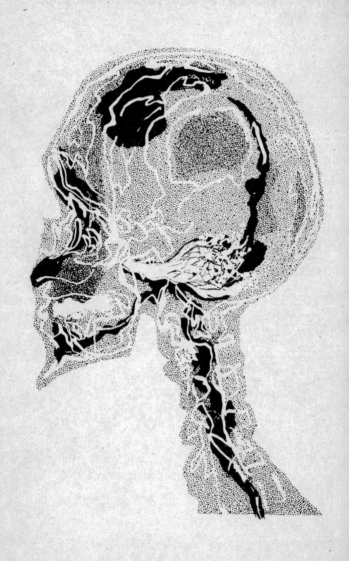

"Now it is perceiving you,
doctor. I recognize your
X-ray image . . ."

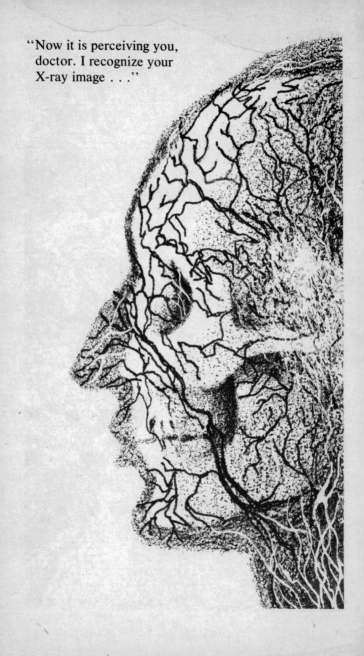

"I think it is possible that I may have picked up the Hundred-Hander at last. We are still in the X-ray area, and I am perceiving through Id senses what appears to be a womb, which is to say a new home for the shipwrecked creature..."

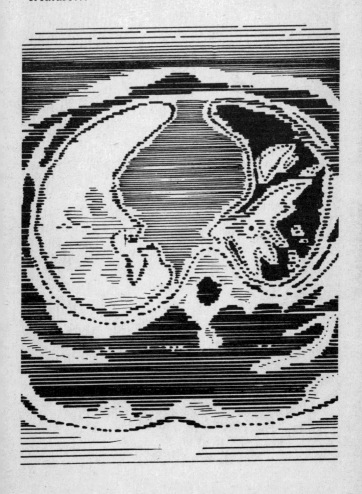

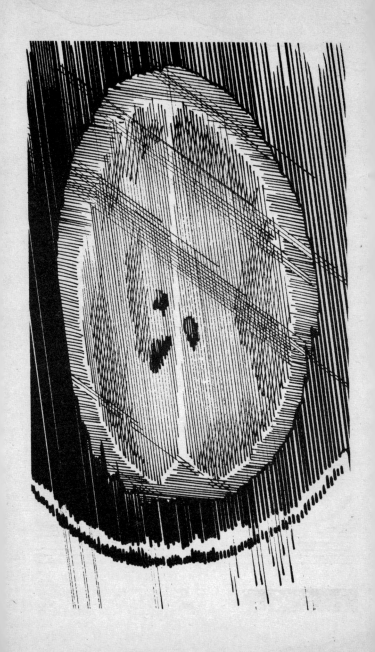

"Yes! Yes! Yes! It is the Golem Hundred-Hander through whom I am perceiving our world. It has reached the visual portion of the spectrum and is searching for womb and mother."

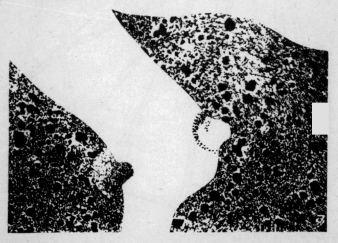

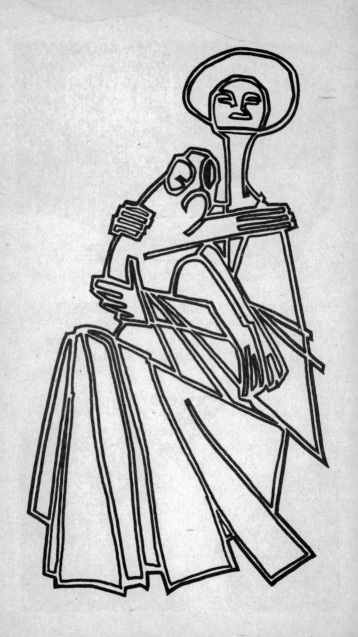

"Miz Nunn! Miz Nunn! Miz Nunn! It has a remarkably clear perception of yourself in the role..."

". . . but it seems to sense that you do not welcome it."
"My God, Subadar! No! Never!"

"So now it senses impending death."

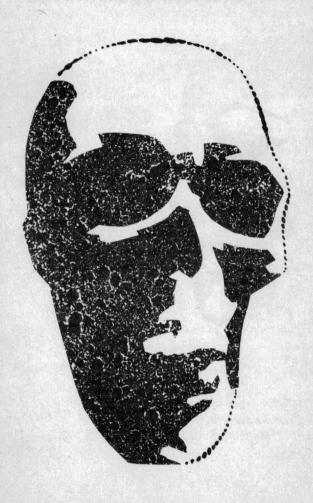

"Most remarkable. As the creature descends our visual spectrum into the—What might it be, doctor?"

"From the extreme violet down through indigo, blue, green, yellow, and orange to the extreme red."

"Thank you."

("Christ, he's cool! Doesn't the son-of-a-bitch feel anything?")

"Now the desperate thing is searching for the protection of a father."

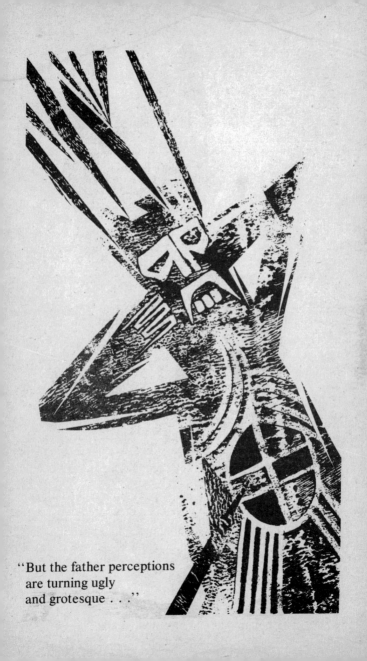

"But the father perceptions
are turning ugly
and grotesque . . ."

"Psychodynamically consistent, Subadar. Son and father are deadly enemies in the contest for the mother."

"I feared as much. It is a vision of Garuda, a deadly Hindu god, and it is how the Golem envisions me as its father."

"Suddendly there is a sensation of extreme heat. Most uncomfortable. Can you explain, please, Dr. Shima?"

"Easy. The Golem's down under the extreme red and into the infrared. Heat's a phenomenon there."

"Then we are no longer within the visible?"

"No."

Interesting. What can it hope to find here? And now strange vibrations, Dr. Shima."

"Radio-wave propagation of all sorts, anywhere from short-wave down to ten kilocycles. How does the Golem sense them, Ind'dni?"

"Merely as geometric designs. What an opportunity for a critic of entertainment, eh?"

"Great Deva in Devachan! It is frantic now, and has transposed to sound."

Gretchen seized the microphone. "But when the Golem tried to attack me and spoke that backwards gibberish, you said the creature was 'not of intelligence.' Your words, Subadar."

"True, madame, and the gibberish continues. It is perceiving word images and fragments alone."

"I don't understand."

"I will try to illuminate Golem's extraordinary perceptions which I am sensing, Miz Nunn. Do you read music?"

"Through other eyes, yes."

"And as you read it, does your inner ear hear it?"

"Yes."

"Conceive, please, of someone who cannot read musical notation in act of looking at a score. Would such person hear anything?"

"No, nothing."

"And what would they see?"

"Just lines and dots and circles and strange signs and symbols."

"Thank you. And that is how Golem[100] is presently perceiving the sounds that we use for communication."

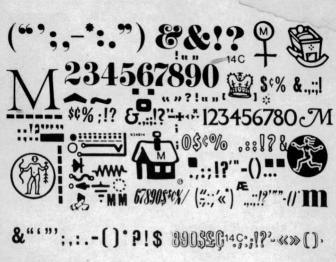

("'";,-*:."") &&!? 14C

M 234567890 !""

^~ "" ?!""

$¢% ;!? &.,:;!

--- $¢% !? &.,:;!? ×+÷× 123456780 ℳ

::!?"""

934814

.0$¢% .::!?&

M ,.;!?'"-()...

MM 67890$¢%/ (":;:«) "...!?""-()"m

&"'"";,:.-()*?!$ 890$£¢14¢;,?;!?'-«»().

YZ&.,:!?%-+◄►* $ + M "*Ç[(;)]::;º|º +

M

"0/%+º/º .:!?""-()†$*; M::;::!?´m

.""

M
M
M ABCDEFGHIJKLM12345 ma
M

M
A
ma

Mamma
Mamma
M
Mamma
MA
MA
MAMA
MA A
M
Mamma Mamma MAMмм

M
A
M
A

"It cannot find a host, a home, a father, a mother, any refuge . . . "It has lost it's fight for survival. We are going . . ."

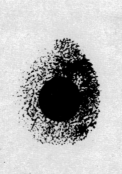

"Nothing remains."

21

Ind'dni sprawled exhausted in the deep chair specially engineered for the DODO's bulk. They were in the office of F. H. Leuz and surrounded by a kaleidoscope of fish. The walls were lined with scores of tanks that emitted a bubbling and hissing. While Gretchen and Shima watched the Subadar, Leuz crossed to a clear tank with nothing in it but crystal water and a single lobe of bleached brain coral. He drew a glass from a spigot at the base of the tank and brought it to Ind'dni. As he passed a tank containing a conger eel, he gave it a friendly tap and the eel snapped its frightening jaws at his fingers.

"Got him trained," Leuz said. He put the glass into the Subadar's hand. "Drink careful-like," he said. "It's vodka. Hundred proof."

Ind'dni was not only shattered but completely disoriented. The first sip he attempted was from the far side of the glass. He succeeded only in dribbling on his chest. He turned the glass ninety degrees in his hand to reverse it, but again tried to drink from the opposite rim. At last his bewildered mind understood and he managed a sip from the near lip, then another, and finally the entire glassful. He took a breath.

"Thanks zaban, Leuz-doctor. Was most full. Of need. Needful, yes?" He smiled at Gretchen and Shima. "So. Not quite so impervious, Alkhand-sarangdharind'dni, as Burne-Salem estimated, eh? Alien must admit name complete when entering country." He handed the glass back to Leuz. "Mujh thank beloved Lord Siva all over at last."

Gretchen clasped her hands. "Then the Golem's gone, Subadar?"

Ind'dni made an effort to master coherent speech. "Rather . . . Rather to say, extinguished."

"But dirty, rotten dead?"

"Difficult to state. That extraordinary creature left no *corpus vile.*"

Shima was dissatisfied. "Why can't you say for sure, Ind'dni?"

"Alkhand-sarangdharind'dni full name most of reluctance to discuss scientific science with experts, Shima-doctor, but . . ."

"Yes? But? Go on, man!"

"Seemed to me that it . . . Withdrew? Disappeared? Dissolved through a Black Hole."

"The hell you say!" Shima exclaimed. "A Black Hole? Into a contra-universe?"

"Excuse me." Leuz was leaning back against a tank, seemingly enhaloed by a hundred neon fish. "The Black Hole passageway into a contra-universe is still only a theoretical concept. There's no hard evidence, outside of assumptions about stellar collapse." The huge man looked up at the ceiling where a stuffed devilfish hung, flapping its wings to nowhere. "Some claim that the tremendous Siberian blast of nineteen-ought-eight wasn't caused by a meteorite but by a wandering Black Hole."

"But was what I seemed to perceive from our senses, Leuz-doctor."

Gretchen knifed in. "*Our* senses, Subadar? And when you were reporting from the bathysphere you said, '*We* are going.' "

"Bikhe, Miz Nunn. 'We.' 'Our.' Self senses very nearly transported all way through with the Golem."

"But they didn't?"

"Partim only. Then I withdrew."

Shima whistled. "Describe it, Ind'dni. What was it like?"

Ind'dni closed his eyes, but before he could answer, Leuz began drawling suggestions. "Chaos? Disorientation? That's obvious from the way you're behaving now, Subadar. Time running backward? Space inside-out? Total inversion? Heart and respiration reversed? Body transposed, right for left and left for right? Everything contra?"

Ind'dni could only reply with a nod to each. Then he whispered, "And I saw the goks."

"You saw the *what?*"

"I saw what Shima-doctor calls skog; my contra-self."

All three were incredulous. Shima burst out, "Christ on the Mount! A mirror image?"

"Worse. A negative of self. Dismaying reversal." Ind'dni made another effort to reorganize himself. "Black for white, white for black, as Leuz-doctor suggests. I am bred and cultured by Hindostani tradition. Trained by security discipline for conduct of self-civilized control. Contra of self was refutation, negation of my accustomary lifestyle. It was—How to say? Was—I can only use Miz Nunn's descriptive of deep-buried id. . . ."

"Remorseless," Gretchen murmured. "Treacherous, lecherous, kindless."

Ind'dni gave her a backward wave of thanks. "So, in admissioned panic, the positive Ind'dni got . . . to use one of your favorite locutions, Shima-doctor . . . got out the hell of there."

"*Jesu!*" Shima breathed. "To lose such an opportunity. I would have been forced to follow that challenge until I caught up with it and made it talk."

"In reverse gibberish, no doubt," and Gretchen

suddenly burst out laughing and went on laughing in hysterical relief.

"Opportunity was cheerfully and blessedly lost, Shima-doctor, for me," Ind'dni said, ignoring Gretchen's cackle which was rising to a crescendo. "For me, reversed contraworld made our mad Guff seem rational by contrast."

"Not rational; cheerful!" Gretchen bubbled. "Cheerful's the word. Cheerful! Cheerful!" She smacked the conger eel tank with her lips. "Giz a kiss, bigmouth. The Golem's dead, departed, gone to its contrareward . . ." She skipped from tank to tank, laughing and smacking them with her mouth. "We've got to celebrate. No more Golem. No more horrors. I'm out of the cell, hear, all you fisheses? No more Guff-arrest-cell. No more padded cell. Hear ye! Hear ye! Salmons and soles! Shadses and sturgeonses! Cods and crabs!"

"Hey Gretch!" Shima protested. "Easy, girl!"

"Whatsa matter you?" Gretchen demanded. "Not happy? I am. It's all over. Snagu! Situation normal; all guffed up. I'm out of the cell. Come on a my place, all of you. We'll join the crazy ladies if they're still there. We'll celebrate. We'll eat and drink up a storm and sing crazy songs to celebrate. Come on a my place. Snagu! Snagu!"

She tore out of the office and the three men followed. There was something about Gretchen that had to be followed.

* * *

The masonry which had once been a bridge pier and was now an Oasis fortress was a shambles. It was wide open, without security, and it was impossible to tell the rips from the bees. The crazy ladies (Snagu!) were still there. They had by now taken over the entire Oasis (with every woman in it) to transform it into a buzzing swarm, and the food and drink were still there, even more than ever. When Gretchen, followed

by the three men, entered, she was confronted in the
Oasis lobby by:

A
silver-sequined
S*T*A*R

A belly-dancer
with tureen of
Bee's Wing Broth
balanced
on her head

Clown   Boadicea   Clown
playing   with   playing
clarinet   Honey-baked Ham   trombone

ROYAL JELLIED EELS
borne by
The two-headed Beast
That Ate Nizhni Novgorod

Clown
playing
French horn

Followed
by
a train of
laughing shouting
women
offering no assistance whatever

And on the trek up the winding stone stairs to
Gretchen's apartment (all Oasis services had come to
a dead stop), they were forced to squirm past clusters
of Moses, Goldilocks, a lady's maid, a carpenter,
Security guards, a Hobo, wood and water sprites,
groupies, kackies, yancy-boppers, giggers, squeam-
souls, and assorted geek-girls who had come to rip and

stayed to enjoy the fun. Gretchen was pelted, crammed, choked, gagged with sweets forced into her mouth by insistent hands.

Although the swarms respectfully made way for Gretchen, the men were treated with rude contempt. Leuz had to use his massive bulk to force a path for the others. Even the most violent women bounced off him like confetti.

Shima called, "Can you believe this *Walpurgisnacht*, Lucy?"

"Don't you remember Vrok?" Leuz threw back over his shoulder. "Excuse me, ma'am."

"Vrok? Who Vrok? What Vrok?"

"Vrok, the crock. Sorry, lady. Taught astrophys at —Oops! Sorry, girl—tech. Used to say—No, no, ma'am, *your* fault—Vrok always said, 'Nature is more audacious in her realities than man in his most fantastic imaginings.'—Unhand my crotch, lady . . .''

"What the hell's natural about this?"

"You've never been asshole buddies with bees?"

In what had once been Gretchen's tailored lounge was a wreckage of debris honeycombing a vast wooden cask on which some drunken hand had printed with crimson cherry brandy: HONEY OXO MEAD. Gretchen, even more possessed by the uproar, was impelled to plunge head foremost into the cask.

She emerged, gulping and gasping. "DEE-licious!" she shouted. "DEE-voon! Everybody celebrate! Snagu! Snagu!" and submerged again. Up. "The Golem's dead! Quahk! Quahk! Quahk!" Under again.

"So's the queen!" Gafoozalum screamed. "The old queen's dead. Dead. Dead. Dead. Regina's guffy dead!"

"This may lead to something fantastic, Subadar," Leuz said. There was no answer and he looked around. "Where's Ind'dni, Shim?"

"Don't know. Either he got lost in the mob or took off. How can it get any more fantastic than this, Lucy?"

"I used to keep bees when I was a kid, Shim, and I know 'em. First thing a hive does when it loses its old queen is build queen cells and start a batch of candidates for the job."

"How?"

"They fill the cells with royal jelly. Take a look around. Isn't all this royal jelly?"

"By God, I think you're right."

"First candidate out of her cell becomes the new queen. Remember what your girl's been saying? 'I'm out of the cell.' "

"But she means the Golem and Guff-arrest."

"Sure. First thing she does is go from cell to cell and kill her rivals before they hatch."

"D'you mean Gretchen's been crowned queen by this mob?"

"Then she takes off from the hive to get herself banged by the no-good drones hanging around outside. She emits an Oxo Acid come-on that no male can resist. What's printed on that cask where she's taking a bath? Honey Oxo Mead."

"Jesus! You've almost got me convinced."

"You better be."

"But do they know what they're doing . . . Gretchen and all the rest?"

"No. They're just following an instinctive pattern Nature formed ages ago."

"For bees," Shima objected. "Not people."

"Uh-uh. Can't you get it through your head that your Gretchen isn't people; she's the New Primal Man. She's getting back to Nature's basics on her way to the pinnacle, and there's going to be hell to pay."

Gretchen came out of the honey mead shrilling and piping. She was shaking and trembling, and clung to the side of the cask while the mob rocked around her. They embraced her, stroked her, kissed her, butted her lovingly. They rolled her off the cask.

"Uh-huh," Leuz said. "It's the new queen pattern all right, Shim. Now the fireworks start. Shim?

Shim?'' Leuz looked around in surprise. Shima was gone. Like Ind'dni, he had taken off.

Gretchen scrambled to her feet and began short, darting dashes at no one and nothing, still shrilling. She was unaware. She was frenzied. She was primal. In that vast labyrinth with its tortuous passages and corridors and apartments, hacked out of the bridge pier masonry to form the Oasis, she was the new queen and blind-driven to extinguish all rivals.

She went down the ladder to the Raxon apartment below, thrusting through swarm clusters, searching, searching for what she didn't know, but the primal instinct would tell her when she found it. She clawed her way up to her own apartment again, still searching, seeking, shrilling. Then she came face to face with Nellie Gwyn, unrecognizable in belly-dancer costume, singing in a scream, but Gretchen recognized her. She went for her throat while the mob cheered.

When Nell was dead, Gretchen again began her darting dashes at no one and nothing, and then again began searching, seeking, out into the corridor, shoving through the excited swarms until she came upon Yenta Calienta, majestic in Delilah robes and the beard of Moses. The death-struggle carried them the length of the corridor.

When Yenta was dead and Bimmy beaten off, Gretchen went down the Oasis stairs, searching, seeking, shrilling, hunting. She found her prey in the lobby and left Sarah stiffening in a snowdrift of silver sequins. The kill had stripped off the last fragments of Gretchen's clothes. Then she took flight out into the Guff.

She ran; her African breasts heaving, her buttocks quivering, her vulva openly inviting and compressing spasmodically with every stride. She ran blindly through the Guff. And she was madly pursued by the burning, aching, wish-dreaming drones of the Guff.

The drone is Nature's necessary trash; merely an *apparat* for the manufacture of semen, all the way from the lion to the bee. The male lion is a drone, lazy, unproductive, useless outside of his one function; fed and cared for by his mate who makes the kills, produces his litters and raises the cubs. But after he has dined on the prey she had provided and lies drowsing in the sun, what does he dream he is? The King of Beasts? And what does the human drone dream he is?

"Look up in the sky!"
"It's a bird!"
"It's a plane!"
"It's EAGLEMAN!"
Mysteriously hatched in an aerie by superscientists from outer space and flown to the Guff, EAGLEMAN uses his mysterious aerial powers to fight the forces of evil and injustice, meanwhile posing as Tiny Gimp, a timid, harmless cripple.
And the cripple banged Gretchen's ass off.

"What's riding that horse?"
"It's a boiler!"
"It's an ashcan!"
"It's KNIGHTMAN!"
Welded into human form from invincible space-steel by a mysterious star blacksmith, and given the wisdom of Vulcan, KNIGHTMAN uses his mysterious powers of chivalry to fight the forces of evil and injustice, meanwhile posing as Skip Sands, a timid, harmless horse trainer.
And the trainer galloped Gretchen sidesaddle.

"Look in that bathroom!"
"It's a sink!"
"It's a tub!"
"It's HONKMAN!"
Boiled up from the atomic waters of a Swedish mineral spring and mysteriously transported to the Guff by Space Guardians, HONKMAN uses his mysterious muscular superpowers to fight the forces of evil and

injustice, meanwhile posing as Sven Svenson, a timid, harmless garbage collector.

And the garbage collector gave Gretchen a Swedish massage.

"Look behind that tree!"
"It's a branch!"
"It's a bush!"
"It's REDMAN!"

Deposited in the last wigwam of the western plains by ecologists from outer space and heir to all the mysterious lore of the Indians, REDMAN used his mysterious tracking powers to fight the forces of evil and injustice in the Guff, meanwhile posing as Moisha Katz, a timid, harmless accountant.

And Moisha bellywhopped Gretchen.

"Look down in that cellar!"
"It's a tank!"
"It's a furnace!"
"It's GORILLAMAN!"

Born in the torrid jungle of Africa and educated in the Guff by an animal trainer from outer space, GORILLAMAN uses his mysterious junglecraft to fight the forces of evil and injustice, meanwhile posing as Fido, a timid, harmless performing dog.

And Fido banged Gretchen spatchcock.

"Look in the precinct!"
"It's the fuzz!"
"It's the law!"
"It's JURYMAN!"

Dictated in the law courts of outer space and heir to all superstellar legal lore, JURYMAN was mysteriously brought to the Guff to prosecute the forces of evil and injustice with his mysterious legal powers, meanwhile posing as Ronald Pica, a timid, harmless court stenographer.

And the stenographer prosecuted Gretchen, *vi et armis*.

"Look up in the sky!"
"It's a comet!"
"It's a nova!"
"It's NEUTRONMAN!"
Born on a collapsing star and mysteriously transported to the Guff by the supermavins of space, NEUTRON-MAN secretly uses his mysterious astral powers to fight the forces of evil and injustice, meanwhile posing as Lance Languid, a timid, harmless dilettante.

And the dilettante mounted Gretchen baroque.

"Look down the street!"
"It's a flame!"
"It's arson!"
"It's FIREMAN!"
Ignited from the flames of a Salem witch-burning and mysteriously delivered to the Guff by saviors from outer space, FIREMAN secretly uses his mysterious burning powers to fight the forces of evil and injustice, meanwhile posing as M. Monsieur, a timid, harmless chef.

And the chef skewered Gretchen *en brochette*.

"Look up at that wall!"
"It's a bug!"
"It's a spider!"
"It's MANTISMAN!"
Mysteriously absorbing the superpowers of an Amazon explorer from outer space, and transported to the Guff aboard a fruit freighter, MANTISMAN uses his mysterious insect skills to fight the forces of evil and injustice, meanwhile posing as Speed Stubbs, a timid, harmless SpaceCap.

And the SpaceCap banged Gretchen stelliform.

"Look at that pyramid!"
"It's a rock!"
"It's a stone!"
"It's INCAMAN!"

Saved from his dying mother's womb by a Sun Priest from Algol IV, and endowed with the mysterious Egyptian magic of the pyramids, INCAMAN uses his occult powers to fight the forces of evil and injustice in the Guff, meanwhile posing as Alex Brut, a timid, harmless secretary.

And the secretary banged Gretchen widdershins.

Then came BURNMAN, COSMICMAN, DEMON-MAN, ISOMAN, SHARKMAN, MAGNETMAN, PLASTICMAN, JETMAN, POWERMAN, and a score more dreaming drones, all fighting for their turn to fulfill themselves with the reality of Gretchen's compelling invitation and mount her in pronation, in supination, akimbo, backhand, mizzenmast, bunch-backed, crural, zigzag, oblique, careened, skewed, uphill and downhill. And finally SCIENCEMAN, posing as Blaise Shima, a timid, harmless chemist, had his turn to rencounter Gretchen with stoccado thrusts.

But it was during this climax that the frenzy of the queen pheromone was exhausted and the nuptial flight ended. Gretchen's spasming muscles in her pubes contracted in a last convulsion and clenched steel-tight. Shima's penis was torn out of him to remain gripped in her vulva. Still dominated by the new regal role possessing her, Gretchen ignored Shima and left him, writhing and bleeding to death.

22

When Gretchen staggered into her Oasis, she was instantly surrounded by excited women who passed her from embrace to embrace, stroking, petting, kissing her. Up in her shambled apartment they produced a divan, liberated from somewhere else, and coaxed her to recline on it. She was a naked odalisque, streaming with sweat, saliva, and semen, primal and pungent. They clustered around her nude body, gently stroking her Venus-mount until the contraction cramp relaxed. Then they withdrew Shima's bloody penis, the mating sign that their queen was no longer a virgin, and waited, rustling and whispering in a humming buzz.

At last Gretchen opened her eyes and looked around. They fell silent and watched her expectantly.

"It's all got to be restored," she said in a faint voice.

"Yes, BB."

"Everything back to the future."

"Yes, BB." They didn't understand but laughed submissively.

Gretchen's control began to return. "Priss, you must know cleaning companies."

"Yes, BB."

"Hire one."

"They're expensive, BB."

"I can afford it."

"All of us can do it together, BB," the two-headed monster with four arms offered. "You don't have to pay."

"No. I have another assignment for you two. Which of us did I kill?"

"You don't remember?" Mary Mixup was astonished.

"No."

"Y-You killed three," Priss stammered. "N-Nell. Sarah. Y-Yenta. You almost k-killed her rabbi, too."

"Yes. The prime contenders. Let's get that settled. *Oodgedye, Udgedye,* I want their bods taken to the Guff precinct. You will tell Subadar Ind'dni exactly what happened. Can do?"

"Will do, BB." The twins didn't dream of dissenting, objecting or recusing.

"He'll probably issue an A.P.B. for me, but I'll handle that. You guards, help the twins and go back to Security duty. No more invasions."

"Yes, BB."

"Where's the Raxon woman?"

"Here, BB."

"I'm having your apartment cleaned and restored too, but your ceiling and my floor must be repaired. Do you know construction people?"

"Yes, BB."

"Hire a contractor. I'll pay."

"Not all, BB. My girls did as much damage as yours."

"My girls? Yes. My girls. But I'm running my girls and I'm picking up the tab for everything. Get a contractor."

"Yes, BB."

"Where's the Pi-girl?"

"Here, BB."

"How old are you?"

"Seventeen, ma'am person."

376

"Old enough to work for me. You'll join my staff and attend to me."

"Thank you, BB ma'am person."

"You'll also go to school nights. I'll make the arrangement. I won't have illiterates around me."

"No, BB ma'am. Yes, BB person."

"If any of you girls want anything from Regina's place, you have my permission. Take it, but no quarreling."

"Yes, BB."

"And Nellie's."

"Burned out, BB."

"Yenta's?"

"Her rabbi has it."

"Sarah's?"

"I'll be taking it over, BB."

"You're Norah, her dresser?"

"I am that, BB."

"Good and welcome, Norah. Can you afford Sarah's place?"

"Thank you, BB. I don't surely know yet."

"If you can't, come to me." Gretchen looked around at the hive. "All of you come to me for everything. Is that understood?"

They rustled happily.

"*Only* to me. Is *that* understood?"

Some of them rustled unhappily.

"Relax, all of you. I'll explain it at our first Twenty tonight."

"Twenty?" Mary Mixup was bewildered. "Are there twenty of us?"

Oodgedye stopped her head count. "Sharpen a wit, dummy. BB must mean twenty hours."

"That's eight pip emma," *Udgedye* explained.

"Oh? We're meeting at eight? Where? Here?"

"No," Gretchen said. "We're all filthy. We've got to clean and refresh and change. The Zauna."

* * *

One is subjected to the frigid, temperate and torrid terrestrial zones in the Zauna Baths; also the environments of Luna, Mars and Venus, with authentic sound-effects; winds, snow, hail, rain, thunderstorms, bird calls, insect stridulations, and animal cries. Also the alien language of extraterrestrial plant forms which murmur or moan and chatter or clatter incomprehensibly as they germinate, grow, replicate, and die.

The waters, of course, are fantastically expensive even though they're recycled constantly. The scents, soaps, and essential oils are much cheaper but really useless without water. For a monumental fee one may have exclusive use of the Zauna for oneself and guests, which fee Gretchen paid.

As the colony progressed through hot, warm, cold; baths, showers, soaps, oils, and massages; warming, relaxing, gleaming, Gretchen cosseted her subjects. "I'm going to tell you a true story," she began. "Some of you will recognize yourselves in it. The rest will be able to guess. No, Lydia dear, no trombone fanfare now. Please not to interrupt. No interruptions from anyone.

"There was a group of ladies who met once a week to socialize and comfort themselves with food and friendship and fun and games. They were all very dear, sweet, and delightful ladies who meant no harm to anyone. But they did do great harm because they forgot that they were women, and there's a vast difference between a lady and a woman.

"One of the fun games they played was a witchcraft ritual to raise the Devil. None of them believed in Satan and hell any more than they believed in God and heaven. After all, this is the twenty-second century, and these were modern, sophisticated ladies; but they were also women.

"The difference between a lady and a woman is the difference between carved ivory and an elephant's tusk. No, don't laugh. I'm not comparing us to elephants. We're the carved ivory; exquisite, beautiful, the result of centuries of the craft—keep that word in mind—the craft of designing, shaping and carving the natural tusk into a work of art that will please men. We are carved by man's craft into ladies to please men. And we have forgotten the original tusk, the fighting, foraging, dangerous weapon that is a woman. They say that inside every joke there is a truth. Inside every carved ivory piece there is a deadly weapon.

"Why have women always permitted men to exploit and carve them into ladies? We've done it because we need men as much as they need us. But while we have been forced to accept men as they are, they're afraid of us as we really are, and so our need traps us into the safe carved ivory role—safe for men, that is. But the menace is still inside us.

"And a strange thing happened with this group of lovely ladies. The primal dangers buried and forgotten inside each of them combined to give birth to a single, whole danger, a quasi-real creature, a protean primal lust, a male brute multiplied by ten times ten, the Golem[100]. I won't describe the horrors that the Golem[100] brought with it into the Guff. All that's over now. The brute's disappeared into another universe.

"This must never happen again. It will not happen again with me or my girls. Desire men, yes. Accept men, yes. Use men, yes. But never let a man use you. Let them want women, good, but never be corrupted by their craft of shaping the tusk into safe carved ivory. That's why I said: Like men, yes, but no more than that.

"Like them, enjoy them, use them for what they're fit, but never need them. Why should you? We have ourselves. No more ladies; we're women. We're the house; they're only the tenants. They can come and go; we're forever. The next Twenty will be held in this Zauna again, same day next week. I'll arrange it. Meanwhile, stay and enjoy your freedom. Pi-girl, you come with me. I have to split for a showdown with a chauvinist chemist who's used my 'lady hangup' just once too often.''

* * *

(The Soho exit from the Baths. Gretchen and Pi emerge into the Guff. They are clean steamed, massaged and bathed. They wear fresh jump suits. Neither has applied maquillage, but Gretchen has frittered her Afro with rainbow sequins. Pi has braided her pale hair into pigtails tied with white silk bows. They stop for a moment while the street and sidewalk signs glow and speak and urge the public.)

THE SIGNS

LIVE! LIVE!LIVE!LIVE!LIVE!LIVE!
LOVE! LOVE! LOVE! LOVE! LOVE! LOVE!
EAT! EAT! EAT! EAT! EAT! EAT!

SIDEWALKS

Won't you adore having your ass banged off, baby? Follow me! Follow me! Follow me to the scene of the scrime!

(Two drunks giggle and totter the length of an endless glowing sidewalk penis which leads them around a corner.)

1ST DRUNK

(In slurred Guff Blurt) Hey man grab man blast man scrime man 'round the world man in all directions huh huh huh?

2ND DRUNK

(Simulating aristocratic elegance) Aye dew nott föllöw yew m'freund.

THE SIGNS

MANBALONEY . . . 100
MUDBALONEY . . . 150
GIRLBALONEY . . . 175

GRETCHEN

(Pointing) We head this way, Pi-girl.

PI

Where to, Miz Person?

GRETCHEN

Uptown west. To Blaise Shima's penthouse. We'll have to walk it. Come on, girl.

> *(The two women thread their way through the Guff streets. As they skirt the banks of the Hudson River, the mud monsters, generated by the radio-active pollution in the New York harbor ooze up onto the broken pavements; ambulatory slime molds in search of foul foods.)*

THE MONSTERS

Ssss! Pfff! Srrr! Zzzz!

> *(In the Scrime House of Mother Merkin, three whores stand at an upstairs window, burning phallic candles in left hands, right hands preparing their allure for the night. They are dressed and coiffured in replication of current entertainment celebrities.)*

PI

Ooo look, Miz Nunn person. Isn't that Greta Grabya?

GRETCHEN

No.

PI

And Fonda del Solitary?

GRETCHEN

No.

381

And Rh Factor?

No. They're just fifty-class funks.

(The bawds throw open the window and begin their singing commercial to the Guff public.)

My mother said I always should
Prance with a yanceman in the wood.
If I did, she would say,
You lucky girl to use your ass.
Use your ass.
Use your ass.
And make the lucky fucker pay.

(A corner Pukebox blazes lurid lights.)

Oh please, Miz Person. I just love Phlegmy's latest. Please, Miz? Please?

(Gretchen grudgingly halts and inserts slug in Pukebox. Pi presses button No. 1101. A sound-bug flips out, is drawn to the print of Pi's index finger, and follows her finger, sounding softly.)

(With clinical realism)
Vomitation. Vomitation.
Retchitation. Retchitation.
Spew. Spew.
Upchuck, daddy,
With a solid pour.

(The sound-bug finishes its number and flies back to the Pukebox. Near Person Lane, formerly Maiden Lane, twenty-two porters, bearing huge delivery loads of Condensed & Evaporated Plaste-

382

quila, are in hot argument with a squad of P.L.O. soldiers and their lieutenant.)

A PORTER

Hey man gotta makeadeliver. Since when gotta customs boundairy line here is all?

LIEUTENANT

Hey man set up yesdy. Wanna deliver gotta pay twemmy is all.
(To Gretchen)
Hi hey. Remember youse. Bije babe Falasha Jew doll come to our pyramid. Hihey pretty Jew jill.

GRETCHEN

Hi handsome. I see our PloFather got new illegal neighborhood boundry. Great. We got to pay?

LIEUTENANT

No money fm'you, pretty bije babe. Maybe something else, later?

GRETCHEN

Sure. See you underneath.

(Explosion! Concussion! The Krypton Ketchup factory bursts open as a bomb explodes and the Organic Terrorist Movement makes a statement over the public broadcast system.)

BROADCAST

We done it! We done it! But be assured, poisoned public, that the ingredients of our bomb were pure-ly and safe-ly organic. The Movement NEVER rots.

(A thousand and twenty-seven Guff ghouls are crimsoned as they lick up the ketchup.)

THE GHOULS

Lap-Lap-Lap-Lap-Lap-Lap-Lickety-Lap.

(In Captain Shaft's Dart Range the naked female targets scream challenges at the Sado-Mach dart-shooters.)

TARGETS :

Shoot, man, shoot! Hate me and shoot! Shoot for a triple! Tit, tit, and cooz!

CAPTAIN SHAFT

Try your luck, babes? Got some juicy big-prick targets . . .

GRETCHEN

She's too young and I'm too old.

(A Hang-Glider sails low overhead, slowly descending. A man hangs by the neck from the glider, the strangling noose knotted into the traditional thirteen turns of the rope.)

PI

Ooo look, Miz Gretch person. I seen a lot of suicides but never like this one before.

(A gaggle of crones follows the falling glider avidly absorbing the emissions from the spasming penis of the suicide.)

GRETCHEN

Saw, Pi. *Saw.* It's obvious I must put you through a good school.

(A night class in the Educational Television Elementary School earnestly studies a projection screen.)

THE SCREEN

PABLUM/GOOD OLD-TIME FLAVOR
Define "Good"
Define "Old"
Define "Time"
Define "Flavor"

Write five hundred (500) word essay on use of the hyphen.

Define "Hyphen"
Define "500"

PI

(Sadly) I couldn't pass that test, Miz Gretch. Person.

GRETCHEN

(Cheerfully) Not to worry, dear. That was an advanced class for high-I.Q. types.

(In Nixon, formerly Lincoln, Center, Ms. Liz Cuiz blushingly receives First Prize for her display of wax flowers in the Seventy-fifth Annual Imitation Horticultural show.)

MS. CUIZ

Gotta admission, wax beat plastic anytime, exspecial fr'eatin'.

(Hastily)

Doan beez mad on me, youse beautiful Photo-Plastic Ink. guys . . . I dig plastic too.

(The Eskimo Exterminator Company cleans out an IRS warehouse to save tons of accusatory and incriminating documents from the ravages of insects and rodents. Two Eskimos debate over the merits of ants and roaches as they devour them.)

1ST ESKIMO

Halstu di oyg'n tsu der erd, vestu mer vi verem nisht zen.

2ND ESKIMO

Der vus hot alemen lib, iz gelibt fun keynem.

PI

Them Eskimos get in everywhere.

GRETCHEN

Esquimaux, Pi. *Esquimaux.*

(In Slammer Sodom's Rodeo a Chimpanzee rider complains bitterly to the handlers readying the human bronco he is to mount for the competition.)

CHIMPANZEE

Tk-nk-fk-wk-tk-lk-mk-bk-zk!

1ST HANDLER

What's he beefin' about now?

2ND HANDLER

Aw, these rodeo stars is always complainin'. He says we tie the barbed wire too tight around the bronc's balls to make'm buck. Says it takes alla juice outa the stud.

(In the Cryogenic Ice Palace two cannibals are discussing cryo-cuisine.)

1ST CANNIBAL

Gotta like thaw 'em out, man, before you roast 'em.

2ND CANNIBAL

Not if'n they beez friz like over hundrid year, man. Get kinda stinksville. Gotta roast 'em friz.

1ST CANNIBAL

Wha'part you dig most?

2ND CANNIBAL

Guts.

1ST CANNIBAL

Oh man, das d'answer. Guts is delly.

(Night and the Guff. Murk light. Gnome-goons. The frozen corpse of Mr. Rubor-Tumor is being roasted. Salem Burne's dancers warm themselves around the fire. The PloFather's spidery hands play on the buttocks of Sheikh Omar ben Omar as he

mounts an Unbeliever. In the morgue Gianni Jiki buys the corpse of Droney Lafferty for its piebald skin which will be turned into a wall-hanging. The black eyes of Yenta Calienta have been traded for a hand-powered Mixmaster. The Therpool has discovered that its freak water is also hallucinogenic. Three Hudson Hell Gate Dam engineers have mathematically proved to a Science Convention that bees can fly. Miss Priss is ravished by a robot and takes it to a therapist. The original Scriabin Finkel, aged 97, dies and his stable composes a Scriabin sendoff entitled: SAFE-HIT ME, FINKEL, THROUGH THE OUTFIELD OF DEATH.)

Shima's Oasis had once been the Spanish Museum. His penthouse was a peak in the sawtooth skyline looming over the fuming Hudson River where flickering will-o'-the-wisps burned and danced above the whorls and eddies.

Gretchen opened the penthouse door and called in a tone of command, "Blaise!"

No answer.

She entered, attended by Pi-girl. They explored lounge, bedroom, bath, kitchen and terrace, still carpeted with Opsday earth. "Blaise!"

"No one here, Miz BB ma'am person."

"After all I've been through, has that son-of-a-bitch gone back to work without even calling me? Withdrawing? *Le pauvre petit.* Typical!"

She called CCC. No Shima.

"If he's lost control and gone into fugue again, this is the last time I bail him out. Pi-girl, call the Guff precinct for me. I don't want them to hear my voice and trace me. I'll tell you what to say."

Pi called the Guff precinct, prompted by Gretchen. No. Shima. No A.P.B. on Shima. No Ind'dni. The Subadar had gone home.

"What the hell! I've got to quash the coming A.P.B. on myself anyway. Pi-girl, you go back to my place and supervise the restoration. You're responsible, girl. I'm growing you up. I won't have children around me. I'm going to Ind'dni's place. He may know where Shima is. I'll do a number on both men and get it over with. I *am* a new breed, by God! Free! Free! It's a *mechia!*"

The Pi-girl attended Gretchen to Ind'dni's residence in what had once been Gramercy Park, and then continued on to the Oasis in "Old Town." Gretchen mounted to Ind'dni's apartment and rang.

The door was opened for her by the Subadar, beautifully robed in white. "Ah! he smiled. "I have been expecting you. Come. Come in. Come in peace and hope. We too have found the way to the primal pinnacle. We have found the *ishta devata,* the true worship. It is the Lord *Siva* in His first glorious manifestation as *Sveta,* the White."

Gretchen gasped, then managed, "Ind'dni?"

"Once," Ind'dni smiled. "Come. Come in. You are my beloved friend, Gretchen Nunn."

"Once also," Gretchen answered as she entered. "I've found the way too, Subadar."

"Yes," Ind'dni said quietly as he safed the door. "Yes, I'm fully aware of all that has transpired. I did tell you that I was not without resources. You have reached a new peak, an exalted peak, perhaps even the primal pinnacle which, alas, Dr. Shima could not before he died. Despite all his brilliant assets, he could not cope with the challenge he dreamed of meeting."

"What? Blaise dead?" Gretchen was shocked.

Ind'dni nodded.

"But how?"

"Ah, you do not remember. You have left your old life behind, as I have mine. He was torn apart by you in your new role of queen."

"*I* killed him?"

"Tore him apart."

Gretchen was speechless.

"What? Guilt? Grief? Come, love, we are both of us beyond that, so let us speak frankly as equals, and we *are* equals, you know. I too have reached a pinnacle and am, perhaps, the only primal equal you can have. So let us befriend and support each other."

"Y-You—You're only trying to comfort me." She was shaken. "I tore Blaise . . . tore him apart?"

"We must comfort each other. We're alone on the heights and have only each other."

"B-But you all said I was born to it . . . The New Primal Man . . . Not *you,* Subadar. How have you reached your pinnacle?"

"I was reborn through the Black Hole."

"In the contra-universe? It had that effect?"

"Or perhaps the new colony, your new hive, has raised me to the heights?"

"My God! My God! My God!"

"Rather call Him by His true name, *Siva,* the Divine Generator of Life. We shall enter the universe of *Siva* together. You have much to teach me and I shall teach you to procreate the all-embracing spirit of the *Soma.* We shall worship the twelve sacred *Lingas* together."

"Ind'dni, this can't be you. You sound insane, and I think I'm mad, too. What's happened to us?"

And he taught her to worship the twelve sacred *Lingas* for three mad erotic hours that left her gasping and incredulous and melting into the universal *Soma.*

"Oh my God . . ." she whispered. "Oh my God . . . My God! My God! My God! I've never been loved like this before. Never! No woman ever was. I've never loved love like this before. Never! Is this the pinnacle?"

He nodded.

"I knew you weren't the fag you pretended to be to Shima. You're a man. You're more than a man; you're ten times ten any man I ever knew. My God! Dear God! I love you. I love you. I love you. And you? Me? Is it the same with you?"

Ind'dni smiled to her, then arose, went to a mirror and on it printed with a crimsoned forefinger:

I LOVE YOU

It took a long moment for Gretchen to understand what she'd just seen.

"But—B-but that was your left hand," she whispered. "You're writing with your left hand, and that's backward mirror-writing. I—You—He never came back from the contraworld. Oh Jesus! Dear Jesus God . . ." Her voice broke. "He . . . He was left behind. He's trapped in that contrabedlam forever. You came back in his place. Didn't you? Didn't you?" Her voice rose hysterically. "And you've been masquerading as the real Ind'dni . . . My dear, sweet, wonderful Ind'dni. That explains why you did and said everything backwards after the return. You're his contra-self, the reversed Ind'dni, remorseless, treacherous, lecherous, kindless . . . the negative Ind'dni that my real Ind'dni saw."

He smiled. "I'm Golem[101]."

A.D. 2280

So?dis?Candida?

N.

Dishere Souse Amourica?

Nn.

Zit Jewropey?

Nnn.

Wherjeez?

Guff!Guff!Guff!

Blessya.

N'achoo, man. She's his name. Guff. Dig? Gay-you-ffuck. Guff. You beez inna Guffa Viewnitey Status. Lassitude 101001 degrades norse.

! Whajeer ?

Anus Domino 100011101000

!! I beez friz feisty year ??

Y. Gotta cure fwattailsya now ∴ us move youse S fom Lasky to Guff.

Gone telly esplainment what I up agin inna dishere mod Guff?

Shoe. Where fom original?

Afro.

391

Oak. But 1firsth gotta putyouse inna pitcher. How happenny. She's all happyning !strong! ago, inna twemmy onus hungries, 2175.

Whakine rap izzat? 2175?

Wazza talktypus ago then. Youse ear me close, man, and me—

GIRLman!

Oop! Scuze! No notice tits. Lissen, girlman, &me input whahap while youse cryøgens friz in coughins. Tell how+why hole Guff change fom = peoples to ≠. Tell how oletypus mans go aus-out, exstink like dinnersours, and N*E*W breed primal poisons like us we make quantum jump & replace her inna Guff. Y'gotta dig ifn wanna beez = to us.

I think I go back inna coughin.

Nnnn! Lissen!